TREASON IN THE SECRET CITY

TREASON IN THE SECRET CITY

A Libby Clark Mystery

Diane Fanning

This first world edition published 2016
in Great Britain and the USA by
SEVERN HOUSE PUBLISHERS LTD of
19 Cedar Road, Sutton, Surrey, England, SM2 5DA.
Trade paperback edition first published
in Great Britain and the USA 2016 by
SEVERN HOUSE PUBLISHERS LTD

British Library Cataloguing in Publication Data
A CIP catalogue record for this title is available from the British Library.

ISBN-13: 978-0-7278-8615-6 (cased)
ISBN-13: 978-1-84751-716-6 (trade paper)
ISBN-13: 978-1-78010-777-6 (e-book)

Typeset by Palimpsest Book Production Ltd.,
Falkirk, Stirlingshire, Scotland.

*With love and appreciation to my first reader and
best friend, Wayne Fanning*

ONE

In the early hours of May 30, 1944, an unknown noise roused me from sleep. I listened to the silence for a moment, uncertain whether I had actually heard something or merely dreamed it. When I heard nothing out of the ordinary, I fluffed my pillow and rolled over to my other side. A sharp sound of knuckles on glass brought me to full alert, sitting straight up. I looked up to the high window by my bed and saw a face. I opened my mouth to scream in terror, but stifled it when I realized the face was very familiar.

I pulled a blanket in front of my pajamas as I stood up on the mattress. 'Marvin, what in heaven's name is going on? You scared me to death.'

'Sorry, Libby. Sorry. I just didn't know who else . . . I'm sorry. Go back to sleep,' he said, turning away.

'Marvin, you get back here right now. Don't wake me up and then tell me to never mind. What did you want to say? Is something wrong in the lab?'

'Oh, no. No, no. It's nothing that can't wait.'

'Marvin! You obviously didn't think that a couple of minutes ago.'

'Uh, uh,' Marvin stammered, appearing as if he might flee without warning. 'Uh, Europe? Does it worry you that we're getting less solid news out of there than out of that theatre in the Pacific lately?'

'I've noticed that, too. I don't know what it means, Marvin, none of us do. But I hardly believe that you woke me up in the middle of the night to get my opinion on what might be happening on the other side of the Atlantic. What's the real reason?'

Even in the dim lighting, Marvin's reddened face shone like a beacon as he once again stammered senselessly, then said, 'It's kind of personal.'

'Go around to the front door. I'll make a pot of coffee. OK?'

Marvin nodded and disappeared from view.

I sighed as I slipped into my full-length blue chenille robe
and slid my feet into the matching bedroom slippers. Walking
to the door, I wondered if Marvin was a lovelorn sad sack looking
for advice about what to say to the girl of his dreams. So many
of these young chemists had their noses in books all the way
through college and were terrified of approaching a female. I
keep telling them that the men are so outnumbered by the women
here, they could probably say anything and still get a date. It
was rare for any woman here on the reservation to be overloaded
with male attention; there were a few but most of the girls went
hungry.

After letting Marvin inside, I went into the kitchen and filled
the percolator with water and coffee and set it down on a burner
on the stove. While fixing a tray to carry everything into the living
room, I asked, 'So, Marvin, what brought you out at this hour?'

'There's a box of sand behind the chair in the living room.'

I bit back a sharp retort about his blatant equivocation,
wondering if the progressive diminishing of my patience was
simply a part of growing up or if it was caused by the stress of
work or the fact that we were at war – I was weary of waiting
for it to end. I leaned on what little reserves I had remaining and
tolerated Marvin's evasiveness until we were both seated with
coffee in hand. 'That's for G.G.,' I said.

'G.G. visits you here?'

I laughed out loud – first sucker. I admit, I was looking for
that kind of reaction when I decided on that name for my little
kitten. In my defense, I originally thought of it because of my
respect for and gratitude towards General Groves – the original
G.G. If I'm being honest, though, the deciding point in its favor
was my perverse desire to sow momentary confusion. Still chuck-
ling, I walked out of the kitchen. 'Not that G.G. Here, kitty,
kitty.'

A black kitten with white whiskers, chest and paws bounced
out of the bedroom, coming to an abrupt halt when he saw a
stranger. He arched his back and hopped sideways in the comical
way that all kittens think is menacing and awe-inspiring. Then
he darted into the kitchen.

'That's G.G.,' I said. 'I'll give him some food and then we can
sit down and talk.'

'Don't you want to put him out?'

'No. There's skunks and weasels and heaven knows what else out there, particularly after dark.'

'We always had cats in the barn but if one ever slipped into the house, Mom would have a fit. She'd grab her broom and chase it around until she got it outside. I never thought of doing anything else.'

'A lot of people keep their cats inside now. They live a lot longer and stay a lot healthier. People keep dogs in their houses, too.'

'I knew that. We didn't with ours, but I know a lot of regular folks have made them house pets. I guess it's the cat's turn now. You ever wonder if they really like it better or if they miss their freedom?'

With the coffee poured and doctored, I leaned back in the chair and said, 'That's a pretty serious question considering we're in the middle of a war to protect our own. But there's a reason food, water and shelter are called our creature comforts – it's a basic need and an undying yearning that we share with all the animals. Enough philosophy – let's get to the reason you're here.'

'I had second thoughts once I saw you in the window. I'm scared and confused, Libby. I need to be sure I can trust you.'

'Really? How can you doubt that? Haven't we been through enough together? Didn't I keep your name and those of the rest of our group from Lieutenant Colonel Crenshaw?' I asked, referring to the Walking Molecules, our secret gathering of scientists formed to talk science without censorship, which had gone beyond their original mission and defied the authorities and solved a murder, earlier that year. 'Spill it, Marvin.'

Marvin exhaled a jagged breath. 'First, let me say, Frannie is not a spy, no matter what anyone says. She was tricked. She thought she was helping the war effort. She had no idea . . .'

'Hold up. Who's Frannie?'

'Oh, my cousin, Frannie. Frannie Snowden. She works switchboard. She's a good girl. She always follows the rules. She doesn't make trouble. She was a Civil Air Patrol volunteer before she got her job here.'

'So what's the problem?'

'She's been charged with treason.'

'Treason?' My stomach somersaulted over the implications; this was no silly problem. It was deadly serious for anyone and everyone who was involved in it. 'Has she been arrested?'

'Not yet. And not ever if I can help it.'

'Do you know where she is?'

'Yes. I have since the day that they came for her and she slipped away. See, she helped this scientist named Hansrote make some phone calls to some guy named Raymond. She said he told her that other guy was a spy delivering information to help the allies and she fell for it. She realized too late that the scientist had lied to her – that he was actually the spy and he was giving information to the enemy. Inadvertently, Frannie gave herself away. Once he knew that she knew, he reported her as a spy to save his own skin.'

'OK, Marvin, I want the whole story. Start from the beginning and tell me everything you know on your own and all the details she shared with you.'

'I'll start with my meeting with her after she was in trouble. A couple of nights ago, me and my roommate Jubal went to dinner and we were talking about how disappointing the baseball season was with so many of the major league players enlisted or drafted to fight in the war. On the way back, we were debating which one was the biggest loss to the sport and had narrowed it down to Hammerin' Hank Greenberg, Joe DiMaggio and Stan Musial.'

'Get to the point, Marvin.'

'OK, we heard somebody say something – thought they were offering an opinion about baseball at first. Then I realized that it was my cousin Frannie hiding in the shadows. Of course Jubal thought it was a girlfriend but I set him straight on that and told him to get lost since I could tell Frannie seemed upset. I figured it was some silly girl thing or some stupid family squabble. Oh, I'm sorry, Libby. I don't think that just because you're a woman that you get upset about silly girl things, but my cousin – well, she's another story.'

I nodded and with as much patience as I could force into my voice, said, 'Yes, Marvin, go on please.'

'Then, she asked me if she could stay in my dorm room. I thought that was loco and I told her and warned her we could both lose our jobs. Then, she told me what had happened and I knew it was not a silly problem at all – it was deadly serious.'

I listened as Marvin recounted the elaborate and detailed story that Frannie had shared with him. It sounded incredulous at first but with each added detail, the credibility of the story strengthened in my mind. If it were true, the fact that it was happening here was nothing short of shocking.

TWO

The sun had slipped below the horizon by the time Frannie had finished her shift at the switchboard and walked outside. The soft darkness creeping over the ridges surrounding Oak Ridge and laying claim to the streets one foot at a time was very peaceful and pleasant.

'It was so nice,' she told Marvin, 'I decided to walk back to the dormitory rather than catch the bus. I wasn't worrying about a single thing. I had no personal problems to fret over at all. I was trying to decide if it would be worth my while to go into Knoxville on my next day off and then I made up my mind to do it. You know me, Marvin, I love to shop even if I don't buy a thing.'

She said that she was humming under her breath and enjoying the evening when out of the corner of her eye, she saw a stealthy movement in the shadow of the buildings to her right. Then she heard, 'Miss Snowden' whispered in the dark. She turned to look at the emerging figure, and felt goosebumps run up her arms. 'I saw a man wearing a hat with the brim pulled down low. Then I was really nervous, it felt like there was this hard knot in my chest. I wanted to turn and run but my feet wouldn't – couldn't – move. I was frozen there. I swear Marvin, if he were a snake, he could have bit me and left me for dead.

'The man said, "Ms Snowden. Don't be alarmed. You know me." He sure didn't look at all familiar. I finally got my feet to take a couple of steps backwards but I felt like I was in a gangster movie and I was the one with cement shoes – my legs felt so heavy. And then he laughed – sort of like that chuckly laugh my dad does when he can't believe I did something too silly to be true. You remember the way Dad always did that, don't you, Marvin?'

'Sure, Frannie, but then what happened?'

'The man said, "Oh, I'm sorry. You've talked to me on the phone but have never seen me face-to-face, have you?" He stuck out his hand. "Dr Hansrote. Edwin Hansrote." So I said, "Oh, Dr Hansrote, you gave me a fright." But I was thinking that even though he was acting a little scary, he couldn't be all bad – not many men offer to shake hands with a woman. I took that as a good sign that he respected me. I said, "Good evening, sir. Is there something I can do for you? I won't be back on the switch-board until tomorrow morning."

'Then, he asked me an odd question. "You are a good American, aren't you, Ms Snowden?" And I said, "I like to think I am, sir." And he said, "You want to do your part to win the war, don't you?" I told him that was why I was here and that's when he asked for my help. I sure couldn't think of anything I could do to help anyone but then he said, "I need to talk to someone without the censors listening in."

'Well, of course, Marvin, I told him that I couldn't do that. It was against all the rules and I could get in a lot of trouble and he would, too. But he kept on me. He said that I had to help him – that the future of the whole country was in my hands. I still said no and then he told me something that turned every-thing upside down.

'He said that he was hoping he didn't have to tell me the whole story that I'd just take his word for it and believe what he was doing was vital for the war effort. He said that it was really top secret but if I was going to help, I probably deserved to know what was going on. I asked what he was talking about and he told me that there are enemy spies right here in Oak Ridge. I started looking around – I mean if they were here, they could be spying on the two of us right at that moment, couldn't they? But Hansrote did one of Dad's chuckles again and said that they were not where I could see them and even if I could, I wouldn't recognize them because they were so crafty. He said, "Believe me, Ms Snowden, they are here and they are helping the enemy every day. We need to stop them from getting infor-mation to the Axis by setting a trap for them."

'I thought that sounded pretty dangerous and I told him. He didn't deny it but he said, "Good Americans have to be willing to stick their necks out to make sure the right side wins this war. I am willing to take risks for my country, aren't you?" What could I say to that, Marvin? Just hearing him say that made me want to stand tall and salute,' Frannie said, straightening her spine and bringing a hand to her forehead. 'I told him that I was willing to do anything for the United States of America. I reminded him again, though, that he was asking me to break the rules. That I was specifically forbidden to get off the line, that I was supposed to monitor it unless I had to turn it over to a censor because it sounded suspicious.

'That's when he said, "There are exceptions to every rule, Ms Snowden. And this is one of them. I'm going to tell you more but you have to solemnly swear that even if you decide you don't have the courage to help me, you must keep everything I'm saying to you a secret." So I told him, "No loose lips, here, sir."

'Then he said, "Good girl. I am in contact with someone who is working for us, behind enemy lines. He is taking a great risk to give me information about the work they are doing and helping us identify and expose the spy in our midst. But he is very cautious. If he ever heard a suspicious click or unexpected sound of any type, he would stop talking to me. And you know how it is. Those little sounds you hear in the background when you're talking to your mom. You know someone is listening in – you just know it. That's why I have to have an unencumbered line. He needs to know it's safe to tell me the things I need to know. And that's where you come in." By that time, I was so nervous about the whole idea, I had gnawed on my lower lip until it hurt. I told him that I wanted to do the right thing but I wasn't sure if it was. I needed time to think about it. I didn't tell him that a big reason I wanted to buy some time was because I wanted to talk to you about it before I decided.

'But he was so insistent and so genuine, Marvin. When he said, "There's no time, Ms Snowden. Every hour, our boys are being killed and wounded. We need to win the war as soon as possible before there are no boys alive left to come home." And then he said, "Things are not looking good right now. U-Boats are taking down our ships as fast as we can send them out. And Africa? You only hear the good news on the newsreels. It's looking gloomy in the Dark Continent. Once all our ships have been taken out by U-boats, how will our boys over there get the supplies they need to survive? There's not a minute to waste, Ms Snowden. The only question for you is are you with us or against us?"

'Oh, Marvin, I wasn't sure what to do. Everything was simple – all black and white – during orientation and training. But at that moment, I felt lost in a big, grey cloud. But, I guess that's the world of spies – nothing they do is above board, is it? I thought maybe he was right. We did need to play it their way and break some rules to beat them. What if I didn't help him and we lost the war? I'd never know if it was my fault or not. I'd feel guilty for the rest of my life.' She exhaled a wavering breath.

Marvin asked, 'You believed him?'

'Absolutely,' Frannie said.

'What did you do?'

'He had it all planned out. He gave me a piece of paper that had the number that I needed to actually connect for him but said when he called, he would ask me to dial the other number he'd written which was his mother's telephone. That's how I would know it was him. I thought that was a little silly because there was no way he could know that I would be the one to pick up his call. He insisted if it wasn't me, he would either hang up or else he'd talk to his mom for a bit and then try later.

'It seemed like a lot of wasted time to me – not that I think it's a waste to telephone your mom just that if you needed to talk to someone else, it wouldn't make a lot of sense. I told him that all the girls on my shift were all good Americans and I could convince them to help. He got a bit upset at that. He said, "No, no, no, Ms Snowden. You promised to keep this conversation secret. Weren't you listening to what I said? There are spies in our midst. Maybe one of them has already compromised one of the other girls."

'I had to admit that I hadn't thought of that. I mean, it's so hard to believe. They all seem so nice, some of them are even my friends. But I hadn't known any of them for that long and I couldn't swear that one of them wasn't a dirty spy. He convinced me when he said, "You just don't know, Ms Snowden. I was very careful when I selected you. I learned everything I could about you and knew you were a very special young woman. With a threat to our freedom and liberty at stake, there's not enough time to check them all out. You understand that, don't you?"

'I told him I did but I could ask them before I said anything. He said, "You can't exactly expect them to tell the truth if they are part of a spy ring, can you?" That made a lot of sense to me, so I told him that I would help him and I would not tell a single soul about it. Before he left, he told me to memorize the numbers he gave me and burn that piece of paper that night. I swear, that paper felt as hot in my hand as if he'd already set it on fire.

'Before he walked away, he said, "We're all counting on you, Ms Snowden. Don't let your country down." And you know, Marvin, that's the last thing I wanted to do, ever. Yes, I was afraid of what could happen to me for breaking the rules but, honestly, I could feel a little sizzle inside. It was so exciting to know that I – little Frannie Snowden – was now a part of the secret spy world. It sounded so romantic. It made me feel like a movie star, only better.'

'How long have you being doing this, Frannie? And how many calls did you make?' Marvin asked.

'I guess maybe half a dozen or ten or so over these last couple of months. I was always really scared when I did. I kept expecting someone to come in and jerk my headset off and take me away. But I kept doing it because I believed it was really important – that what I was doing would help end the war. I didn't have any doubts that I was doing the right thing until the day when I was called upstairs in the administrative building to see the big supervisor. Oh, Marvin, I was terrified. I was afraid someone had seen what I was doing and turned me in. I thought I was about to get fired – or worse.

'By the time I walked into his office, I was trembling inside, my palms were all sweaty, and was fighting to keep tears building up behind my eyes from running down my cheeks. I was so upset, Marvin, that it took me a moment to understand what he was saying – that I wasn't in trouble at all. I was just being assigned to train a new receptionist. I was so happy that I almost jumped up and kissed the man.

'Walking back to my station, I realized that I would have to get hold of Dr Hansrote right away. After tomorrow, I wouldn't be able to make any sneaky calls for him until I finished training that girl 'cause she'd be watching every single move I made.

'After my shift was over, I caught a bus down to Y-12. I waited outside for Dr Hansrote to go home for the day. It was nearly an hour later before I saw him walking out of the building with two other men in suits. I waved to him to get his attention. He looked at me, and it was like he was looking through me, and then he turned away. I kind of whispered his name, but in a loud way. He turned his head slightly and gave me this cold sideways glance that felt like he'd thrown a cup of ice in my face. Then he moved on, laughing at something one of the other men said. I felt like a piece of rain-soaked trash he'd just stomped into the mud. And I didn't know what to do.

'I tossed and turned late into the night trying to figure out what it all meant. I finally fell asleep when I decided there had to be an explanation – maybe he didn't trust those men he was with. The next day was Thursday – the day he usually placed a call. If he did, I would give him a hint that there was a problem before connecting him. If he didn't call then, I'd just have to ignore rings from his line and wait for him to find me and ask what the problem was.

'But when I woke up the next morning, I felt awful like something really bad was about to happen. At first, I didn't understand why I was feeling that way. Then, I remembered Dr Hansrote's brush-off. My idea didn't seem so smart any more. I had half-a-mind to avoid answering any of his calls that day. Three hours into my shift, though, I saw his incoming call, snatched the line to plug into the hole and just blurted out, "I will be training a new operator starting tomorrow." And he almost growled at me when he said, "Just place my call."

'I tell you, Marvin, no one has ever talked to me in that nasty tone of voice before – Daddy wouldn't have allowed it. I started getting really upset about it but I stopped and remembered that I was new at this spy business and maybe he was just surprised or confused by what I said or he was acting irritated to cover up for some reason. I thought that maybe it's all for the best. Now he knows that I won't be able to help him for a while and that's all that matters. I didn't know what to think anymore. Once I put him through, I stayed on the line – just hoping to understand things a little better.

'I listened to that faraway ring – I might have even been holding my breath. I almost choked when I heard Dr Hansrote say, "Raymond, here is my report for the week. The processing of the uranium is moving forward but the pace of accumulation of the sample is driving G.G. crazy. He wants more, faster. They are also now building what is supposed to be a more efficient processing plant that will use a gaseous diffusion method."

'I won't even pretend I had any idea of what he was talking about – it made my head hurt when I tried to figure it out. But one thing that was simple to understand was that Dr Hansrote had lied to me – he was not getting information, he was giving it. Dr Hansrote was the spy he warned me about. I know I've done some really dumb things in my life but this was the worst. I was helping a spy and thinking I was doing my patriotic duty. I even daydreamed about getting a medal when the war was over. What a cheesy sap I am. Honestly, Marvin, I just wanted to die. And then, it got even worse. The girl next to me bumped the arm of her chair into my funny bone and I yelped. She leaned toward me and said, "Sorry, doll," and I'm sure they could hear that, too.

'It was all quiet on the phone. I kept listening until both lines went dead. I pulled the plug and excused myself to go to the little girl's room. I didn't know what to do. I didn't know how to make it right. I thought I should tell an army officer or some big shot in the administration, but I was afraid I'd get in trouble. I thought about writing an anonymous note. But most of all, I was afraid of Dr Hansrote.

'I figured you might know what I should do, but you already thought I was dumber than bricks and I thought you'd laugh at me. Instead, I decided to talk to the smartest woman I knew – Mildred Frank. You probably remember her, Marvin. She went to our church back home. Now she's the boss of a group of those Calutron girls. Anyway, the rest of my shift seemed to last forever and ever. I just kept to myself, pushing and pulling plugs, saying as little as possible. I didn't even answer the girls when they asked me to go with them to Joe's for a beer before dinner.

'I went straight to my room, dropped off my purse and told my roommate, Clara, that I was going up to the third floor for a bit. But, of course, Mildred wasn't there. I talked about movies and things with a few of the girls on her floor and then I got tired of waiting. When I got back to my room, Clara was hysterical. Her eyes jerked from one side of the room to the other as if she thought someone would sneak up and grab her. I asked her what was wrong and she said, "I told them you stopped at Joe's for a beer with the girls. But I know they'll be back soon."

When I asked her who she was talking about, she said the military police had been there. She was scared they'd come back, find me there and know that she lied to them. She told me I had to get out of there.

'I asked her what they said to get her so upset and she said, "Something about you working for the enemy. I know you couldn't be. You aren't are you?" Of course, I denied it. What else could I say? And she said that they threatened her. They told her that since I was a spy, if she helped me, she could be put in the slammer with me. They told her they'd lock her up until the end of the war and then ask questions. She asked, "What have you done, Frannie?" I told her the truth 'cause I couldn't think of anything else. I said, "I trusted the wrong person, Clara. He used me. And now I'm on my own." Silly Clara turned white as a sheet – I guess there was only one way she thought a girl could get in trouble so she asked, "You're not in the family way, are you?"

'If Clara hadn't been so frightened – and me, too, actually – I might have laughed. Me and Dr Hansrote doing that? It was not something that would ever, ever cross my mind – not with him. I told Clara as much in a very nice way then asked her that if the MPs came back, she should tell them she hadn't seen me. She was still in a tizzy and all worried that someone else might have seen me come in and give her away.

'While I threw some personal things and a change of clothing into a bag, I told her to tell them that she'd gone to the bathroom and heard something but never saw me or to tell them she'd been asleep. I told her as long as she never admitted that she saw me come back to the room, she wouldn't get in any trouble. I said that no one will know you did see me unless you tell them. I saw the look in her eyes and knew she might panic and tell them the truth. So I reminded her that as long as she kept my secret, I would keep her secret about her high school art teacher and how her posing for him had turned into other things. I could tell by the way Clara's face changed that she wouldn't spill the beans. Clara sure didn't want her mama to know what she did. She promised not to give me away and I went down the stairs and out of the building as quickly as I could. I've been hiding ever since waiting for you.'

THREE

'And that's what she told me,' Marvin said.

'When did you say this happened?' I asked.

'A couple of days ago. She spent the last two nights in my closet.'

'She slept in your closet?'

'Yeah and I brought food back for her and all but Jubal was getting fresh with her when I wasn't in the room and we – me and Frannie – got worried that he'd turn her in once he figured out the score.'

'So, your roommate knew she'd been charged with treason?'

'Oh no. I told him she was hiding from her parents.'

'Where is she now? Not outside?' Until I knew more the last thing I wanted was a suspected traitor inside my home. I fervently hoped Marvin was not going to beg me to let her sleep here.

'You mean outside – you mean outside your door – here?'

'Yes.'

'Oh, no. I walked her over to the hutments tonight.'

'Your cousin is a colored girl?' I asked. Heavens! Could it get any more complicated?

Marvin jerked back his head and said, 'No. No, absolutely not.'

'You're going to have to explain. The more you tell me the less sense you are making.'

'It was Hannah – Frannie knew her from back home. Her mama cleaned their house and sometimes Hannah came with her to play with Frannie. Hannah said Frannie could get a hot meal and a night's sleep in her hut. She told the other gals that Frannie was passing for white and got caught and now she's in big trouble.'

'And they believed that?'

'Yeah. Hannah told them she knew Frannie's parents and that was good enough for them. And she wasn't lying about that. Hannah told them that Frannie needed someplace to stay until she could get hold of her brother to come take her home. That's why I need your help.'

'OK. I'll listen to what you want me to do, but first, I need another cup of coffee. How about you?'

'Sure. Thanks,' Marvin said and followed me into the kitchen.

While I refilled our cups, I asked, 'Two days ago? On Wednesday?'

'Yeah, that's right.'

'I wonder if that's why the switchboard was down for the past two days.'

'I don't know but I thought it might be.'

'And I heard a couple of Calutron girls complaining about their rooms being searched.'

'I'm sure that's because of Frannie. Good thing I got her out of my room. I imagine the men's dorms will be next.'

'How long, I wonder, before they get to the hutments?'

'I figured the last place they'd look for a white girl is in the hutments. But they'll get there eventually. That's why we need to act fast.'

I handed him his cup and said, 'OK, sit down and let me hear what you think I can do.'

'Everybody – well, most everybody – in our group will do most anything you propose. Me? I can do OK one-on-one but presenting in front of a table full of other scientists, my tongue would be bound to get tied around my eye tooth. But you – you can do it. You are a proven commodity. So, I want you to convince them to help me find the proof that it was that scientist, not Frannie, who's guilty of treason.'

'How certain can you be that she didn't just fashion this story to get out of trouble?'

'She's not very smart, Libby. And she doesn't have much of an imagination. I mean, when we were kids, she never even saw animal shapes in the clouds until I stood right behind her, pointed her head in the right direction and outlined them with my finger. And no matter how many times I showed her the Orion constellation in the sky, she could never find it on her own. She struggled in school and—'

'OK, Marvin, I get it,' I interrupted. Was he underestimating her? 'Don't forget, some people not considered intelligent in the traditional sense can still be very crafty. And manipulative. Survival instincts can bring out superior performance in anyone.'

'But she's just not that kind of a girl. She's not a traitor,' Marvin pleaded.

'I know you don't think so. I know you want to believe her story. But fact is, you grew up with the girl, you cannot be trusted to be objective. You know that.'

'But I need your help. I need everyone's help. Please don't turn me away.'

'I'm not, Marvin. But I am saying this: I need to talk to her face-to-face. I need to observe her and draw my own conclusions. Can you make that happen?'

'Yeah. I think so. But I don't think it would be a good idea for you to go to the hutments.'

'No, I don't either. So, where?'

'It'll have to be out in the woods. Every day, just before the sun comes up, Frannie sneaks out into the woods. There's a dilapidated shed out there where she hides out for the day. Hannah gave us a potato chip tin from the kitchen to keep crackers and apples and bread safe from animals overnight so Frannie has something to eat during the day. Then, after it grows dark, she goes back to Hannah's place to sleep and get her only hot meal of the day. I'm supposed to meet her there after work tomorrow. I guess that's today now. Could you come with me?'

'If I can get away, I will try, Marvin. Find me or send word to me when you're ready to leave.'

'Probably won't be till late since most days I put in ten or twelve hours right now. But Frannie won't leave the shed and go to the hutments until after I get there.'

'OK, go home, Marvin. Try to get some sleep. We'll both need it to get through the coming day.'

That advice was easier to give than to follow. The idea of another hostile encounter with the military and the administration made me feel uncomfortable, anxious and a little frightened. What if Marvin was wrong about his cousin? If I talked to Frannie Snowden and didn't believe her, what would that do to Marvin? How would he handle it? Would he try to push the issue with the Walking Molecules without my support? Would the cohesiveness of the group crumble under the assault of the inevitable conflict between me and Marvin?

I calmed down enough to take my mind off of the Marvin/Frannie worries, but as soon as I started to slide into slumber, my eyes popped open and the bigger worry intruded. Spies here? That was obviously true. Whether Frannie was telling the truth or simply trying to hide her guilt by pointing at someone else, there was at least one spy here – maybe more.

Could I have talked to that person? Laughed with him? Danced with him? Often the biggest evils were hidden behind a facade of commonplace banality. Traitors, monsters and criminals didn't come with identification tags.

Was Frannie really the Dumb Dora, Marvin thinks she is? Or was that just a mask she wore to conceal a devious, deceptive mind? And when I met her – when I talked to her – would I be able to tell the difference? I know my Aunt Dorothy could do that but I didn't know if I'd absorbed enough instinct from my perceptive, intuitive relative to make a sound judgment on my own.

FOUR

The strange night had worn me out. I didn't feel the least bit rested as I trudged to work that morning. I could have caught the bus but didn't want to wait for it. So, of course, the bus passed me on the way and got there long before I did. Usually, I liked the long walk because it gave me time to think and transition into lab mode, but this morning, I wasted the time fretting about Frannie and spies. As Y-12 came into sight, I struggled to inject optimism into my thoughts. If I didn't put on a good front, I'd drag others down with me.

In January, they'd all celebrated the resolution of the problem of oil contamination and arcing in the coils only to face another series of problems that at times seemed insurmountable. Now at the end of May, four Calutrons were running and producing enriched uranium. I stopped myself in my tracks – I couldn't ever say that word out loud so better not even think it. Enriched tube alloy.

General Groves said he needed them to produce one kilogram of ninety percent pure tube alloy each month. Sadly, by the end of February, we only had 200 grams – a lousy forty teaspoons full of the pretty teal crystals and its purity was at a lowly twelve percent. It seemed like a waste of the gold that lined the small nickel shipping container. Not exactly awe-inspiring. I prepared it for shipment anyway, delivering down to the bunker with an armed guard by my side. Wherever it would go from there, I didn't know. But I was well aware that the scientists on the other end were screaming for some amount of product – any amount – to use in pursuit of the gadget. Although I was working behind the scenes with some of the top scientists in the nation, I used a language foreign to the scientific nomenclature I had grown accustomed to at the universities. Product. Gadget. It was as dumb-sounding as the name of my little merry band of scientists, the Walking Molecules. At least, the guys had an excuse; they had been tipsy when they named it.

We had all worked long hours in the lab and on the floor to modify the Calutron that became functional in January and bring the new ones into production and improve their efficiency. The last sample product I ran through the spectrometer generated excellent results. I didn't really trust it, though – it seemed too good to be true. After weighing, analyzing and extrapolating, the result was sixty percent. I hoped it was right and it was sufficient progress to delay any plans G.G. might have to pay a visit and personally address the issue of the lagging quality and quantity. I knew if he came, he'd seek me out for answers and solutions. Unfortunately, I had no confidence that the ninety percent product he wanted was even possible to achieve.

The sense of urgency infected me today as it did every day when I entered the building after flashing my badge at the guard. I didn't dawdle but went straight to my lab station and plunged into my work. I was too intently focused to notice anyone else's arrival but when I came up for air, I sensed that something didn't seem right. A solemnness hung in the air like an oppressive storm cloud. The scientists all looked listless. Where was the usual hustle and bustle? Had something catastrophic occurred while I wasn't paying attention, did the race tracks fail again?

'OK,' I said in a raised voice, 'what did I miss? Do we have another Calutron problem?'

'No,' Gregg said with a sigh. 'The equipment's fine.'

'Then why all the sad sacks?'

Tom said, 'It all seems so futile.'

'Winning the war seems futile to you?'

'No, thinking we can do anything that would lead to that outcome. We're just sitting here trying to improve our production for a purpose we're not allowed to know and the only thing we do know is that we're obviously failing miserably.'

'Failing? Why do you say that?' I said, biting my tongue to keep from blurting out the news of the vastly improved quality and quantity, because I knew Tom was not considered to have a 'need to know' for that information. I'd come to hate that phrase.

'We're working long hours and everyone keeps telling us to pick up the pace, work harder, make more. No matter how hard we try, it's never enough. Give me one good reason we shouldn't all just give up.'

'Because we need to keep pushing ourselves to do our best day after day, because if we don't, the Germans will clearly surpass us. We don't really know what the end result of their endeavors will be, either, but I, for one, don't want to find out.'

'Sometimes, I hate this place. It's already taken the life of one little girl here. How many more have to die before we realize we are wasting our time?' Tom snapped back.

'Tom, don't tell me you're still agitated about little Virginia Elam? Aren't you over-reacting?' I asked. 'That little girl was killed in a traffic mishap. Accidents happen everywhere. Children die needlessly – sure it's sad, but we don't have a monopoly on tragedy here in Oak Ridge.'

'No, we don't. But we do have a monopoly on secrets, that's why what's happening here makes it so much worse. Somewhere that little girl has grandparents – people who love her. Were her parents allowed to tell their family she was gone? Did they make Virginia's parents lie to their own parents to cover up her death? Or will they just forbid them from communicating with family outside of the fence? If they disobey, will they be locked up until after the war? The army doesn't ask questions, they just make assumptions.

'And the underground network of informers – the creeps – seem to be everywhere. I think some of them are just people like us who've been convinced it's right to spy on their neighbors, but I think there are others who are pretending to be just regular folks but who are really working for the FBI or some agency like that. It's not just that we have to keep government secrets, we have to keep our own lives secret from everyone out there who cares about us.

'Did you know if you died, no one would send your Aunt Dorothy a death certificate explaining why? I'm not even sure they'd let her know you're deceased. Maybe, she'd just stop hearing from you. Poof! You're gone. If she inquired, she'd probably be investigated. She won't know until after the war. If that ever ends – and the pace we're keeping here sure isn't going to do it.'

That kind of attitude was exactly what worried me; we couldn't allow it take root and grow into apathy. We all had to keep working hard and with determination. 'Tom, we've faced problems before and solved some of them. Things aren't perfect but everything is constantly improving. We can lick these problems if we keep our focus.' I walked over to Gregg's station and motioned Tom to follow. 'Listen, guys, maybe all of our crazy little group should share family contact information so if something happens to one of us, we can get the word out. I know it would be a risk but it's one I'm willing to take.'

'It's worth some discussion, Libby. Why don't you bring it up in the next meeting? I don't think Tom will have an objection, will you, Tom?' Gregg said, teasing him about his notorious reputation for fighting against every new idea anyone ever presented in the group.

'Funny, Gregg,' Tom sneered. 'No, I won't object. And Libby should be the one to bring it up – family concerns are women's business, aren't they?'

I rolled my eyes. 'Fine. Let's get back to work. We've got a war to win and we're not going to do that standing around and grumbling like a bunch of gouty old men.'

Tom opened his mouth to snap off a reply, but Gregg's laugh at my comeback stopped him. I was smiling as I returned to my station. One day, someone will get through to that Neanderthal.

FIVE

.

I got word from Marvin just before seven that evening that he was leaving in five minutes. After the previous night's interrupted sleep, there wasn't much of me left to do anything for anyone. All I really wanted to do was go home, play with my kitten and go to bed. I'd love to wriggle out of my commitment to meet Frannie that night, but the situation was volatile and procrastination could be fatal. I wrapped up what I was doing as quickly as I could and joined Marvin out on the boardwalk ten minutes past the hour.

As we walked through town, I heard Marvin nattering about his cousin's good character but I wasn't paying much attention to anything he said. I worried, again, about my ability to tell the truth from a lie, to ask the right questions, to pick up on any telling verbal clues or facial expressions. I probably was most concerned that Marvin was right and Frannie was nothing more than a pawn in a sinister game. The security of the project did not have to override the needs of the individual, but often it did. Innocence could become irrelevant once you got caught in the jaws of the security bureaucracy.

Stepping off the beaten track, Marvin turned to me and put a finger to his lips. 'Ssssh,' he said as if I were the one talking non-stop. Entering the wooded area, we followed a barely visible animal trail. I doubt I could have ever found the shack without Marvin leading the way. It sat in what was once a clearing, but now it was filled with scrubby brush and young trees, one of them so close to the rickety wooden structure that it looked as though another two seasons of growth might force the little building to lean over to one side or maybe collapse all together.

'Wait here,' Marvin said. 'I need to let Frannie know about you before she sees you, gets scared and maybe runs off.'

I listened to the quiet murmur of voices while I swatted at pesky mosquitos trying to dine on my arms and legs. Finally, the door of the shack, missing the bottom hinge, scraped and wobbled back open. Marvin stuck his head out and waved me inside.

It took a moment for my eyes to adjust to the gloomy light in the dark cabin. When they did, I spotted Frannie standing near a corner, her brow furrowed like a fresh plowed field, her teeth nibbling on her fingernails. Frannie's curly brown hair was poking in every direction and her skirt and blouse were soiled and disheveled with little bits of dried leaves sticking to nearly every inch from her head to her toes. For an awkward moment, none of us said anything.

Marvin spoke first. 'Why don't we all have a seat?' he said as he scooted the potato chip can and two apple crates into a triangle.

I sat on the nearest box, eager to get off my feet. Marvin was next and then Frannie approached the remaining can with obvious trepidation and eased her way down, appearing as tense as a performer with severe stage fright. Watching her, I still wondered if it was all one big act.

'Frannie,' I said, 'Marvin told me your story but I'd like to hear it in your own words.'

'Yes, Frannie,' Marvin said. 'I told her about Hansrote approaching you and—'

'Please, Marvin,' I interrupted, raising a hand. 'I really want to hear it from Frannie.'

Frannie looked at me with pursed, quivering lips and then turned her gaze to her cousin. Marvin nodded. Frannie exhaled a huge sigh.

As I listened to her retell the story, I paid attention to all the details to make sure everything lined up with what I had heard from Marvin in the early-morning hours. I didn't take my gaze off her face as I searched for any little sign of duplicity. I saw nothing to cast doubt on her honesty. She made eye contact with me, but didn't hold it for overlong, she looked up and away as she recalled the events she shared.

When Frannie finished her tale, she asked, 'Can you help me?'

Still, I hesitated to make a commitment. How did I know it wasn't one big, clever lie? Then I saw the tears welling in Frannie's eyes – a frightened young woman or a good actress? It was so

hard to tell. 'What do you do in your spare time, Frannie?' I
asked, hoping an unconnected, seemingly harmless question might
catch her off-guard if she was prevaricating.

'I like to go dancing and shopping and to the movies,' Frannie
said with a sniff.

'I mean, now. What do you do while you're passing the time
out here?'

'I try not to get scared.'

'You don't have anything to read?'

Frannie jumped up off the chip can and dug around inside of
it, pulling out a raggedy copy of *Photoplay*. 'I have this,' she
said with a lopsided grin. 'I've read it cover to cover a few times.
I sure hope you can fix things up for me so that I can get back
in time to see the new Cary Grant movie,' she said opening to
a page with his picture on it. 'I haven't seen him since *Bringing
Up Baby* came out before the war. And he's just so dreamy,' she
added as she pulled the tattered magazine tight to her chest, a
gesture that had Dumb Dora written all over it.

When I asked Frannie if she would like a book to read, Frannie
crinkled her nose and shook her head. 'I don't read books – not
since I got out of school. But I sure would like the new issue of
Photoplay or maybe *True Confessions*.'

Oh dear, she probably was as vapid as Marvin insisted. The
possibility that she was indeed a duped innocent shifted to
the top of the list. I tried not to allow my instinctive distaste for
her choice of reading material to show on my face and said, 'I'll
see if I can pick them up for you before I come out to see you
again.'

'When?' Frannie said.

'I don't know right now. I just know I certainly will need to
ask you some questions after we start digging into this.'

'You're going to help Frannie?' Marvin interjected. 'Will you
present it to the Wal—?'

'Don't name it, Marvin, please,' I interrupted him quickly.

'What?' Frannie asked.

'The less you know about who we are, the safer we all will
be, Frannie. I'm sorry, but right now, you do not have a need to
know,' I said, cringing at my own words.

'But you believe her, right? And you'll help her, right?' Marvin begged.

I paused for a moment. The two of them were very convincing and the Marvin I knew didn't have a dishonest or devious bone in his body. 'Yes, I will, unless and until I learn something that changes the equation. If the group disagrees and don't want to take it on and it's only you and I, I won't give up without solid answers. It may be harder for the two of us alone but we can do it if necessary. We can't allow Hansrote to frame Frannie and continue his undercover treachery undetected.'

SIX

The next morning, I pulled a small sample from the latest batch of green salt and ran the test again. Much to my surprise, the end result indicated that we'd reached a sixty-five percent concentration of the desired product. I found it hard to believe so I did the mathematical calculations one more time. At the current speed of production, I'd have another 200 grams ready to go – I might even be able to send two shipments in June. The progress was exhilarating yet I knew that G.G. would not be satisfied. We were still far away from his goal in both quantity and quality.

However, I could not answer the question of whether or not G.G.'s ninety percent purity demand was an essential one because I did not have any data on the latest research by Fermi, Oppenheimer and all the other scientists at the forefront. Was it their conclusion that it was a critical level needed to initiate the chain reaction that would make a war-ending weapon of destruction? Or was the figure just an approximation by the military brass? Worst of all was that it was a question I was not comfortable asking in a straightforward fashion because I'm not even supposed to be thinking about the ultimate 'function of the gadget'.

The need for a compartmentalized security structure was frustrating but G.G.'s rule was clear: 'Each man should know everything he needed to do his job and nothing else.' That thinking seemed to be in step with military structure but definitely defied the basic character and values of most scientists – sharing of ideas and solutions was an integral part of our world. When it was stifled, the science – and the scientists' morale – suffered. How do we combat that and maintain a productive environment?

Maybe I could get clearance to give a progress report to the chemists. Those defeatist attitudes I'd seen in the lab this week would vanish in the bright light of positive numbers. I'd probably be smacked down for even suggesting it, but I had to try.

As usual when he wasn't in a meeting, Charlie Morton, the head of the Analytic Chemistry department, left his office door wide open. I rapped my knuckles on the glass pane before stepping across the threshold.

Charlie looked up from his desk, his smile contradicting the furrows on his brow. 'Good news? Or another problem?'

'Good news,' I said, returning his smile.

'I think I heard some hesitation in your response, Libby. I guess it's not unadulterated good news.'

Charlie and I had reached a fragile peace after his refusal to stand up for me earlier this year. After events turned in my favor, he seemed to want to decipher my thoughts and uncover my unspoken words. The way he studied me was unnerving at times. And he was usually right, just like he was now. Frankly, I wish I weren't so easy to read.

'Yes, Charlie, I do have two related concerns.'

'Give me the good news first.'

'My analysis of two recent samples put us at sixty and sixty-five percent respectively. And the quantity of product seems to be rising at the same rate as the quality.'

'Excellent, Libby. But what's bothering you?'

'The first thing is a question I don't believe you can answer but I will trust you enough to ask.' I saw a look of protest on his face over my obvious doubts about his reaction but waved them away as if they were irrelevant. 'I don't know if the goal of ninety percent is a figure the military pulled out of a hat or if it is an essential quantity based on scientific research.'

'You're right, Libby, I can't tell where the number originated, either. Even if I knew the answer to your question, I probably couldn't tell you. But this time, I have no idea. But no one but the two of us will know that you asked. What's your other concern?'

'Morale, Charlie. There's a negative mood in the lab – a sense of futility.'

'Who's the instigator?'

'Charlie!'

'Sorry I asked.'

'We're scientists, Charlie. It's natural for all of us to want to find answers, but we're working in a vacuum. We are betraying our basic character as scientists. We can't evaluate data we don't have. I want to tell the chemists about our progress. I'm certain it would restore hope.'

Charlie was shaking his head before I finished the last sentence. 'We can't be totally open. You know that. We do that today, we're gone tomorrow. And we might take some of the others with us.'

My shoulders slumped and I turned away.

'Wait, Libby. I'm not saying that you can tell them nothing.'

I faced him again. 'What are you telling me then?'

'Let me think a minute . . .'

'You want me to come back later?'

'No. Just a minute,' Charlie said as he closed his eyes and lowered his head.

It seemed to me, at that moment, Charlie was trying to find a way to tell me not to say a thing to anyone without getting me angry. When he spoke, it wasn't what I'd been expecting.

'Okay, Libby, tell the chemists that we have had a substantial improvement in quality and quantity – just don't give them any numbers. And tell them it's not to be repeated outside of the lab. We don't have any creeps in there, do we?'

'Oh. I don't think so, Charlie. But, although I can vouch with certainty for some of them, I can't for everyone. Honestly, I think it's worth the risk.'

'Will that satisfy you?'

'You know those guys. Most of them trust numbers more than words. Without precise information some of them won't be happy, but hopefully enough of them will to make a difference to the overall attitude.'

'If anyone is credible with that bunch out there, Libby, it's you. Since Thanksgiving, you've been surprising them all in one way or another. Lieutenant Colonel Crenshaw might have ordered silence but some news spreads organically despite admonitions to the contrary.'

It wasn't exactly what I'd wanted, but I'd accept it. With the matter of Frannie Snowden hanging over my head, I needed all the friends I could get.

SEVEN

Tonight was our regular meeting of the Walking Molecules at Joe's. I decided to unleash my news about our progress to the group first and then to the rest of the chemists the next day. I was also going to bring up the issue of exchanging our private information about next-of-kin, as well as the Frannie Snowden dilemma; it was this which required good moods all round.

When I arrived in the back room, Teddy, Joe and Marvin had already placed an order for three pitchers of Barbarossa beer and ten glasses. The waitress returned with Rudy, Gregg, Gary, Stephen, Dennis and Tom right on her heels. Everyone passed around the pitchers and filled their glasses.

Gregg called the meeting to order and said, 'Libby gave me three items for our agenda tonight but I haven't heard from anyone else. Is there something I need to add?'

'Three?' Tom sniped. 'Is she in charge?'

'Tom, you can add anything you want and we'll discuss it,' Gregg said.

'With a full schedule already, I imagine anything I suggest could be tabled for the next meeting,' Tom grumbled.

Gregg looked as if he were getting rather annoyed with Mr Negativity so I jumped into the fray. 'Tom, two of my items should be short and sweet – one is just an announcement and the other is the exchange of information that you suggested I bring up.'

Tom rolled his eyes, slouched back in his seat and, in a voice dripping with sarcasm, said, 'I yield the floor, Madame Chairwoman.'

I ignored his dig and moved straight to the next-of-kin name and phone number exchange first. After summarizing the need to inform our families in the event of a traumatic event, I asked if anyone had any questions.

'What idiot would have questions?' Tom asked.

Gary, Tom's little disciple piped in, 'Yeah, you're the woman. This is family stuff. You're supposed to know best about that.'

I ignored their snide attitudes and let Gregg take the lead. 'If there are questions, ask them. Otherwise, let's vote.' He looked around the table. 'Hearing no discussion, raise your hands if you're in favor.' Nine hands went up in the air immediately. Gary shot his upward after making sure Tom's was already in the air.

'That settles it,' Gregg said. 'Who will be the keeper of the document? I don't think Teddy or Libby should since they are the two individuals in the group who have come to the attention of the military and civilian authorities.'

There was a dead silence in the room as everyone looked down into their glasses or on the table. I was beginning to understand the military policy of ordering a soldier to volunteer. 'Guys, this is not a huge responsibility,' Tom pleaded.

Joe spoke first. 'I think it should go to one person who is responsible for making a copy and giving it to you, Gregg, as a precaution.'

'Built-in redundancy?' Tom mocked. 'Joe, you really think it's something someone would want to steal?'

'No, Tom,' Joe said. 'I for one care about my family and want them to know if anything untoward happens to me. But what if the keeper of the document was the one with relatives that need to be contacted, what then?'

Tom shrugged his shoulders and said, 'Are you offering to do it?'

'Yes,' Joe said, 'I am.'

'Well, that's settled,' Gregg said. He'd obviously anticipated that outcome because he produced and passed around a piece of paper divided into four columns with headings for name, relative's name, phone number and address. He filled in the top line with a flourish and passed it along to the next guy. 'Libby, are you ready for item number two?'

'Yes,' I said with a nod. 'Gentlemen, I am proud to announce that we have made excellent progress in producing vast improvements in quality and quantity of the product.'

'What does that mean?' Dennis asked.

'It means that since March our purity is higher and our quantity is greater.'

'How much higher?' Teddy asked.

'How much more?' Gregg added.

If I could tell anyone in the group, Teddy and Gregg were the first two I'd pick. But I couldn't say anything about the numbers. I looked down at the table, took a swallow of beer and saw nine faces staring at me, waiting for answers. 'I'm very sorry but I don't have clearance to say anything but that the increases are significant.'

'Have we hit the goals – whatever they might be?' Tom asked.

I wasn't sure if I was crossing a line but I answered anyway. 'Not yet.'

'Can we believe you, based on that vague response?' Tom pushed.

I closed my eyes trying to think of some assurance I could make but before anything came to mind, Teddy spoke. 'Tom, when Libby was in a lot of trouble, she didn't spread the blame around. She kept your name – everyone's name – to herself. If you can trust her to stand up to the powers that be, you can trust her for anything.'

God bless, Teddy, I thought. He's been so persistent and I've been so prickly. I refused to go out with him more than once a month and still he stands up for me. I told him I wasn't certain that I was ready for a serious relationship and yet, he's always there when I need him. I knew I wouldn't have his patience if the shoe was on the other foot. I valued my friendship with him and I was attracted to him, but I had to feel confident that he wouldn't want to stifle my independence or interfere with my career before I'd make any commitment to him. He'd passed every test I'd thrown his way but still, I wasn't there yet. After his little speech, the room went quiet.

Then Gregg brought the issue to an end. 'Well, it is good news. Excellent news. We probably won't know how good it is until after the war and we're going to have to live with that and keep pushing to improve. Libby, you have something else?'

I glanced at Marvin who looked like he might be sick at any moment. He gave me a pleading look and I began. I explained the story of Marvin's cousin Frannie from beginning to end with Marvin nodding his head every time I glanced in his direction. I wrapped up by saying, 'What I am asking from all of you is help to get to the bottom of this situation. If Frannie is as inno-cent as I believe – and Marvin believes – if she is, we need to help to prove it. We need to learn everything possible about Dr Hansrote and anyone else that might appear in his orbit. We need to unmask him for the security of the project and for justice for Frannie. Will you help?'

Tom snickered, 'What are you, Libby? The patron saint of lost causes?'

'That would be Saint Jude, Tom,' Joe chimed in.

Tom rewarded him with an overly dramatic eye roll. 'You have an answer for everything, don't you, Joe?'

'Not really, Tom. In fact, right now, I have a question.'

'What's that, Joe?' I asked.

'Actually, I wanted to ask Marvin. Do you know your cousin well?'

'We lived in the same block growing up, so yes.'

'As an adult, Marvin. Do you know her now?'

'I'm not sure if I'd consider her an adult yet, Joe. She's just twenty years old and a very immature twenty at that. But yes I do.'

'Do you have any doubts about her story?'

'No,' Marvin said, shaking his head.

'Libby, how about you?' Joe said, turning in my direction.

'You know me, Joe. I'm a scientist just like the rest of you. I doubt everything I cannot run through a mass spectrometer and weigh on the balance beam. I can't do that with Frannie Snowden. So, yes, I have some doubts and I analyzed them seriously before presenting this problem to all of you. But know this: whatever the group's decision, I will accept it. Without your assistance, it will be more difficult, but Marvin and I still plan to work on verifying her claim and clearing her name.'

'That's good enough for me. I'm in,' Joe said.

'Me, too,' Teddy echoed.

'Are we ready to vote then?' Gregg asked.

Positive murmurs went around the table.

'I'll go first,' Gregg said. 'I propose that we help Libby and Marvin gather the facts and pursue this matter. All in favor raise your hands. Eight hands shot up without hesitation. Eight pairs of eyes turned toward the two hold-outs. 'Tom, Gary, are you opposed?'

'I abstain,' Tom said.

'Yeah, me, too,' Gary echoed.

'Abstain?' Gregg asked.

'Why not,' Tom said. 'If this all blows to smithereens in our hands, I don't want to go on record voting for this plan. You don't need our votes to pass this, so what's the problem? And for that matter, what's the plan?'

'No problem at all, Tom,' Gregg said. 'What *is* the plan, Libby?'

Oh dear, I wasn't as prepared as I should have been. Stalling was my only option. 'I was hoping to get the group's input on formulating a course of action.'

'It seems pretty obvious to me,' Teddy said. 'We need to find out anything we can about Hansrote. Who he works with, who he works for, where he comes from, who he eats with, who he drinks with, if he's married, if he has a girlfriend, everything.'

'We're not supposed to ask questions about scientists – particularly not those up higher in the chain of command than we are,' Tom objected.

'Be subtle, Tom,' Gregg said. 'I know that's asking a lot of you, but try.'

'And remember,' I added, 'you're not asking about a scientist, you're asking about a spy.'

'Easy to say until you get caught,' Tom objected.

Angry, I said, 'Oh, for heaven's sake, Tom. Don't do a thing if you don't want to help. Just remember that, if they come for you next.'

'That's why we keep a lady in the group. We need some dramatic element to make us complete,' Tom sneered.

'Oh, put a lid on it,' Teddy snapped.

'I'll tell you what I plan to do, Tom,' Rudy said. 'I'm going to say that Hansrote asked a friend of my sister for a date and I was checking to make sure he wasn't married or trouble.'

'What if they ask for the girl's name?' Tom asked.

'I shrug my shoulders and say, "How do I know? It's my sister's friend. They all look like pests to me." And if you don't have a sister, say a cousin or say somebody you met at a dance, anything.'

The room fell to silence again. After two minutes, Gregg said, 'Okay. How about another round so we can drink a toast to our newly improved product?'

The boys all cheered while I fretted. I hoped I hadn't dragged them into a situation that would prove the undoing of us all.

EIGHT

I spent the following morning bent over the desk running equations and working out calculations trying to find a solution to maximize the quality of the production. When I finally pushed away from the desk, the lab was nearly empty. I looked at my watch and realized it was lunch time. Just knowing that made me feel instantly hungry.

Dashing into the restroom, I saw an envelope taped to the mirror over the sink. It was addressed to me and covered with Xs and Os. For a moment, I just stared at it, blinking my eyes, waiting for it to disappear. Then I tore it down, ripped it open and started to read.

> I hope the envelope didn't embarrass you too much. I figured if I said it was a love letter, it would be easier and safer to convince a secretary to leave it for you. The reason I thought this was necessary is that I am concerned about Marvin. He hasn't been in the lab this morning. No one seems to know where he is. Maybe he's sick today and I'm just being paranoid. But the coincidence of our talk last night and him not showing up this morning is making me nervous. Would you ask around and see if anyone in your area knows where he is?

It was signed 'Teddy'.

Oh, heavens. Maybe he is senselessly paranoid but that now makes two of us. I hope we're both being silly. In the cafeteria, I picked up my food and headed straight for Gregg's table. Sliding my tray into the one empty spot, I smiled at Gregg who responded with a quizzical look. I raised my eyebrows and I think he got the message. I was certain of that when he finished his lunch and just sat there as the others got up and left. He moved over to the seat directly across from me.

'Do you have something on your mind, Miss Clark?'

I grinned at him. 'I certainly do.'

'Tell me,' he said, planting his elbow on the table and resting his chin on his palm.

'Have you seen or heard from Marvin today?'

'No,' Gregg said, 'but why would I? He's in the other lab.'

'Teddy's over there, too. He said that Marvin didn't come to work today.'

'Is he sick?' Gregg asked.

I shrugged my shoulders. 'Do you know who he rooms with? All I know is that his first name is Jubal.'

'No. Maybe we should have gotten that information from everyone last night when we got the family contacts.'

'Teddy is concerned about the timing of his absence. Frankly, so am I.'

'It's probably too soon to panic but I'll ask around. The coincidence does not sit well with me, either.'

Returning to the lab, I shifted between working on solutions to our problems with the product and asking around about Marvin. Between me, Teddy and Gregg, we probably talked to every non-managerial chemist in Y-12. It was Gregg who found his roommate, Jubal Cain, a South Carolina boy with an accent so thick it made me sound like a Yankee. I imagine if he ever met a girl from Maine, they would need a translator.

Gregg introduced us and said, 'Jubal said that Marvin never slept in the room last night.'

'Are you sure?'

'Marvin said he was going to meet some of his pals at Joe's. When he didn't return, I figured he got ta drinkin' and couldn't get hisself back to the room or he coulda gone all out and met a girl at the bar for an excellent night.'

'He does that often?' I asked, wondering if I needed to reassess my image of him.

'Marvin? No. His idea of relaxin' is to drink one or two of those watered-down beers, but he never touches the harder stuff. And truth be known, I don't know if he's ever touched a girl, either. But even a blind hawg finds an acorn now 'n then,' Jubal said with a chuckle.

'If you see him or hear from him, would you tell him to come see me or Gregg just as soon as he can?'

'Will do. Y'all let me know if you find him first, awright?'

Gregg patted him on the back and said, 'Sure, Jubal.'

Jubal moseyed off – really there was no other word for it – with a deliberate, loping pace that looked right out of *Huckleberry Finn*.

'It's hard to believe someone who talks like that is actually a scientist,' Gregg said.

'Don't let the southern accents fool you, Gregg. We, southerners aren't all slow-witted illiterates.'

Gregg winced. 'Sorry, Libby, I forgot you were from Virginia. But you just don't sound that southern.'

'So, you were taken in by my Pennsylvania veneer, Mr Abbott?'

'Oh, there you go, it still does sneak out. How many syllables are there in "my"?'

'Oh, hush,' I said with a grin. 'You ain't heard nuthin' yet.'

'Al Jolson, 1927, from *The Jazz Singer*.'

I laughed out loud. 'I won't even ask why or how you know that.'

'It's a long story – I'll tell you after the war,' Gregg said with a wink as he walked away.

Yeah, right, like everything else. But maybe now it was about to come true. Maybe we were on the verge of invading France by the sea. Or maybe it's just a scare tactic the allies are using to distract the Nazis. Add another thing to the long list of information I do not need to know.

NINE

The moment I stepped outside at the end of my work day, I spotted Teddy pacing on the boardwalk running alongside the building. I walked up to him and he swooped me in his arms and whispered in my ear. 'One of the guards has been keeping a close eye on me. If he sees a romantic rendezvous, he'll forget about anything that made him suspicious. And besides, I like this,' he said as his lips met mine.

I had to admit I liked it, too. And I had to agree his cover was a good one. But still, it made me uneasy. I wasn't sure I understood all my feelings about him and I wasn't sure if I trusted any man to keep his word after he had a legal document in hand – my stepfather being a case in point. Until women's careers were considered as important as men's, making a marital alliance with any man was a gamble. *Why am I even going down this road?* I had put up enough barriers that he'd never go so far as to propose unless I cleared a path for him.

To continue the ruse for the soldier's benefit, I held his hand as we walked away from Y-12. He leaned towards me and whispered, 'I checked with the secretary. Marvin did not call in sick.'

'So he never came in all day?'

After Teddy shook his head, I updated him on what Gregg and I had learned from Marvin's roommate and asked, 'I wonder if he went out to Frannie's hiding spot.'

'Could you find your way there without him?'

'Maybe. I sure could try. But the sun's starting to set. We'd never get there before she left for the hutments tonight.'

'But if he's out there, he might stay there overnight.'

'Marvin? Not exactly the outdoorsy type. I never figured out how he managed to do the Dossett Tunnel dare to get into the group.'

'That was before my time, Libby, but I heard he chickened out the first time and begged and pleaded for a second chance and barely managed that. So, I guess he is a bit yellow, but that still doesn't explain why after we all agreed to help him, would he run off like that without a word to anyone?'

'I don't know, Teddy. The possibility that he disappeared of his own free will doesn't make any sense to me. But if he's not there and Frannie's not there, we won't learn anything.'

'All right. Tomorrow at daybreak. Why don't we try to find that little shack then? I'll meet you at your place.'

'Okay. See you then. Right now, I have to run to Town Square and see if I can pick up any magazines for Frannie and then I want to make it an early night. It might be a good idea if you do, too. If I can't find the hideout right away, we might get lost in the morning.'

'I'll walk you as far as Town Square. Once we get through this mess, I'd like to talk to you about what your plans are after the war.'

'I don't know when that will be, Teddy, and I have no idea where my career will take me after this job. There's no way I can make plans right now.'

'If the stories about an upcoming invasion onto the European continent are even part true, the war might be over sooner than we think. The project, the product and the gadget might be outmoded before we can get the job done. And if I am right about what I think the gadget is, the world would be a better place if we never accomplished what we are trying to do.'

'Teddy, don't say that out loud, again. There are creeps everywhere.'

'I wouldn't say it to anyone but you. Now that we are on the subject, I want you to know that although I do want to keep working in a lab after the war, it's not like I am motivated by ambitious career plans. It's just that I like that kind of work and I know I need to work – so that's it. If it came down to it and I got married to a woman with a career, I'd be willing to follow her anywhere she needed to go to make the most of it. I could get a job anywhere and it wouldn't bother me in the least if in doing so, I went down the ladder instead of up if it helped her succeed.'

I had to admit that was a surprise – a welcome one. I still wasn't convinced he'd stick with it when push came to shove, but maybe he would. 'I thought you said we'd talk about this after we got this problem with Frannie Snowden all settled.'

'I did. But then. Oh, horsefeathers, we're already at Town Square. I guess I'll see you in the morning then.'

'Yes, till then,' I said and surprised him more than a little when I landed a small kiss on his lips before heading off. I turned back once and saw him staring after me. The thrill of the current passing through me made my fingers and toes tingle when I caught sight of him just standing there, keeping his eyes on me as long as he could. I wiggled my fingers in his direction and took off for the shops. *Maybe Teddy, by the time the war is over, you'll have me convinced. Maybe . . .*

TEN

In the morning, I pulled on my Chippewa ranger shoes for the trek into the woods and packed my knapsack with nicer footwear for work, a few pieces of paper and a pencil, along with the magazines for Frannie. As an afterthought, I opened the box in the kitchen I call my treasure chest and pulled out one of the two remaining Hershey's bars my Aunt Dorothy had sent to me the month before. I suspected the half dozen she sent were black market buys but that wasn't a question I wanted to ask.

I'd no sooner stepped out of my front door when I saw two guys walking up the boardwalk in my direction. One was Teddy, whom I'd expected. The other was Gregg. I was not comfortable with both of them going to see Frannie; I thought she was going to be skittish enough with just one.

Gregg put my mind at ease when he reached me and said, 'Don't worry, I'm not coming along unless you think you need me for some reason. I just happened to meet Teddy on my way over here. I wanted to tell you that Marvin didn't show up at the dorm last night either. And you had said you were going out to see her again so I thought you might find my compass useful.'

'That's terrific, Gregg, I'm sure I will and the update on Marvin is very timely. I'm already worried about Frannie's reaction when I arrive with Teddy, so it's probably best that you don't join us.'

'I thought that might be a problem. Also, I thought if you guys are held up for some reason then I can cover for you in the lab,' Gregg said.

'I'm glad you'll know where we're going, Gregg,' I said. 'With Marvin missing, we should have thought about telling someone about our plans so if we get lost and wander around in the woods for a few hours, there won't be a panic. And with the compass in hand, I still might not find Frannie's hideaway, but I'll sure be able to get us back here.'

In just a couple of days, the growth on the weeds and bushes was astronomical. Several times I had to stop and get my bearings. There was one spot where Marvin and I had walked with ease, but now a blackberry bramble threatened to block the way. Teddy and I detoured around that and trudged forward. I hit one place where I made a decision to veer to the right, but in about fifty yards, it looked all wrong. We retraced our steps and went in the opposite direction.

We reached a point where I no longer could see even the vaguest of pathways. 'I did something wrong somewhere, Teddy.'

We both looked around in every direction but I saw nothing to indicate where we needed to go. Then Teddy pointed down the hill. 'Look, is that it? Did we circle around it?'

'Maybe,' I said, as we stumbled in toward the building. We took the most direct route which had us fighting vines, ducking branches and stubbing toes on rocks. We made enough noise for a herd of elephants, probably terrifying Frannie.

Once we were within twenty feet of the structure, I knew it was the right shack. I opened the rickety door and spotted Frannie huddled in a corner with wide, terrified eyes. She exhaled loudly when she saw me. Then, she bristled back and looked for an escape route. 'That's not Marvin!'

I reached towards her and patted her arm. 'It's okay, Frannie. It's Teddy. He's a friend of Marvin, too. Look,' I said, slinging the knapsack off my back. 'I brought you magazines and a special treat.'

She snatched the latest *Photoplay* and *True Confessions* out of my hands the second they cleared the bag. 'Thank you. Thank you. Thank you. I was getting sick of looking at that same old magazine.'

'I've got something else,' I said as I pulled out the Hershey bar.

Frannie's mouth dropped open and she looked about ready to drool. 'For me? Really?'

I placed the candy in her hand and she stroked it as if it were a baby bird. 'Can I open it?'

'Yes. It's all yours,' I said as I smiled at her delight.

She ripped through the outer wrapper, then carefully folded open the inner layer. She broke off a square with great care, stared at what was left, then, with great reluctance stretched it toward us and said, 'Would you like a piece?'

Teddy and I both shook our heads and she slid the chocolate into her mouth and moaned with delight. As she savored it, she took care to cover up the remainder and put it in her potato chip tin. When the last bit melted in her mouth, she sighed and said, 'Thank you, again.'

'Frannie, when did you last see Marvin?' I asked.

Her eyes squinted and she said, 'Why do you ask?' She looked as wary as a puppy encountering his first black snake.

'Tell me when, Frannie, and I'll explain.'

'I haven't seen him since you came out here with him – two, three days ago, I guess.'

'I was afraid of that,' I admitted. 'We were hoping he was out here with you. We haven't seen him since our group meeting two nights ago. We agreed to help him look into your situation and try to find evidence that Hansrote is the guilty one. We are worried because he hasn't been to his dorm room either. Where do you think he might have gone? Could he have gone home?'

'And leave me out here? I don't think he would do that. At least not unless he felt he had to get help for me, but you said that you were going to help him.' Frannie's eyes were darting in every direction. Her breath grew too fast, too shallow.

I wrapped an arm around her as she collapsed into my body. I made soothing noises as I stroked her hair. Once she showed signs of settling down, I said, 'You need to keep as calm as possible, Frannie. It might mean nothing at all. Teddy and I and the rest of the group are digging into the background of Hansrote. If we can get to the bottom of your problem, I'm sure we'll find Marvin, too.' I can't say that I was totally convinced of the latter but I tried not to show it.

Frannie let out a shuddering sigh, pulled back and asked, 'What can I do?'

'If I remember correctly, Hansrote had you memorize the number he was calling, is that right?'

Frannie nodded.

'Do you still remember it?'

'Yes,' she said. 'CA6-4410.'

I pulled a pencil and notebook out of my knapsack and jotted it down.

'You're not thinking of going through the switchboard to make that call, are you?' Teddy asked.

'No. I'll have to go into Knoxville. Maybe from that phone booth at the drug store on Gay Street. That phone is so busy, there's always a waiting line. No one will know who placed the call.'

'What will you say to whoever answers?'

'I'm hoping when I call, the person identifies the number in some way. I don't intend to talk to anyone.'

'You could ask for Raymond and see what happens,' Frannie suggested.

'I'll keep that in mind and see how it goes,' I said. It might be a good idea but then again, it could be disastrous. 'I'll try after work this evening. The car has been idle for a while, it needs to run.'

'I'm going with you,' Teddy said.

'I'd like the company, but that's not necessary.'

'Under the circumstances, I'd say it is.'

On that ominous note, Frannie burst into tears. 'You've got to find Marvin. He was an Eagle Scout. He worked very hard at it. And he's really smart. He would have left you a clue if something happened to him on his way out here. He earned a badge for that. I know he'd mark the trail. You've got to find the signs he left. You've got to find him. If you can't come out here, just go to the cafeteria and tell Hannah to tell me that my cousin is doing fine – then, I'll know. Okay?'

'Yes. We'll do that, Frannie. I really hate to leave but we need to get to work before somebody starts asking questions.'

I turned back once as we walked away and saw the forlorn young woman standing in the open doorway. She gave a feeble wave. I shot my hand in the air and we walked out of sight.

ELEVEN

After the end of our workday, Teddy and I piled into the 1932 Buick Coupe that I had on extended loan until my former roommate's brother Hank got back from the war. As we drove into town, I noticed that a newer black Buick was driving the road behind us. We parked and I saw that same car – or one very much like it – pulling into a space half a block back.

Inside the drug store, there were only three people in line ahead of me – that is considered lucky, believe it or not. Teddy and I chatted while we waited making sure that we did not touch on any topic that could label us as being from the city behind the fence. It was probably a futile gesture, though, since Teddy's accent was a dead giveaway that he wasn't a Tennessee boy. My voice could still pass for a southern girl who got her education up north – not something a good rebel gal would do, but still I wasn't automatically considered an outsider.

When I finally took a seat, I dialed the operator and asked for Manhattan CA6-4410. I deposited the amount of coins she instructed and soon heard a phone ringing far away. I heard the click of someone picking up the receiver at the other end, but no one spoke. After waiting for a moment, I said, 'Hello.'

Still no response. 'Is anyone there?'

I could hear breathing but whoever was on the other end said nothing. 'Raymond, are you there?' I asked.

'Who is this?'

Pulling a name out of nowhere, I said, 'Edith Thomas. Is that you, Raymond?'

I heard the sound of disconnecting and then dead air. I clicked the lever in the cradle several times until the operator came back on the line. Teddy handed me more change and I filled the phone and listened to it ring. That was all it did. Over and over. I held on until the operator said, 'Your party is not answering.'

I said, 'Thank you,' and ruefully heard the coins falling back out of the phone.

'Maybe it was a female voice that bothered him,' Teddy said. 'Let's come back tomorrow and I'll try the number.'

Sounded like a good idea to me. So did an ice cream soda. But when I looked over at the soda fountain, I saw a sign that read: 'No Sugar. No Coke. No Ice Cream.' All those ads Coca Cola put in magazines sure made their drink look like a part of everyday American life. It seemed as if every G.I. was walking around in foreign countries handing them out like there was an unlimited supply.

Teddy must have read my mind because he stretched an arm around my shoulders and gave me a squeeze. 'It can't be much longer before the war is over and everything is normal again.'

'Maybe,' I said. 'Then again, maybe after the war, what we learn to call normal won't be anything we would have recognized a few years ago.'

Emerging from the store, I saw a figure in a dark suit and fedora hurry away from the window and head straight for the black Buick. I pulled my car away from the curb and looked in the rear-view mirror. The Buick pulled out, too. I made a right at the first intersection and then turned right again at the next one.

'Where are you going?' Teddy asked.

'Look behind us. Do you see a black Buick?'

'Yes. Why?'

I made a last-minute left turn. 'Still behind us, isn't he?'

'Yes. What's going on, Libby? Do you think we are being followed?'

'Definitely,' I said. 'I thought I was just being paranoid when he was behind us all the way into town. I saw him fast-walk away from the drug store when we came out.'

'Did you see what he looked like?'

'No,' I sighed. 'Just a suit and a hat – nothing else. But it makes me even more concerned about Marvin. If we're being followed, maybe he's been nabbed.'

'If the military picked him up, there's no way for us to find out – unless you think Lieutenant Colonel Crenshaw will talk to you.'

'Ha! Yes, sure, Crenshaw will *talk* to me – and probably tell me one lie after another.'

'There's got to be something we can do, Libby. Marvin is one of us. We can't just forget about him.'

'Of course not. But, we have to find out where – the exact spot – he was last seen. When we get back, it'll be about the same time of night that Marvin and the rest of us left Joe's. We need to walk from there to his dormitory and talk to anyone we see along the way. Maybe somebody saw something that evening.'

The black Buick was still following us as we approached the gate. My stomach clenched tight as I feared I would once again be pulled from the car and taken for questioning. I didn't breathe easy until we sailed past with a flash of our identification cards. The car was still behind us.

I drove to Joe's and parked in the lot. The Buick parked several spaces away. We got out of our vehicle and did our best to appear relaxed and unworried. Entering Joe's, we moved toward a window and saw the man with his head down and brim pulled low over his brow walking our way. We rushed through the kitchen and out the back door.

Using other buildings for cover, we circled around until we could see the front of the bar. The man was there peering in the window, shifting his body from one side to the other. Then, he made the move I had hoped he would: he stepped up to the entrance, pulled open the door and slipped inside. I stifled the urge to run as we walked quickly down the hill and headed in the direction of the dorms.

'Do you think we lost him?' Teddy asked.

'Looks like it, but we can't assume he won't figure out what we've done, so keep your eyes peeled,' I said. 'I suspect though that he'll go back to his car and wait for us to return to ours.'

There were still a lot of people walking the boardwalk, some out for a casual stroll while others moved with more urgency. I approached a tall man wearing thick-lensed glasses while Teddy stopped someone else. 'Were you out here two nights ago?'

His eyes squinted and a frown replaced his initial smile of greeting. 'Why do you want to know?'

'It's my boyfriend,' I lied. 'We had a little spat and he stomped

off and I haven't heard from him in two days. I'm trying to find
out if he was meeting another woman. He's not as tall as you.
But his hair is about the color of yours and he has a very notice-
able nose and Adam's apple.'

The man grinned. 'Sorry. I was out here walking – I do most
evenings. But I didn't remember seeing any guy meeting a girl.
Good luck,' he said and walked away.

I tried the same line a dozen times with the same kind of
reaction and response before we reached the dormitory. Teddy
hadn't had any luck either.

We walked inside the door and a thin young man with freckles
and screaming carrot-top hair behind the front desk jumped up
and went bananas. 'No females allowed! You will have to leave.'

'I just wanted to ask a question.'

'Get out or I'll call and have you removed.'

We stepped out front and Teddy went in alone while I paced
the boardwalk. Teddy trotted out looking excited. 'Here's what
I learned. Marvin does live in this dorm—'

'We knew that,' I objected.

'Yes, but he didn't know we knew it. I didn't tell him Marvin
was missing or anything. I said you were his cousin and wanted
to leave a message for him. He said that would be okay if I
brought it inside – not you. He must have said that three times.
Anyway, I told him the two of you had an argument about a
family problem on Tuesday night and asked if he saw him
returning then. He said, 'Sure did. He came through the door
and there was a man right behind him.'

'What did the man look like?'

Teddy shrugged. 'He didn't know much. He said that he was
wearing a suit and a hat with a low brim that hid his face. I
asked if he heard anything they said and all he got were a few
words.'

'What words?'

Teddy blew out a big exhalation. '"Frannie" was one – Marvin
said that a couple of times. He also said, "I don't understand"
in a loud voice more than once. He thought Marvin looked very
upset but after a few minutes he left with the man.'

'I wonder if it was the same man who was following us tonight.'

'It had to be.'

'But was it spies or was it some secret security thing? We're going to have to go back to Joe's and if he's still there, we'll ask him.'

'Are you serious, Libby? That could get us hauled in, too.'

'We can't find out anything if we don't take any risks. And there's two of us and one of him – sounds like a good odds to me.'

'You'll do this with or without me, won't you?' Teddy said.

'Definitely.'

'Okay, I'm with you all the way.'

When we got back to Joe's, the black Buick was still parked in the same spot and I could see the man with the hat sitting behind the wheel, his head turned in the direction of our parking space. I headed straight for his car hoping he wouldn't see me approaching from the opposite direction of where I'd left mine. But he did. His head jerked back, then forward and the engine started when we were about twenty feet away.

I broke into a run but he peeled out of the lot before I could reach him. 'Hey. Hey. Wait. Wait!' I shouted. He continued driving away at a speed that made his Buick lurch from side to side as it encountered one mud hole after another on its way up the street.

TWELVE

I woke up Saturday morning with a sense of foreboding and a feeling of helplessness. Teddy and I decided an emergency meeting of the Walking Molecules was essential and both committed to trying to get everyone together at Joe's that night. But before that, we had to get through another long work day and make a run into town so that Teddy could call the number we got from Frannie. No time today to go out to see her, but hopefully she'd be occupied with her new magazines and not be too anxious about spending the day alone.

I drove Hank's car to work that morning so Teddy and I were able to take off for Knoxville as soon as we both finished in the lab. The whole drive into town, we worried about every vehicle moving in the same direction as we were. It got pretty funny when we pondered the possibility that a farm tractor that pulled out behind us was a reason for concern.

At the drug store, Teddy climbed into the booth and requested to be connected to the number in New York. Moments later, Teddy pulled the phone back from his ear when the receiver emitted an obnoxious sound. Then I heard the operator's voice. 'I'm sorry, sir, but that number is no longer in service.'

'But my sister called it yesterday. Did he forget to pay his bill?'

The operator repeated, 'I'm sorry, sir. That number is no longer in service. I cannot provide any further information.'

Teddy hung up and stared at me for a bit too long. The gray-haired woman next in line cleared her throat, getting our attention. 'If y'all want to stare into each other's eyes, could you please step outside the booth and let someone else make a call?'

Back in the car, Teddy said, 'Well, horsefeathers! The one solid piece of evidence we had to help Frannie just went up in smoke. We'll never get her off the hook.'

'Don't panic. The FBI, the police, all those people have ways of finding out where that phone was connected even after it's no longer in service. They'll be able to tie it to someone. It still matters. But now I wish I'd never called yesterday. I should have thought first and known a woman's voice might be unexpected and his reaction would not be predictable.'

'Too late to cry over spilled milk, Libby. Let's get to Joe's. Between all of us, we should be able to come up with something.'

Gathered around the table in a back room at Joe's, Teddy and I told the group the bad news about the phone number. Tom criticized me for what he called my Dumb Dora decision to place the first call and Teddy came to my defense. I interrupted before the confrontation could escalate. 'Did anyone find out anything about Hansrote?'

Joe spoke up first. 'He was a physics professor at Columbia University before coming here to Oak Ridge. He is married to Henrietta Rockefeller, a distant relative of the most prominent members of that clan, but she came with her own tidy fortune. Word has it that although Hansrote married her for her money, he is a bit resentful of it and driven to build a fortune of his own.'

For a moment, all I could do was stare at him open-mouthed and blink my eyes. How did he dig up that level of personal information? Then I, and everyone else, started bombarding Joe with questions more quickly than he could possibly sort out and answer. He held up his hands. 'Please. I can't understand anyone.'

Everyone quieted down after a final grumble from Tom. 'Libby,' Joe said, 'you first.'

'How do you find that level of personal information about a scientist here without getting hauled in for questioning?'

'That's easy. My older sister, Gertie, went to the same finishing school in Switzerland as Henrietta. I thought I recognized Hansrote's name the other day but didn't want to say anything until I talked to my sister.'

'Oh,' Tom sneered, 'so you're rich and mighty, too. I'm surprised you deign to sit at the same table with us and drink our peasant beer.'

Joe sighed. 'My family *had* money – and notice, please, the past tense. My sister is twelve years older than me. They lost almost everything in the crash when I was ten years old and spent a few years selling off the assets and trying to maintain an image of prosperity. It paid for my education, but by then, nothing was left but just enough to keep my parents housed and fed. I barely remember that other life.'

'You don't owe us any explanation of your past, Joe,' I said. 'Let's get back to the important questions – which are, I remind you all, about Hansrote. Is his wife here, Joe?'

Joe grinned. 'Her family still has their fortune and would not tolerate their society daughter living in the backwoods of Tennessee – or any other southern state for that matter.'

'Do you know when he left Columbia to come here? Or anything else for that matter?' Teddy asked.

'He studied at Princeton and got a doctorate in Physics. That's about it. Gertie said she could find an excuse to call Henrietta and see if she can learn more without being too obvious. I told her I'd let her know.'

'You never know which tidbit might be useful, Joe. I say it's worth a try. Does everyone agree?' Gregg asked.

Heads nodded around the room and Joe said, 'Consider it done. I should be able to call her tomorrow sometime.'

'Tomorrow – that brings up another concern,' I said. 'Marvin.'

'Have you heard from him?' Gregg asked.

'No. He still hasn't been seen by anyone that we asked. I think tomorrow is a good time for a hike to search for clues,' I said, bracing myself for objections.

True to form, Tom led the charge. 'Sunday is our only day off and you want to run around in the woods like chickens with our heads cut off? We don't even know where to start.'

'Yes, we do,' Teddy said. 'Libby and I saw Frannie yesterday and we can find the way there. We need to scour the trail out to the shack and see if we can find anything that gives us an indication of what happened.'

'Dumb!' Tom proclaimed. 'Didn't you say that Frannie was at the hutments after dark? It was late when we left the meeting and Marvin never made it to his dorm room. He wouldn't go to her hideout if she wasn't there. He went somewhere with a man he met in the lobby. We need to find out who that is and then maybe we'll know what happened to him.'

I laid a palm flat on the surface and placed the other hand

on top of it, as a reminder to remain calm. I leaned forward and asked, 'How do you propose we do that, Tom?'

'Well, we could – we might – well, you blew that chance didn't you by approaching him.'

I stared at Tom until he started to squirm.

'What possible reason would he have to go out to the shack with that man when Frannie wasn't there?' Tom asked in a nasty tone of voice.

'Let's try this scenario on for size, Tom,' I began. 'The man tells Marvin that Frannie is having a problem. Maybe he said that her ruse at the hutments blew up in her face. Maybe he said she was sick. Or she broke a leg. There are a score of possibilities for Marvin heading out there. Whatever the reason, perhaps he believed the man at first. It's possible that on the way Marvin got suspicious and went off in another direction. Frannie told me that Marvin was a dedicated Boy Scout who earned Eagle Scout honors. She is certain that he would have left a clue somewhere if he intentionally went the wrong way.'

Gary laughed with scorn. 'Sounds dumb to me.'

'Maybe not,' Tom said.

'Oh, maybe not,' Gary echoed.

'I say the earlier in the day we do it, the better,' Gregg said. 'All in favor of meeting up at first light and hiking out, raise their hands.'

Every arm reached for the air. 'Okay, Libby, we're all going. You're in charge of this expedition. Where do we rendezvous?'

THIRTEEN

Teddy and I met on the boardwalk in front of my house and set out while it was still dark. This morning, I packed one of my dresses, some undergarments, clean socks, and a pair of pajamas for Frannie whose clothing had definitely seen better days. I figured before the day was over, I'd find some time to go out to the shack. After arguing about possible locations last night, we'd decided against the Chapel on the Hill. Initially, the group leaned toward meeting there because every Sunday morning, a nearly non-stop rotation of services for different denominations took place at the church building. That meant that we could lose ourselves in the crowds going to and fro without raising any suspicions. That idea was dashed when Joe said, 'Personally, I don't want to wear a suit, a tie, and my good shoes to stomp off into the wilderness. I plan on wearing hiking boots, short pants and a knit shirt. I imagine I'd stand out in a group of folks wearing their Sunday finery.'

We eventually decided to meet at a massive, dying ancient oak on the edge of the forested area. As we'd planned, Teddy and I were the first to arrive. We waited, listening to the jubilant songs of wakening birds while the others straggled in muttering complaints about the heat and humidity that was already making the air feel sticky and uncomfortable.

'Everybody got a canteen of water?' Gregg asked. When he got positive responses all around, he said, 'Okay, Libby, lead the way.'

'Before we start, I think I can go straight to the shack without any wrong turns, but if we get close, I'm going to ask all of you to stop while Teddy and I approach Frannie on our own. We won't get that far, however, if Marvin detoured and we find his trail signs. We all need to be on the lookout for any path – no matter how faint – that diverges in another direction. And hope that if Marvin turned that way, he would have marked a tree or rock or something to indicate it. Also look for any dropped items that he may have used instead. Okay, this way.'

When we saw a thin deer trail off to the right, we stopped to examine the area thoroughly. After half an hour of finding nothing more than broken bottles and rusted spent shotgun shells, we moved back to the main trail. We repeated this procedure three more times with the same result. Then we approached a little alcove, about five foot deep in the trees and brush. The grass and weeds were flattened as if a number of people or animals had milled about in that spot. Scattered around were a large number of cigarette butts – scratch a herd of deer off the list.

I think all of us were contemplating the significance of the find but it was Gregg who asked the question: 'Does this have anything to do with Marvin? Could people have stood here waiting to ambush him?'

'If so,' Joe said, 'the man who brought him out here had to know they were lying in wait.'

'Should we push our way through the brush and see what's on the other side?' Tom asked.

'Nah,' Teddy chimed in. 'Look, none of those branches are broken and not enough time has passed for it to grow back that dense if they'd been knocked aside a couple of days ago. I think we ought to move up the main path. Seems like if it was some sort of trap, Marvin would have known it and that's why he would have moved them away from Frannie's hideout.'

After a little back and forth, we all agreed and trudged off in the direction of the shack. Tom headed down the next side path first and in a moment let out an Indian whoop. We all ran up to him. Following the length of Tom's pointing finger, we all saw a huge gouge in the side of a hickory tree. It was a sort-of straight line with a diagonal line on the end as if someone tried to cut an arrow into the bark but had to stop before he finished.

'That, lady and gentlemen, is a scout trail marker. And it looks fresh,' Rudy said.

'Oh,' Tom said in a snotty tone of voice. 'You're a Boy Scout, too.'

'Yeah, I was, Tom. You want to make something out of it,' Rudy said as he jutted out his chin and clenched his fists at his sides.

'I didn't say anything,' Tom protested.

Gregg cast a stern look at him and the friction of suppressed anger in his words seemed to echo in the hills. 'Just cut it out, Tom. We all heard your tone of voice. Someday you're going to have to address that chip on your shoulder. But right now, we need to find Marvin, so let's focus on that and be grateful that someone here knows something about trail markers.'

We walked further up that new path and just as I was thinking we were reading too much into what we had found, Teddy shouted, 'Eureka!'

At a fork in a path, pushed down on the tip of a young sapling set back two feet up the left fork, was a bold turquoise ring. 'Is that Marvin's?' I asked.

'It looks like one I've seen him wearing. I doubt if many people around here have one like it,' Teddy said.

'Yeah,' Dennis said, 'I asked him about it a few meetings ago. He said it was his grandfather's – that he'd picked it up out west, maybe in Arizona or someplace like that.'

We followed in the direction indicated by the ring and walked a narrow path through even denser undergrowth. The trail seemed about to close in on itself but then it opened up into an area that appeared to be an overgrown clearing similar to the one surrounding Frannie's shack. To our left, the remains of an old stone chimney and foundation indicated that someone once lived in this spot. To our right, was a flat area devoid of large trees as if it were once cultivated – the ground lay in the undulating curves of land once tilled. The sun shone full and bright on that section, almost blinding after the gloominess of the light in the denser woods.

We walked through the one-time settlement in silence and caught a whiff of something putrid in the air. 'Is that skunk?' Gary said. 'I've never smelled skunk before. It's really bad.'

I knew better. I'd smelled skunk on many occasions out on the farm. I'd also smelled dead cow in the field. This stink definitely reminded me of the latter. 'Something's dead around here,' I whispered.

Without a word, our motley crew clumped closer together. Although I knew that it was natural for many creatures to die from old age, disease and injury, and decompose in the open, I still worried that it was death from predation. Did a mountain lion take down a deer? And was it watching us right now, waiting to cull the weak from our herd? An uglier question kept knocking for admittance but I fought against acknowledging the possibility: did the clinging, oily odor mean we just found Marvin?

If that was the answer, I didn't really want to know. Still, I kept putting one foot forward after another, my eyes scanning across my field of vision from side-to-side. I spotted an anomaly up ahead – something seemed pressed into the trunk of a large arboreal oak. I took a few steps toward it and realized that pressed was not the right word at all – it was tied with rope, three loops of it, wrapped around the girth of the tree. I could not make myself take another step. I knew it had to be Marvin. I knew his death had to have been hard and ugly and long. I turned my back to the sight.

Teddy was right behind me, staring past my shoulder to the tree. 'Is that what I think it is?' Teddy asked.

'I think it is, Teddy,' I said.

He wrapped his arms around me and we just stood still. I imagined that he was feeling the same numbness that seeped through my body taking possession of my limbs and my throat, wrapping tendrils of fog around my ability to think and act.

I barely registered the others gather round us. I heard the susurration of their voices but could not distinguish their words. One by one, they quieted, too, as their gazes turned toward the tree. We stood there as if enchanted and turned to stone.

Then, Tom cast off the spell and moved toward the tree, picking up speed as he crossed the distance. Gregg, roused by Tom's actions, shouted, 'Stop!'

Tom cast a glance back over his shoulder and said, 'What if he is still alive?'

'The smell alone means that's impossible,' Gregg said. 'Back away. You could destroy evidence. We need to contact the authorities.'

'What authorities, Gregg? The military? Our local police force? I think we are off reservation property. What county are we in? Which authority do we tell? Who will believe that we had nothing to do with this?'

'Yeah,' Gary joined in. 'Why don't we just get out of here

and head back to civilization? It was creepy enough before we found a dead body.'

'Shut up!' Tom snapped.

Gregg looked at Gary with a disgusted curl on his mouth. 'Dead body, Gary? We didn't just find some dead body. That's Marvin. He's one of us.'

'But, Gregg,' Tom continued in a less combative tone, 'we may think that's Marvin, we may believe he is dead, but we don't really know that it's him from this distance and we cannot be certain that the smell is emanating from him without a closer examination. And we need to know what happened to him when he was tied to that tree. Was he left to die? Was he murdered outright? We're scientists. We need to respond like scientists, not like a group of scared little schoolgirls.'

'We're chemists, Tom, not coroners or doctors or pathologists or even biologists,' Gregg objected. 'We can't rush in and stomp all over the area like a bunch of well-meaning but misguided English majors.'

I'd heard enough. 'Tom is right,' I said. 'We need to confirm our assumptions before we even discuss when we report and to whom we report. And, Gary, if you want to go back, go ahead – it's fine. You helped us get this far and that's enough.'

'Go back? Through the woods? By myself?' Gary sputtered. 'You can't make me do that.'

I bristled at his reaction to my suggestion and had a childish urge to snap at him and call him names. 'That wasn't an order, Gary. This is not the military,' I said. 'I would ask all of you to stand back while Tom and I approach the tree and assess the situation.'

'Libby, no, you can't!' Teddy objected.

Is he trying to tell me what to do? I stared at Teddy until he looked away and swept an arm toward the tree as if inviting me forward.

The stench intensified exponentially with every step Tom and I took toward the slumped body. I battled my biological urge, forcing a suppression of my gag reflex, wishing my sense of smell would shut down in protest. Tom handed me a handkerchief he pulled from his back pocket and pulled his shirt tail up and across his mouth and nose. I placed the cloth in front of my face as he had done; it helped but only in a relative sense. The acid in my stomach continued to churn and my knees objected to every bend.

When we stood next to the body, I felt light-headed and repulsed. Tom bent down to look up into the face. 'It's Marvin,' he whispered. 'There's some blood and his eyes and nose look swollen. I don't know if that is an artifact of decomposition or if he was punched. Can you tell the difference?'

That question enabled me to shift my very human repugnance to a compartment and shut the door. I was here for fact-finding and that was what I would do. 'I doubt it, Tom. I have seen a lot of dead livestock and wild animals but very few deceased people,' I said as I bent over to observe. I shook my head. 'No, but look at his legs. They're bent at odd angles.' I reached down and ran a hand lightly down his pants leg. 'I feel a protruding bone.'

'And look at his fingers,' Tom added. 'Someone has bent them in directions they shouldn't go.'

'But what killed him?' I asked. 'There's some blood on the ground but not enough to cause his death.'

'That is a question that's totally beyond my field of expertise. However, I would say it was obvious that he was tortured before he died – and probably for information.'

'About the project? Or about Frannie?' I wondered aloud. 'By the spies, the military, some federal agency?'

'It had to be the spies, didn't it?'

'I want to believe that the spies did this to Marvin. But, Tom, in times of war, governments – even our government – have done much worse.'

'Including what we are probably working on down there in the lab,' Tom said through clenched teeth.

'Let's not get bogged down with philosophical and moral questions right now, Tom. We have to stay focused on this problem – Marvin is dead but a young woman's life is at stake, too.'

FOURTEEN

We sat down, forming a horseshoe-shape, as we perched on the jutting stones of the old foundation. The seats were uncomfortable but so was the conversation. The smell threw a putrid blanket over it all. Gregg suggested reconvening some distance away but to some of us, leaving Marvin's body behind to the vagaries of nature and the teeth and claws of predators felt too much like abandonment in a time of need.

I tried not to breathe too deeply as we talked. It took a little while but we rejected the ideas of doing nothing, of making an anonymous tip, or burying him on the spot. The next point of contention was which authority we needed to contact. After arguing about whether or not we were in Roane or Anderson County, we ruled out the locals. The next divisive point was whether to go to the military or the Tennessee Highway Patrol. The military proponents all feared we'd lose our jobs if we talked to outsiders, the other felt that unless we went to someone beyond the control of the reservation, Marvin's death would be covered up. I opted for a conversation with Lieutenant Colonel Crenshaw. I didn't particularly trust him, though, making me willing to be persuaded to the other side. The biggest issue of all was the timing.

Dennis summed up the 'what-are-we-waiting-for' faction best. 'Have none of you read any detective fiction? You ignore a body and everybody thinks you are responsible for the death. If we don't hurry to report our discovery, we will be blamed for it.'

'Yeah, but what about the possibility that the body would be moved while we are doing that? We've seen that happen in real life,' Rudy said, resurrecting the ghost of Irene Nance, the young woman whose murder we had investigated last winter.

'Somebody is going to have to stand watch and make sure that doesn't happen,' Dennis countered.

Gregg stepped in and said, 'If this is what we decide to do, we need to leave more than one person here. If we report to Crenshaw and someone attempted to move him after that, we'll know the military killed him.'

'Not necessarily,' Tom said. 'There is the possibility of coincidence or someone out there waiting for us to leave.'

'Which is why we can't leave someone here alone. A second person – or even a third one – increases the possibility that we'll get a report back.'

'We're forgetting something – someone – very important here,' Teddy shouted over the ensuing discussion about who should go and who should stay. 'Frannie Snowden. What about her? If Marvin was tortured to reveal her location, her safety should be of paramount importance to us. We plunged into this fraught situation to assist Marvin in clearing his cousin. Now that he's dead, are we just going to forget about her?'

Like the rest of the group, my attention had been diverted away from our promises to Marvin: find out everything we can to enable Frannie to come out of hiding. 'They could be going for her now,' I whispered, barely realizing I said it out loud.

Tom cleared his throat. 'She could be dead now, too.'

The heat generated by our animated discussion dissipated in a flash. I felt chills run up and down my arms despite the warm, muggy day. 'We need to check on her before we do anything else. And we need to figure out how to get her out of here without being detected.'

'She knows you and Teddy,' Gregg said. 'Why don't you go check on her while we stay here?'

'Do I tell her what happened to Marvin?' I asked. For a beat, no one said anything. Then there was a cacophony of divergent opinions. Some felt we had a responsibility to be honest with her. Others said we shouldn't tell her now while she was out here on her own. And once again, we were arguing about timing. For a moment I just listened and then I said, 'I, for one, think it would be cruel to tell her until we get her to someplace safe. She's already frightened and she has a lot of time on her hands. If we feed her fear, it will grow too big to contain and she's apt to do something foolish.'

Joe finally broke his silence. 'Bring her back, Libby.'

'Back here? You want her to see and smell her cousin's decomposing body?'

'No, no, no,' said Joe with a vigorous shake of his head. 'Hear me out. We can't let her see him. We can't make her panic before she's secure. Don't bring her all the way back here. Just to the cut off to this trail. On the way, tell her there's a dead, rotting deer carcass near where you're taking her. With that idea planted, she won't suspect anything else. While you and Teddy go to get her, we'll have to come up with a plan for where to hide her next.'

Grumbles of protest bounced around our horseshoe of plotters. 'Oh, come on. You know every one of us operates better under pressure. We can do this. When we put together a plan, half of us will stay here to watch over Marvin – the other half will meet you at the trail fork.'

'We don't have time to go through all the details,' Tom objected. 'We'll have a half-baked, sloppy course of action, full of risk.'

'The biggest risk, I think, is to leave her out here,' I said.

Gregg cut to the chase: 'Do we need any further discussion? Do we need a vote?'

'Even I can't find any fault with Clark's statement,' Tom said.

I looked over Tom's face and his eyes met mine and they were clear and sharp, with no indication of mockery or irony.

'It's settled then?' Gregg said and after a pause added, 'all right, let's do what we have to do.'

Walking out of that clearing and back to the trail took a lot less time than entering it since we weren't stooped over examining rocks, trees and debris the whole way. After we reached the trail, Teddy asked, 'What will we do if she's dead, too?'

We stopped and looked at each other. 'One of us will have to stay with her. The other will need to go get the others.'

'I'll stay there,' Teddy said. 'I would have an easier time scaring off any intruder. Oh, but wait. What if someone is waiting for us to separate and they follow you?'

'Then, they could just as easily pounce on me if I stay behind and you left. There's just two of us. We have to do what we have to do. Just hope she's still alive when we get there. Come on, we need to move.'

This time, I managed to get us both to the shack without any wrong turns. Frannie's face appeared in a crack in the door before she shoved it open. 'Did you find Marvin?'

'We sure did,' Teddy said in a breezy, off-hand manner.

I swallowed hard at his brazenness, but was equally surprised by Frannie's reaction.

Her eyes narrowed and took on a suspicious cast. 'Why didn't he come with you?'

'He drew the short straw,' Ted said with a shrug. 'He's all tied up while the rest of us finally got out of the lab for a day.'

A smile crossed Frannie's face and she nodded. I tried not to let my jaw drop at his audacity and talent for subtle deception.

'When am I going to get out of here?'

Teddy and I looked at each other. 'Today,' I said with as much cheerfulness as I could muster.

'Have I been cleared?' Frannie said – the sound of hope in her voice was very nearly a tangible thing.

'Not yet,' Teddy said. 'Didn't Marvin tell you this hideout was only temporary? I thought he said you knew you'd be moving soon.'

'I did? Oh, okay. Will I be able to see Marvin?'

A lump formed low and heavy in my throat. 'Not just now, Frannie. It's more likely that he's being watched than any of us.'

'Okay. But I need to tell Hannah I'm leaving or she'll worry when I don't show up.'

'We'll take care of that, Frannie. We really need to go.'

'Can I take my magazines?'

'Of course, you can,' I said as I realized anew the depth and fragility of her innocence and vulnerability. No wonder Marvin felt an intense need to protect her. I was now the custodian of her fate.

FIFTEEN

Frannie changed into the clean underwear and dress I'd brought out for her and I put the pajamas and another change of clothes into a paper grocery sack Marvin had left there on one of his visits. Before we could leave, Frannie fretted about returning the potato chip can to Hannah. 'She has nothing in that little hut – nothing. I'm sure she could put it to good use.'

She frustrated our attempts to get her moving by continuing to fuss about the chip can. Finally, Teddy ended the debate. 'Listen, Frannie, I think Hannah can get another one from the cafeteria if she wants it. If not, I promise you that I will come back out here and get this one to her.'

'Promise?' she asked.

'Cross my heart and hope to die,' he said while sketching an X on the left side of his chest. Pacified, Frannie relented. She headed down the trail, chattering with near-giddy excitement as she related the stories she read about in the magazines I'd brought to her. I found all the gossip and lurid tales rather annoying, but they served an important function: they distracted her attention from the perils she now faced. If the full weight of it all descended on her shoulders, I doubt she could have walked without assistance. At some point, I'd have to tell her about Marvin and that inevitability filled me with dread.

Teddy brought up the rear of our little group and he spent so much of his time looking back, I worried that he'd run into a tree or stumble over a vine. The tension in his posture was extreme and his eyes never stopped moving.

I was equally alert for anything suspicious in the path ahead. My biggest concern was any hiding place where dangerous strangers could lurk waiting to catch us unaware. I belatedly realized that I should have carefully scouted for those possibilities on the way to Frannie's shack.

Gregg, Joe and Rudy were waiting for us when we got to

the cut-off. Gregg pulled me to the back of the group heading down the trail and asked about calling the next-of-kin Marvin listed on the pass-around.

'We have to talk to Crenshaw first and then tell Frannie – she might want to be the one to call the family.'

'Makes sense,' Gregg said and went on to explain their plan for moving forward. The others would stay out here until Teddy and I spoke to Lieutenant Colonel Crenshaw and led him or some of his men out to the location of Marvin's body. Gregg, Rudy, and Joe would lead Frannie out of the woods onto a highway beyond the fence. Gregg would hide himself and Frannie in a concealed location while Joe and Rudy headed toward my house. Rudy would wait there while Joe drove my car to pick up Gregg and Frannie.

The next step necessitated a bit of finesse on my part because I had to convince Frannie to play a major role and I needed her to do it well. And I had to be persuasive without telling her about Marvin.

I trotted up the trail to catch up with Frannie who was now retelling the same magazine stories to Joe and Rudy who both looked like they might be capable of falling asleep and walking at the same time. I wrapped my elbow in the crook of her arm to keep her moving while I explained. 'Frannie, here is what is going to happen next. Up ahead is a point where the trail comes close to a road. I was able to hear the traffic noise each time I reached that point when I walked this trail. You will veer off toward that sound with Gregg and Joe.'

I felt her step hesitate and added a little more pressure to her arm and kept up my pace, dragging her speed back up to meet mine. 'What if we get lost?' she asked.

'You won't,' I promised, hoping I was right. 'Gregg has a compass and he'll get you there. You need to follow his instructions without hesitation. You can do that, can't you?'

Frannie nodded. 'I try to pretend like this isn't all that serious but I know how serious it is. I just don't like to think about it.'

'You don't have to, Frannie, just listen to us and we'll do the best we can. Joe will drive you and Gregg to the Andrew Johnson Hotel. Mr and Mrs Gregg Abbott will check in and go to their room.'

'When do I meet her?'

'Who?' I asked.

'Mrs Gregg Abbott.'

I shook my head – it had seemed an obvious conclusion to me – but Marvin had said that his cousin accepted everything at face value. 'That's you, Frannie.'

She stepped in front of me, making a sudden stop that made me nearly lose my balance. Arms akimbo, she said, 'I will not do it.'

'Frannie, don't worry. Gregg is not going to stay in the room with you. He's just going to go up, get you settled into the room and pick up anything you need before he goes back to his dormitory.'

'How do you know he won't take advantage of me?'

'Gregg knows how important it is to protect you and to find the truth to set you free.'

'Once I'm outside the fence, how do you know I won't run off and leave you holding the bag?'

What an odd question, I thought. 'Frannie, I believed Marvin when he said you wanted your name cleared. If you run off, that will never happen. Everyone will assume you are guilty.'

A harsh tone was in her voice when she said, 'That's true.' Then, it softened to its normal girlishness and she said, 'I will not marry him, under any circumstances.'

'Oh, Frannie, you're not going to really marry him. It's just pretend. It's like you're an actress in a movie. You'll be the leading lady. Isn't that exciting?'

Frannie's face brightened and she flashed a grin. 'That's killer diller, Libby.'

That phrase made me wince. It came too close to the literal truth for my liking.

'I can do that,' Frannie continued. 'Should I go for the Katherine Hepburn style or maybe I'm more a Bette Davis type, what do you think?'

'Pretend that Gregg is Cary Grant . . .'

Frannie crinkled her nose and scowled. 'Not exactly.'

'Just pretend and act like the woman you think belongs at Cary's side.'

'Oh, yes. Katherine Hepburn it is.'

I certainly hoped she didn't ham it up too much. I found it easy to believe that it was child's play for Hansrote to manipulate her.

Teddy and I parted ways with the group and Frannie surprised me with a huge hug and eyes full of tears. 'Thank you, Libby. You're the best friend Marvin ever had.'

I'm not sure she'd feel the same way once I told her what had happened to her cousin. But that day of reckoning was still undetermined. I had to face Crenshaw first.

'It's Sunday,' Teddy said. 'Where will we find Crenshaw?'

'He might be at his office but I think it's more likely that he is at home.'

'You know where he lives?'

'Yes. Mrs Crenshaw sent me a card inviting me to dinner after the conflict between her husband and I was resolved.'

'You went to dinner at his house? You sat down and ate a meal with him?'

'No. I politely excused myself but made a mental note of the street address.'

'How much are we going to tell him?'

'I'm not sure. I tend to think, at this point, we should just tell him we found Marvin's body and leave it at that. We need to have something to implicate Hansrote before we take it any further.'

'Do you have any ideas on that front, Libby?'

'I'm thinking about something. I'm just not ready to talk about it yet.' I was thinking of something very risky. Would Henrietta Rockefeller be appalled enough at the idea of her husband spying on her country to cooperate? I hoped that Joe could uncover more first from his older sister. Until then, I was keeping that option as a last resort.

When we knocked on the door of one of the larger cemesto houses, a gangly teenaged boy answered. I asked for his father and he walked away leaving the front door open. I could hear talking in the distance.

'Who is it?' Crenshaw said. After he pause he said, 'Why didn't you ask them?'

The boy shuffled back to the door and asked, 'May I tell him who's calling?'

From another part of the house, a woman's voice said, 'Please, William. Who's calling please?'

The boy sighed, turned beet red and exaggerating the emphasis on the word 'please', said, 'May I *please*, tell him who's calling, *please*?'

The woman's voice scolded, 'Watch yourself, mister.'

It was such a typical family interaction, it was all I could do not to laugh in his chagrined face. 'Tell Lieutenant Colonel that Miss Elizabeth Clark and Mr Theodore Mullins are here to see him.'

Crenshaw came to the door immediately. 'To what do I owe this pleasure, Miss Clark, Mr Mullins?' He stretched his arm out, shaking both of our hands. 'You didn't find another body, did you, Miss Clark?' he said with a chuckle.

'Actually, we did,' Teddy answered.

The smile fled from Crenshaw's face. 'This way,' he said.

We followed him through the foyer and into the living room where he invited us to have a seat. Mrs Crenshaw was there before we could sit down. 'Dear,' she said, 'can I bring a pot of coffee? Won't take but a minute to fix it.'

Crenshaw looked at us with raised eyebrows. We both shook our heads.

'No, thank you, Martha. If you and William would grant us a few uninterrupted minutes, please.'

'Certainly, dear,' she said with a smile and disappeared into another room.

'I trust that wasn't a joke, Mr Mullins.'

'No, sir. We found the body of a scientist out in the woods, tied to a tree.'

'Tied to a tree?'

'Yes, sir,' I said. 'It appears as if Marvin Gray's legs and fingers have been broken and his face battered badly.'

'Do you know who is responsible?' he asked.

'No, sir,' Teddy and I said in unison and far too quickly.

He looked back and forth at our faces trying to read what was behind our denial. I smiled as sweetly as I could.

'You both saw this body?'

We nodded in response.

'Did anyone else see this body?'

We nodded again.

'And I suppose, just like the time before, you won't tell me who they are.'

'I'm sorry, sir,' I said. 'I made a commitment to the group.'

'Yes, of course you did. What you're telling me sounds like torture. What information would Mr Gray have that would have put him at risk? What was he working on?'

'Sir, I wouldn't know. We don't discuss our work within the group.'

Crenshaw gave a cynical laugh. 'Of course you don't. And you don't debate any theories about the nature of the gadget you are working on, do you?'

Teddy and I both sat in silence. I stared intently at a pencil that had rolled under a nearby chair.

'So did this whole mysterious group see the body? Did they all trample over any evidence in the immediate vicinity?'

'Yes, sir and no, sir,' I said, relieved to have a question I could answer. 'We all saw the body, but from a distance. Two of us approached it to determine if he was still alive and to see if we could ascertain what had happened to him.'

'The two of you?' the lieutenant colonel said pointing his finger from one of us to the other.

'No sir,' Teddy said. 'Not me.'

'I need to know who the other person was.'

'Not at this time, sir,' I said. 'If there comes a point in your investigation where you can convince me that you genuinely do have a need to know, I will talk to that person about coming forward.'

Crenshaw bowed his head and shook it from side to side. 'Very well,' he said when he looked us in the eyes again. 'And you can show me where this body is?'

We nodded again.

'Let's hope nothing untoward happens before we get there.'

'We left men standing guard, sir,' I said.

Crenshaw stood, walked to the phone and barked orders into the receiver. 'Send my driver here now to transport me and two others. And send three or four MPs in another vehicle. Then contact the Provost Marshall General's office and alert him to stand by for a request to provide the service of the Criminal

Investigation Division. Tell them I'll call later today to verify our need or with orders to stand down.' He disconnected the call without waiting for a response.

From the back seat of the jeep, I directed the driver as close as I could to the ancient oak, while another jeep with four military police followed behind us. We set out on foot with Teddy and me leading the way. When we reached the alcove where the ground was littered with cigarette butts, I stopped and said, 'This seems to be the spot where some people laid in wait for Marvin.'

'How in heaven's name did you find this place?'

I kept my eyes away from Teddy, afraid that I'd give something away if I looked at him when I answered. 'I went walking this way with Marvin last week so it seemed a good place to start looking for him.'

'Are – were you involved with this young man, Miss Clark?'

'No sir. I knew him. He had a personal problem and he wanted my advice. We were discussing that while we hiked. He was a friend but that's the extent of it.'

'How much further?' Crenshaw asked.

'Just a little further,' I said and led them to the marked tree. 'You're all going to have to wait here while I give the men guarding the body a chance to conceal themselves.'

One of the MPs objected but Crenshaw cut him off. 'Do as she says, corporal.'

I dashed up the path, explained the situation to Dennis, Tom and Gary and watched as they faded into the woods. Returning back to the turn-off, I warned them all about the horrible smell.

When we were in sight of the body, Crenshaw said, 'You two stay right here,' and motioned for the MPs to follow him. They examined the body for a few minutes and Crenshaw walked back our way. 'Did you remove anything on or near the body?'

'No sir,' I said.

'You didn't remove a rope from around his neck?'

'He was strangled?' I said, feeling nauseous. What a horrible way to die.

He paused for a moment as if deciding whether or not to answer my question. 'It appears so. You didn't remove a rope?'

'No, sir, we did not.'

Crenshaw turned around and said, 'One man – whoever has the strongest stomach or the weakest sense of smell – needs to stand guard by the body. Another needs to take up a position at the end of this cut-off. A third will remain at that area where Miss Clark suggested might be the site of an ambush.'

'Are you just going to leave him there?' I objected.

'For now, Miss Clark. Criminal investigators from the Provost Marshall General's office will arrive as soon as possible. He will remain out here until I get instructions to the contrary from them.'

I didn't want to desert Marvin again. I knew he was dead, but still, I didn't want to turn him over to the military; it felt like betrayal.

SIXTEEN

We told the driver to drop us off at men's dormitories so that we could tell Jubal that Marvin would not be returning. That earned us a lecture from Crenshaw on not revealing any details of the situation to anyone. We listened in silence and nodded in agreement. It was the perfect cover-up for our real motivation in not being given a ride back to my place. I wasn't sure who we'd find there besides Rudy. I was determined to conceal the identity of the rest of the group for as long as we could. Once Crenshaw's driver left, we walked straight to my house. Marvin's roommate could wait.

Tom and Gary were sitting on the steps leading from the boardwalk to my little flattop. Tom spewed out a litany of questions without any pause for answers. 'Did you find Crenshaw? Did you talk to him? Did he believe you? Were you interrogated? Did they lock you up? Did you escape? Did you take them out to the tree? Well, come on, what's going on? We were worried.'

'Is Rudy inside?' I asked.

'Him and everyone else, too. Well, except for that girl. Gregg left her at the hotel. What happened for pity's sake?'

'Why don't we go inside and we'll tell everyone at once.'

When I walked in the door, Gregg bounced up from my easy chair and motioned for me to have a seat.

'Let me make a couple pots of coffee first.'

'Real coffee?' Dennis asked and looked ready to drool.

'Yes. Got a fresh tin from my Aunt Dorothy for my birthday. How she gets her hands on these things I'll never know. She always changes the subject when I ask.'

Teddy sat down on the sofa beneath an open window that brought a welcome breeze. The rest, instead of sitting down and battering him with questions, all crowded after me into the kitchen. Even with just me, and sometimes one other person in there, the room didn't feel spacious but it certainly was roomy enough. Now, it felt like a shrinking box. I didn't object, though. I was rather touched by their obvious show of concern and offers to help.

When the cups were filled and passed around, we all sat down in the next room on the sofa, the easy chair, one of the two dining table chairs or cross-legged on the floor. 'I'll give a brief report on what happened but before I answer any questions, I would like to hear from Gregg about how Frannie has handled herself since I saw her.'

I ran down the sequence of events and, despite my request, queries started bombarding me immediately. I held up my hands and said, 'Wait. Gregg, how did it go?'

Gregg shook his head and laughed. 'I had a very clingy girlfriend in high school, but she was nothing compared to Frannie. She snuggled by my side, touched my face time and time again and kept clutching my hand. I think the young clerk at the front desk was embarrassed by her profuse display. But she was convincing. When we got into the room itself, she backed away from me so fast, you would have thought I was diseased. On the way out, I spoke to the staff in the lobby again explaining how my wife had been very ill and would probably spend most of her time recovering in the room and want room service for most meals. They seemed to accept that, too. So I'd say all went very well.'

'Does anything about Crenshaw have you worried, Libby?' Rudy asked.

'Yes. I think he suspects I know more than I am telling him. Of course he is aware that our group exists and is aware that I won't reveal any names. Beyond that, I can tell he knows I'm up to something. He knows better than to ask me vague questions just fishing for answers but I can tell he's looking for clues to what I'm thinking. He did, Tom, ask for your name but I wouldn't tell him.'

'Me? Why does he care about me?'

'He wanted to know who else approached Marvin's body. I told him that if he reaches a point in the investigation where he can convince me he needs to know, I would ask you if you wanted to come forward.'

'He knows who you and Teddy are and you're doing fine so it probably doesn't matter.'

'Probably,' Teddy said. 'But it is also possible that the only reason we are fine is because he thinks we might eventually disclose all your names. If that happens, who knows what he'll do.'

'Very possible,' Gregg said. 'I think it could be what is keeping you and Libby safe. Give up a name if you have to do so – but not until you have no other choice.'

'The question I have for all of you is, what do we do next?' I asked.

'We need to make sure that Marvin's body is removed from the woods,' Tom insisted.

'I already planned to check with Crenshaw on Tuesday morning about that.'

'Tuesday?'

'Tom, I've got to give investigators time to get here and look over the scene. If I go tomorrow, I'll just annoy Crenshaw and possibly shut the door to any communications from him.'

Tom grumbled and then asked, 'What did you have in mind?'

'Teddy and I were talking as we headed back here. To us, it seemed obvious that we needed to follow Hansrote. He's bound to have found or be looking for someone who can provide him with a clean connection to the outside world and to that Raymond guy in Manhattan.'

'I don't think that he would go with another switchboard operator on the off-chance that Frannie said something to someone before she fled,' Teddy added.

'And I don't think he'll stand in line at the drug store or any other public pay phone. It has to be a private residence,' I added.

Gregg asked, 'Do you think that means he'd go off the reservation, then?'

I nodded.

'So we'd only need to follow him when he goes outside of the fence. That sounds doable, Libby, if you'll make your car available.'

'There's a problem with that,' Gregg said. 'We don't know where he works.'

'But,' Joe offered, 'we do know where he lives.'

'We do?' I said.

'Well, Henrietta knew.'

'How do you know that?' I asked.

'While Gregg was getting Frannie settled in at the hotel, I called my sister. She gave me the address.'

'No one on the outside is supposed to know that information,' I said.

'No, but—'

I cut him off. 'But Hansrote is revealing secrets to the enemy so what difference does it make?'

'Exactly. Anyway, remember when Hansrote came here, Henrietta said she wouldn't come down until he found a suitable home for her and their two daughters. He got one of the larger cemesto houses on Thornton Road, based on the fact that his family would be moving in. When he told Henrietta about it, she asked a lot of questions. He gave her the street address and bragged about how it was one of the best homes here.

'Henrietta told my sister, that he described it to her, that it sounded like a hovel, a cramped little shack, and she didn't know how he thought it was suitable. But, apparently, the final straw was when he told her to pack galoshes or boots for herself and the girls because of all the mud. According to my sister, Henrietta told him, that she was willing to forsake civilization to go to the barbaric backwoods of Tennessee for the sake of winning the war, but that she refused to subject herself and her daughters to primitive, unsanitary conditions. Apparently, it was beneath the dignity of a Rockefeller! My sister said that she didn't think Henrietta ever had any intentions of going but just strung Hansrote along to get him out from under foot. The marriage, apparently, was not made in heaven.'

It was more gossip than hard-fact but it sure was entertaining. And people want to know why I am dubious about marriage. Hard for me to understand why they approach with such eagerness. Focusing on the issue at hand, I said, 'Someone needs to stake out his house.'

'I'd already planned to do that, Libby,' Joe said. 'It sure would make it easier to follow him to work, though, if I could use your car.'

'Certainly, drive it back to your room tonight so you can set out early. You may want to go past his house before you go to the dorm to figure out the best place to park tomorrow morning while you wait for him. While we're talking about the car, I am willing to make it available to all of you for work on this case. We'll have to be careful not to run through the gas ration coupons, but as long as they seem to be holding up, I'll drive to work every day so that if someone needs to continue our investigation, it will be readily available.'

'I need to check on Frannie tomorrow evening. I think she'll need a lot of contact to keep her spirits up and I need to show up there enough to make our marriage believable to the staff.'

'If it's all right, I'll ride in to town with you,' Joe said. 'My sister is having tea with Henrietta tomorrow and I can call and find out if she knows anything more.'

'Agreed,' I said. 'But go immediately after work so that we can meet up at Joe's later and share information. I think I know someone who went to Columbia. I'll try to talk to him when he takes his lunch break, see if he knew Hansrote.'

Teddy said, 'We didn't stop and tell Jubal what happened to his roommate on our way here. I'll go see him when I leave here and see if he knows anything more about Marvin that might help.'

'If anyone can think of a line of inquiry to follow before tomorrow night, please take the initiative if you can. Just be careful. One of us is dead. We don't want to lose anyone else.'

'*And Then There Were None*,' Tom said.

'Excuse me,' I said.

'You didn't read that Agatha Christie story in the *Saturday Evening Post* about five years ago?'

It all came rushing back to me. Murdered one by one. 'But Tom,' I said, 'you are not suggesting that one of us was responsible for Marvin's death, are you?'

'Actually, my train of thought did not run that far down the track. Now that you mention it, though, maybe we ought to keep that possibility in mind.'

SEVENTEEN

The first thought that crossed my mind when I awoke on the morning of Monday, June 5 were Tom's cautionary words. At first I regarded them as nothing more than Tom being Tom – negative and paranoid. But, there was such a long moment of silence after he spoke that it seemed obvious to me that everyone else was considering the possibility. No one laughed at it or objected to it. Even if there was no substance to the idea that one of our own was involved, it introduced an element of distrust that could erode the foundation of our group.

The secrecy imposed by the security demands at Oak Ridge had to be deadly for interpersonal relationships. I thought again of the wives who never heard a word about even the most mundane aspects of their husband's work, who spent evenings watching dinner grow cold without knowing why their spouse had to work late or when he would get home from the lab; how did they cope with that? How could any sense of intimacy thrive when so many shadows lurked in a home?

Entering Y-12, I went by Saul Aiken's work station before mine but he had not yet arrived. I left a note: 'I am thinking about doing some additional post-graduate work at Columbia after the war. If you're willing and able, could you meet me out front at noon to talk to me about the school on our lunch break?' Hopefully, that would work.

The morning passed quickly. The sample concentration level held up to my most recent calculations and the quantity produced seemed to be rising on a consistent curve. I focused my mind on possible process improvements and banished intruding thoughts about Marvin, Frannie and my building paranoia. When I went outside at lunch time, I planned on waiting for up to twenty minutes for Saul but was delighted to spot him already out on the boardwalk.

As we walked to the cafeteria, I asked general questions about the campus and its surroundings. I was subtley moving the conversation towards my intended topic of the faculty, when Saul laughed. 'You just want to know about Enrico Fermi, don't you? That's what this is all about, isn't it? I was a chemistry major and didn't take any physics classes with Fermi but I did attend one of his lectures.'

'You did take some physics courses, right?'

'Sure. A few.'

I took a deep breath and plunged right in. 'Did you ever have a professor named Hansrote?'

Saul crinkled his nose and pursed his lips. 'In a manner of speaking.'

'What do you mean?'

'I took an introductory level physics course with him. But Hansrote only showed a couple of times, his graduate assistant taught most all of the classes. But worst of all, Hansrote had a nasty reputation for theft, or plagiarism, or whatever you want to call it. He had a habit of telling doctoral students that he could get their dissertations published – and he did keep his word on that. The only problem was when they appeared in a journal, the by-line always read: "Edwin Hansrote, Ph.D." and no one else got any credit. If that doesn't outrage you, I'm sure this will: I once overheard him make an ugly comment to a female student that I later heard he made to every woman who took one of his classes. He walked up to her and said, "I understand that you are a physics major." When she said, "Yes, sir," he said, "I want you to know that I will do everything in my power to see that you fail this class, because women do not belong in any field of science – particularly not in physics." I made sure I never took another of his classes and I was very disappointed to learn that he ended up working here.'

'I've never seen him at Y-12,' I said with as much innocence as I could muster.

'I don't think he's working in our building – seems like if he were, I would have seen him coming or going, but I haven't. Listen, I suspect this has nothing to do with any plan you might have to attend Columbia after the war. I suspect you are fishing for information about Hansrote. I don't know and I won't ask what kind of project you are working on, but if you can avoid having him on your team, do so. If you can't, don't trust him for one minute. He has the moral conscience of a rat swarming a garbage dump.'

That disturbing portrait of Hansrote did not surprise me considering what I suspected about him. The question in my mind was how we could use it. I was drawing a blank on a possible answer but hoped someone would have a good idea tonight at Joe's.

I stepped out of Y-12 and planned on trying to catch Crenshaw in his office in the administration building. But before I got more than a few steps, I heard a female voice calling my name. I turned around and saw a young woman standing beside two men in dark suits and fedoras who turned their heads in my direction. I had to remind myself to breathe. Was one of the men Hansrote? I thought about running but knew if they were here for me that would be a futile action that would cause more trouble in the long run. But still, I could not find my voice or move a step.

The tall, whip-thin woman started walking towards me. As she did, the other two men turned away from me and resumed their conversation. Breathing became much easier but still I was wary.

'Why, Libby Clark, as I live and breathe, I can hardly believe I finally found you,' she said.

As she got close enough for me to register her facial features, a glimmer of recognition sparked but did not ignite. 'You've been looking for me?' I asked.

'I certainly have ever since I heard that you were working at a secret place in the middle of nowhere, I knew it had to be here.'

She stood in front of me and I still could not place her.

'Oh, my!' she exclaimed, tapping a palm to her chest. 'Of course you don't recognize me. I'm not the little pudgy thing I was when you left Virginia.'

Then it fell into place. 'Jessie? Jessie Early?'

'The one and only,' she said.

'It's been what? Ten years?'

'Just about.'

'And someone told you I was here?'

'No. But Mama knew I was working out in the middle of nowhere. I didn't tell her where but I did tell her I was in the south and out in the country. Then about a month ago, she said she heard you were in someplace like that, too. So I started looking for you everywhere I went. Then, the other day, I started thinking that as smart as you were, I thought you might be a scientist. I waited a few times outside of the place where I work and never saw you, so I decided to try here. And here you are. Are you a scientist?'

'Yes, I am.'

'I knew it. I knew you'd make something of yourself.'

'Maybe we can get together sometime,' I said. 'Right now, I really need to get to the administrative building before everyone goes home for the day.'

'I'll be glad to walk with ya, Libby. Walking,' she said, running her palms down her side, 'is what made me what you see today. I started walking back home and Mama worried I was pushing myself too hard. But look at me now,' she said, making a little twirl.

'You look fabulous, Jessie.'

We went up the boardwalk while she updated me on the latest gossip about people from my birthplace. As we neared my destination, she said, 'Listen, I know we aren't supposed to talk about our work or anything, but I know where you work and I know you're a scientist, so it's only fair. I have a job at that huge K-25 under construction. I clean pipes all day long. Don't know why. Don't know what they're for. But that's what I do. I really would like to get together sometime, maybe go to a movie or go shopping in town.'

'I'm really busy this week but tell me where you're living and I'll drop by as soon as I can.'

Jessie pulled out a piece of paper and wrote down her dormitory and room number. 'Don't make it too long. We've been strangers long enough,' she said and gave a little wave before walking away.

I sat and waited outside of Lieutenant Colonel Crenshaw's office. I filled the first fifteen minutes or so recalling memories of Jessie Early from my childhood in rural Virginia. I also wondered if I was ready to revisit those times with someone from my past. All my good memories were tinged with bittersweet ruefulness over their abrupt and horrible end: the death of my brother and father in a fire and the arrival of my ignorant stepfather, Ernest Floyd. Then, I grew bored with my thoughts and paced in the little anteroom, distracting and annoying the secretary, a WAC sergeant wearing a severe tight bun under her cap.

At the half-hour point of my wait, she disappeared into Crenshaw's office and returned to stand behind her desk to deliver a message to me. 'Miss Clark, Lieutenant Colonel Crenshaw asks your forgiveness for being too busy to speak with you this evening. He wanted you to know, though, that he really had no new information that he could share with you.'

I stood before her desk. 'Sergeant, I just would like the answer to one—'

Looking at a spot above my head, she said, 'The Lieutenant Colonel has said there is no information he can impart to you at this time.'

I exhaled sharply trying my best to control my annoyance. 'I just want to know if what we found in the woods has been moved to a better location.'

Still staring above me, she said, 'I told you, Miss Clark, there is nothing for you to learn here. Please leave the office.'

I tried not to raise my voice but it inched up. 'I will not leave until I get an answer.'

She picked up her phone and for a moment I thought she was going to ask Crenshaw for an answer. Instead she said, 'Military Police, please.'

I reached over the desk and pressed down on the cradle, disconnecting her call. 'For heaven's sake, woman, would you look at me for just a moment?'

She stood there at rigid attention, receiver still to her ear as she stared at the far wall.

I slammed a palm down on her desk and shouted, 'My friend was murdered, sergeant. I just want to know if his body has been shown the respect he deserves.'

Without making eye contact, she said, 'When a call to the military police is disconnected there are standing orders for them to respond regardless. They should be here any moment.'

I dragged a chair over, stepped on it and then on to the top of her desk to get into her line of vision. 'My friend was murdered. Crenshaw and I both saw the body. Do you want me to describe it to you? He was tied to a tree. There was blood all over his face. His fingers were all broken one by one. His legs were broken. It appears as if a fat rope was wrapped around his throat and—'

Finally, she looked in my face. 'Please. Stop,' she said, raising her hands, palms out. 'I will go in and ask him if the body has been retrieved.'

I stepped down from my perch and said, 'Thank you.' While she was gone, I struggled to steady my breathing and lower my pulse rate. Getting an answer to a simple question shouldn't be so hard. War or no war, we are humans. And no one's life on or off the battlefront is irrelevant. I thought we were fighting to preserve our values but I despaired that none of them would be left at conflict's end.

When the sergeant returned, she once again focused on the air above my head, 'The Lieutenant Colonel regrets not informing you sooner but, yes, your friend's body has been carefully and respectfully moved to the morgue.'

'Thank you,' I said turning away.

She reached out and touched my forearm causing me to look back at her. She made solid, steady eye contact in a gaze that held more warmth than I would have thought possible. 'I am very sorry for your loss.'

I nodded and headed for the door. I had enough time left to grab a tuna fish sandwich at home before heading over to Joe's for the meeting. Hopefully, someone would have the tidbit to break the case against Hansrote wide open. I knew the current situation could not remain stable for long.

EIGHTEEN

I was surprised to see everyone else had arrived before me as all their heads swiveled in my direction as I entered the back room. The first question on everyone's mind was one I could answer. Relief rippled round the table when they learned that Marvin was no longer hanging on a tree in the middle of the woods.

Our conversation moved to Hansrote. I reported first about the stories I had heard at lunch. Gary, of all people, had found another Columbia graduate who confirmed both the paper-stealing and the woman-hating aspects of Hansrote's personality and had another bit of information to add. Hansrote had been caught a few times going through the desks of his colleagues – another interesting piece of data about the man, but we didn't really need to know anything more to dislike him intensely.

Joe related the conversation between his sister and Hansrote's wife, Henrietta. 'She likes to brag about her husband playing an important part in ending the war, but she expressed the hope that he would discover something that could be used afterwards which would make him money of his own and keep him down there in the wilderness. My sister tried to get more details about Hansrote out of Henrietta but she resisted saying, "He's such a bore – let's talk about something else, anything else."'

'Is your sister questioning you about why you're trying to dig up dirt on him?'

'No, she made an assumption that he was personally causing me problems and I didn't disabuse her of that notion.' Then Joe told us that he was able to follow Hansrote from home to work and found that he was employed at K-25. 'If I know anyone else who works there, I don't know who it is. Do any of you?'

'I think I dated a gal who worked there right after the holidays before everything got so intense in the lab,' Dennis said. 'I'm not sure but I could try to get in touch with her again.'

I sat in silence for a moment, stunned by the coincidence. Was someone up there looking out for me, sending what I needed before I even knew I needed it? I almost opened my mouth to say that when another line of thought trickled to the forefront. What if Jessie were the pawn of Hansrote? Or were the military on to me? Is that why Crenshaw didn't want to speak to me directly? Do they suspect me in Frannie's disappearance? In Marvin's murder? Is she the bait in an elaborate plot or am I being paranoid? Finally I said, 'I ran into someone today who told me she worked at K-25.'

'Today?' Gregg asked. 'That's a bizarre coincidence.'

'Or is it really a coincidence?' Tom asked.

'I don't know,' I admitted. 'It was a girl I'd known in grade school back in Virginia. We weren't close friends but I did know her and I was pretty sure it was the same person even though she'd changed a lot since then. She was waiting for me outside of Y-12 today and said she'd been trying to find me for weeks.'

'How did she know you were on the reservation?' Tom asked. 'And how did she know where you worked? And did she really want to find you for old-time's sake or did someone put her up to it?'

'In the last few minutes, I've asked myself all the same questions, Tom. At the time, her answers seemed very credible, but now, I'm not so sure.'

'If she's somebody's puppet, who's pulling the strings? Hansrote? Crenshaw? The FBI? Or a member of some other shadowy agency no one wants us to know about?'

'I wish I knew.'

Gregg asked, 'Do you know how to get in touch with her and would you be willing to do so?'

'Yes and yes. If she did not seek me out for the reasons she stated, the only way we could find out who we're up against is to reengage with her.' I knew I had to do that but even if she were innocent of any conspiratorial motive, I didn't really want to visit someone who knew and reminded me of the past, but I didn't feel I had any choice.

I opened my eyes just before dawn on the morning of Tuesday, June 6, and stayed in bed thinking about what I needed to do in the lab that day and making plans to go over to the dormitories after work to find Jessie. I also needed to make sure that Gregg was making regular visits to Frannie to keep her spirits up and make sure she hadn't bolted off somewhere. Little G.G. rubbed his head on my chin and then danced around the bed meowing.

I went into the living room, turned on the radio and headed to the kitchen to feed the kitten and start the percolator. It was only a few steps but I didn't make it that far. The news on the radio spun me around.

'CBS News, Bob Koss speaking. And again we bring you the available reports, all of them from German sources on what Berlin radio calls "the invasion". Correspondents at our War Department in Washington, D.C. were told: "We have no information on the German report." There has been no announcement of any sort from allied headquarters in London. News reached this country about the German report at 12:37 Eastern War Time. The Associated Press recorded this broadcast and warned us it could be one that the Allied Forces told us to expect from the Germans. The Berlin report began: "This is a special bulletin. Early this morning, the long awaited invasion by British and American troops began when paratroops landed in the area of the Somme estuary. The harbor at Le Havre is being seriously bombarded at the present moment. Naval forces of the German Navy are off the coasts battling with enemy landing vessels." The German-controlled Calais Radio came on the air today with this announcement in the English language: "This is D-Day. We will now bring music for the Allied invasion forces." We must remember that the Germans are quite capable of faking these entire reports. The reason for doing so is to try to smoke out Allied plans and to start a premature uprising by the resistance movement along the channel coast. The French, the Belgians and the Dutch have all been warned about this possibility repeatedly.'

G.G.'s plaintive wails finally broke through my focus on the news report and I hurried into the kitchen to fill up his bowl and start the coffee before rushing back into the living room. I continued to listen to the evidence pointing to the story being German propaganda and to hints of actual Allied action. I wanted to believe it was true but the not knowing with any certainty kept me tuned to the station for far longer than usual. I dressed in a hurry and drove to work.

Along the way, I noticed small gatherings of people engrossed in conversation, including several right along the boardwalk outside of Y-12. I joined one on my way inside. The group was clearly divided in opinion. All I really wanted was confirmation that the invasion had actually begun. I drifted from one group to another but no one had heard anything decisive from our government. That absence made me sense that it was real. If it was false reporting by the Germans wouldn't the Allies have debunked it immediately?

I walked into my lab where the chattering was at a fever pitch. Charlie came out of his office and said, 'Enough! We will learn whether it is actually happening or not when the president informs us. Regardless of whether an invasion is underway at this time or not, the war is still not over. It is far from over. And we have work to do to help bring it to an end. Go to your station and attend to the tasks at hand. If I hear anything definitive, one way or the other, I will share it with you when I am authorized to do so. Now, get to work.'

Everyone stood still for a moment staring at Charlie. Then the rhythm of our labors reasserted itself and everyone got lost in performing their duties. At lunch time the exodus was an epic one with voices raising before they got out of the building. Everyone wanted to discuss, theorize about and agonize over the possible invasion. I was already weary of the debate. I grabbed a sandwich and a milk from the cafeteria and went back to the lab to eat my meal away from the uproar.

Despite the distractions, everyone promptly returned from lunch and jumped into their assigned tasks with solemn fervor. It wasn't much later that we were interrupted by Charlie. 'President Roosevelt is about to make an address to the nation. If any of you want to hear it, come into my office.'

Charlie's office was very tiny and soon we were all jammed at the doorway, crushing one another in our hurry to get in and hear every word FDR had to say. 'Libby,' Charlie said over the tumult, 'I have one spare chair in here, please come in and have a seat.'

Tom snarled, 'Oh Jeez! Always special treatment for the lady.'

'Tom, keep in mind, not only is Libby a professional just like you, but she is second in command in this laboratory. That alone grants her a seat. But let me tell you, just because I accept women

as my professional peers does not preclude me from being a
gentleman. Even if she were the lowest ranking member of our
group, I would have offered the seat to her. Grow up, Tom.'

Tom mumbled under his breath but didn't make any comment
anyone else could hear. I settled into the wooden chair just in
time for the beginning of FDR's address. 'My fellow Americans:
last night, when I spoke with you about the fall of Rome, I knew
at that moment that troops of the United States and our allies
were crossing the Channel in another and greater operation. It
has come to pass with success thus far. And so, in this poignant
hour, I ask you to join with me in prayer: Almighty God, Our
sons, pride of our Nation, this day have set upon a mighty
endeavor, a struggle to preserve our Republic, our religion, and
our civilization, and to set free a suffering humanity. Lead them
straight and true; give strength to their arms, stoutness to their
hearts, steadfastness in their faith.'

The president went on to pray for their blessings for the soldiers
against the perseverance of the enemy. 'They fight to end
conquest. They fight to liberate. They fight to let justice arise,
and tolerance and goodwill among all Thy people. They yearn
but for the end of battle, for their return to the haven of home.
Some will never return. Embrace these, Father, and receive them,
Thy heroic servants, into Thy kingdom.'

He then asked for help and strength for the families at home.
'With Thy blessing, we shall prevail over the unholy forces of
our enemy. Help us to conquer the apostles of greed and racial
arrogances. Lead us to the saving of our country, and with our
sister Nations into a world unity that will spell a sure peace
a peace invulnerable to the schemings of unworthy men. And a
peace that will let all of men live in freedom, reaping the just
rewards of their honest toil.'

I hardly breathed through his prayer and my heart was heavy
with the knowledge that many families would soon hear the hard
and cruel news that their sons, fathers, brothers and husbands
would not be coming home. When the President said, 'Amen,' his
final word echoed in whispers all around the room. I looked at all
the scientists gathered in that small space and everyone appeared
to be deep in thought, some heads remained bowed. Even Tom
seemed moved. But now, it was time to get back to work.

NINETEEN

I had Gregg drop me off in front of Jessie's dormitory before he took the car into Knoxville to make sure Frannie had heard the news. Again, Joe rode with him – this time simply to talk to his family about the day's events.

When I reached my old classmate's floor, the noise was deafening. Nearly every door along the hall was wide open, with music blaring into the corridor from multiple radios and phonographs creating a jarring cacophony of mixed melodies. I stepped into Jessie's doorway and she spotted me right away.

'Libby!' she shouted. Holding up a tin cup, she bellowed, 'God bless you, Libby Clark, and God bless America!' She put the cup to her lips and downed the contents in one swallow. 'A drink for my friend! A drink for my friend!'

Another young woman staggered over, handed me a cup and slopped a clear liquid into it. It smelled like home-brewed splo and I wasn't about to take a sip.

'To Libby Clark and the merry band of scientists at Y-12!' she said raising the cup in the air.

I put mine to my lips and just allowed the liquid to brush them – even that was harsh and apt to lead to nausea. I smiled, though, and added another toast. 'To the girls slaving away all over this reservation.' Again, I pretended to take a sip and sloshed a little out of my cup as I brought it down. No one noticed. Not a single one of them was capable of swallowing without considerable spillage. Sober as I was, I still seemed to fit right into the celebratory antics, probably because they were all too sauced to tell the difference.

Jessie came to my side and leaned against me. Her breath was so liquor-laden, I wondered if I'd get intoxicated by inhaling the fumes. 'Well, old school chum, tell me. What brings you here tonight?'

She certainly was beyond any kind of conversation this evening so I made an abrupt change of plans. 'I wanted to invite you to come to my house tomorrow evening for dinner. I don't know what I'll fix but I'm sure to find something at the market.'

'Super dooper,' she said.

I knew she wouldn't remember in the morning so I asked for paper and a pen and wrote out a reminder for her and stuck it into the frame around her mirror in the bathroom. Hopefully someone wouldn't grab it and use it to wipe their mouth or anything else.

At home, I fixed a cup of tea and listened a report of the invasion on the radio news. 'Our aircraft met with little enemy fighter opposition or anti-aircraft fire. The naval casualties, the communique concluded, have been very light, especially when the magnitude of the operation is taken into account. The reports of the land fighting, necessarily vague at this early stage of the invasion, indicate that American, British and Canadian troops who landed on the French Normandy coast this morning to open the western front, have forced their way a mile and a half inland to the ancient and important rail city of Caen and allied operations are developing along a sixty-mile front stretching north from the Cabourg peninsula. There have been no reports, as of yet, that the Germans have recovered sufficiently to engage in a counter-attack.'

It was heartwarming to hear our troops were moving forward successfully with their battle plans; but it saddened me later in the report to hear of the wounded being shipped over to England. Where there are wounded, there are also the dead. I turned off the radio and sat back down to read *A Tree Grows In Brooklyn* before heading off to bed.

The next morning, I started the coffee and fed the kitty before turning on the radio. I listened intently to the latest report from the European front. 'Here is the latest on the allied invasion. British sources report that the British Sixth Airborne Division has captured and is holding bridges north of Caen in the Cabourg peninsula. The division was landed at the opening of the invasion and was reinforced last night. American fighter pilots returning to their base in Britain report that allied invasion forces have established a bridgehead from five to six miles deep in France. And this is borne out by German communications.'

Further in the broadcast, I felt real fear when they announced that Field Marshal Rommel himself was leading the German forces sent to respond to the invasion. Rommel's tactical military skills demonstrated with the Afrika Corps earned him the grudging respect of our allied generals. I shivered at what his arrival might mean to the men on the ground.

The typical attitude at the lab, however, was total faith in General Omar Bradley who was leading our troops in Normandy. I had great respect for his ability, too, but it seemed that so many of my male peers were underestimating the determination and ferocity of the Germans. I was far less sanguine. For now, I didn't know who was included in the high-risk venture of the invasion. Could there be any of the young men I knew as boys when I was growing up in the country outside of Bedford, Virginia? Might a dance partner from my high school or college days now be lying prostrate on the beach, dead, dying or wounded? Until I had these answers, I could take nothing for granted.

TWENTY

After work, I found a couple of nice sirloin pork chops at the market and rushed home to get dinner started. I had some very lucky additions in my pantry to add to the meal. Back in January, Dr Bishop, disgraced when his wife had killed his mistress, had sent over the contents of his pantry including the family's home-canned goods before he left Oak Ridge. From that bounty, I could serve green beans and apple sauce for side dishes. The latter, with its precious sugar, was very difficult to find.

I opened the door at the first knock and welcomed a smiling Jessie inside. She seemed in awe over the little flattop but she was even more impressed with the dinner I set on the table.

'Apple sauce? What a treat,' she said as she slid the first spoonful in her mouth. 'Oh, and this tastes homemade. It's every bit as good as my mother's – maybe better.'

'I thought you'd like it,' I said, pleased with her delight. All the while we ate, I searched for an opening to pose a question about the real reason she wanted to contact me. I found it when we cleared the table.

Walking into the kitchen, she said, 'A bit ago, I sure wouldn't have imagined us breaking bread together. I'm ashamed to say you hadn't crossed my mind in years. But this has been fun, so glad we met up again.'

Trying to sound off-hand, I asked, 'Whatever made you think of me again? Was I the topic of conversation?'

'Yes, when your name was mentioned, it all rushed back.'

The words sounded innocent but her averted gaze and the bright red flush on her cheeks told another story. 'So, Jessie, did someone push you to seek me out?'

Keeping her head down, she changed the subject. 'Do you want to wash or dry? Probably, I ought to wash on accounta I wouldn't know where to put away the dry dishes.' She turned on the kitchen faucet and added detergent before loading the dishes into the sink.

I put both my hands on her upper arms and turned her to face me. 'Who, Jessie, who told you to befriend me?'

She jerked away and said, 'What a peculiar thing to say.' She grabbed the dishcloth and applied it to the surface of a plate with intense concentration.

I felt the ripples of anxiety draw tight around my chest. I plucked the cloth out of her hand. 'We have to talk, Jessie. Let's sit back down at the table.'

We walked toward the table and she said, 'I really need to get back to my room. I promised my roommate—'

'No. Sit, Jessie. Now.'

She wilted into the wooden chair and I sat in the other one. Still her eyes were focused downward.

'Who sent you after me? Dr Hansrote?'

Her head popped up. 'Dr Hansrote?'

I nodded.

'Hansrote? Why in mercy's name would I have anything to do with that fancy drugstore cowboy? He's nothing but trouble. Besides, he's already got a mistress.' She spit out that last word like she would a gnat that had zoomed into her mouth.

'Really?' I said. 'He's a married man.'

'Don't I know it. But that wriggly serpent has been after all the girls for a coon's age. He even cheesed up to me once, but I put him in his place real quick like. But that silly Mabel Cruthers fell hook, line and sinker. Now she's quit her job and is a "woman of leisure", she said. He was setting her up in her own apartment in town, she said. He even promised her a telephone – and no party line either.'

The crackle of excitement made me want to grab her and plant a kiss on her cheek. However, I knew it wouldn't do to appear overly enthused. 'Do tell, Jessie. Did he do that or was he just toying with her?'

'He did it all right. She sent me a letter from her new address in Knoxville. She asked me to come visit her sometime. Mama would skin me alive if I called on a woman like that.'

'Does he come to see her often?' I asked.

'She said once a week – sometimes more, but usually that's all. She said when he arrives, she has to leave the apartment while he places a top-secret phone call. Then, when she comes back, she . . . well, you know what mistresses do. She said I ought to try it. She said it sure beats working all day then having a husband pestering you every night when all you wanna do is go to sleep.'

I was nearly trembling at this revelation and struggled to keep the emotion out of my voice. 'Did you save her letter?'

Jessie crinkled her face. 'I probably shouldn't have but I did. Every day after work, I think about writing back to her but then Mama comes to mind and I don't. I guess I oughta throw it out when I get back to my room tonight before I give in to temptation.'

'Do you remember the address?'

'Not off-hand, but I could bring it to you next time we get together.'

'I've got an idea,' I said. 'I'll give you a ride back to the dormitory and I could go in and get it from you this evening.'

'Sounds all-fire important, Libby.'

I shrugged and said, 'I just hate to see scientists behaving so badly. I'd like to report him.'

'Oh my, that would make Mabel pretty mad,' she said with a twinkle in her eye. 'And I sure would like to get a ride home.'

'That's settled then. Now, come on, Jessie. Who was it who pushed you to find me?' I held my breath while I waited for an answer.

Jessie sighed. 'Listen, Libby, I did start looking for you because she asked me but when I ran into you, it was so nice to see you again. You never teased me for being so chubby like a lot of the other girls. And you seemed so nice. And I liked having someone to talk to who remembers home.'

'Who, Jessie?'

'Mama. It was Mama's idea. Sort of. Actually, it was your mother who talked Mama into it.'

'My mother? She writes to me at Christmas and on my birthday and that's it. I never hear from her the rest of the year and she wanted you to contact me?'

'Honest, Libby, I was going to wait until I figured out whether or not you wanted to talk to your mom before I even mentioned it. And if you never brought her up, I was fixin' not to say anything at all.'

'Fine, fine, Jessie. That's not the point. What is my mother up to now?'

'She wants you to come home. She wants to divorce Ernest but she wants to stay on the farm. She needs your help to get rid of him and to run the farm once he's gone.'

'So she thinks I should sacrifice my life and my career on the altar of her helplessness. I made the decision to reject that possibility long ago and I'm not going back,' I said. 'Why does she suddenly want to rid herself of that lazy, incompetent, ignorant husband after all these years?'

'He pulled Ernie Junior out of school to work on the farm.'

'She didn't seem to mind when he pulled me out of school. I can't believe that selfish woman would fret about what happens to Junior. What has he done to her?'

'It's not good, Libby. The tobacco crop that used to earn nearly enough money to maintain the household all year long is disappearing before your stepfather gets home from the auction. Your mother knows he's drinking far too much but she doesn't know what he's doing with the rest of the money. A couple of times, she made the mistake of questioning about where the money is going when Ernest had had too much to drink and he smacked her around.'

'So that's her concern,' I said. 'Not Junior, not the farm, but her pin money and her bruises.'

'It's more than bruises, Libby. The last time, he broke one of her ribs.'

My mother, Annabelle Clark, was a self-centered coward. Still, she was my mother and now she was a victim and calling out for my help. My resistance to returning to my childhood home drenched me in a flood of guilt. For a moment, I felt as if I couldn't breathe. I had to go. And I had to convince Aunt Dorothy to go with me. Since she owned half the farm, she would add the needed legal weight to drive my step-father off of it. Jessie sat quietly with her head bowed as if ashamed of being the bearer of bad news.

'Jessie, thank you. I did need to know this and I do need to pay a visit to see what I can do. But tell your mama this: I am involved in a literal life-and-death problem right now. It involves more than individuals, it is connected to the war. I can't say anything more except that it goes beyond my work in the lab. I will go back to the farm as soon as I can. I will do what I can to get her out of a bad situation but I cannot stay and run the farm. My mother will have to find a way to cope or to actually do something to deal with her problem until I can get there.'

'I wrote Mama a letter early this morning. An army boy from Lynchburg who's going on leave tomorrow offered to drop it off to Mama when he goes past her place on a trip to the mountains with his family. I'll add your message to it tonight. And I'm sorry, Libby – in lots of ways.'

I patted her on the arm and she enveloped me in a hug. I returned it, surprised by the warmth I felt toward this voice from the past. When I pulled away, I said, 'Let's go now so you can get started on it and see if we can find that letter from Mabel.'

I clutched the piece of paper with Mabel's address in my hand as I straggled into Joe's a little while later. I wasn't the last one to enter the back room but I was late enough that the waitress was already in there, setting the pitchers and glasses on the table.

Everyone shared bits and pieces of the news they'd heard that day through the radio and the grapevine. 'Does anyone else wonder if everything we have been doing here is now going to be irrelevant, that the troops are going to win this war without any help from us?' Teddy asked.

'The invasion has only begun, Teddy,' I said. 'It is far too early to declare victory.'

'Yeah,' Tom chimed in. 'And don't forget, there's more than one front to this war and those Nips seem to embrace the idea of dying for the cause. The Krauts want to win but the Nips want to die trying.'

'Really, Tom? Yes, they are the enemy but they have mothers at home just like we do,' Gregg said.

Tom lurched to his feet, hands balled tight at his sides. 'Don't you compare my mother to those Jezebel Krauts or those kamikaze geishas.'

Gregg rose up from his seat, too, jutting out a chin in Tom's direction. 'They're people, too, Tom. All people have feelings. All mothers have hearts that break.'

I stood and walked to the head of the table and smacked on the wood with a fist. 'Both of you, cut it out, now. Sit down and remember: the enemy is not at this table. Period.'

'"For what is a man profited, if he shall gain the whole world, and lose his own soul?"' Dennis said.

All heads turned toward him and stared bewildered and silent.

'It's from the Bible. The New Testament. Matthew 16:26. I often think of it when I think of the war, of the Nazi aggression in Europe, the Japanese occupying forces in China and across the Far East. And it is also brought to my mind when I contemplate the work we are doing on the gadget and the coarsening of our attitudes toward our fellow man. Jesus said we are to love our enemies and we have reduced them to sub-human instead. It certainly would be foolish to win the war and lose our souls in the bargain.'

'Oh, jeez, we've got a holy-roller in our midst,' Tom said as he slumped back into his chair.

Gregg sat down and said, 'Don't you think you've done enough name-calling for one night, Tom?'

Tom's posture turned rigid as a dark cloud of fury crossed his face.

'Oh, please, let's not start up again,' I said.

'Sorry. Sorry, Libby. Sorry, Tom. Let's just call this meeting to order,' Gregg said. 'Our little project, Frannie Snowden, is certainly a needy young woman. She complained about being cooped-up, about not hearing from Marvin, about all the people celebrating the night before while she was stuck in her room not knowing what was going on. So I went out and bought her a radio to keep her occupied. I'm worried she's not taking this seriously enough. Libby, I think it's time she knew what's happened to her cousin. Otherwise, I'm afraid the temptation might be far too great and she'll wander out on her own.'

I sighed. I realized I had been avoiding that conversation without giving any thought to my motivation. I should have talked to Frannie before now. 'I'll go see her tomorrow after work. There is something else I need to attend to in Knoxville but it will have to wait. I flattened the lightly crumpled piece of paper with Mabel's address on the table and explained the situation.

'I'll visit her Friday evening. I think I should go alone and talk to her woman-to-woman.'

'Too much risk,' Teddy said.

'I surely can deal with a girl without the assistance of a man,' I objected.

'But what if Hansrote shows up?' Tom asked.

'The odds are against it. He usually only visits her once a week. I'll listen for a male voice before I knock and I'll work to build a girl-to-girl connection with her immediately, so if he shows up, she won't mind hiding me in a closet or somewhere.'

'I don't like it,' Teddy said.

I knew he was only concerned for my safety. I knew he was not ordering me around. Still, I felt the stifling effect of being in a room of men telling me what to do and I bristled. 'If you don't like it, Mr Mullins, then you can lump it. And that goes for all of you. I've made up my mind and that's final. I go alone.'

I glared at them as they snuck nervous glances at one another. Then Tom stood, raised his beer glass and said, 'To Libby Clark and the success of her mission!'

'Here! Here!' went around the room as glasses were raised in a salute. Then Tom couldn't help himself. He had to add a sarcastic finale. He stepped back from the table and doffed an imaginary hat as he bowed low and said, 'Anything further, madam?'

For a brief moment, it stung like a slap in the face. Then, the humor of it all struck me causing me to burst out laughing. Everyone at the table joined me. The merry band was merry once again. What an odd group we all were. In the back of my mind, I could hear Tiny Tim saying, 'God bless us every one.'

The laughter died down, a pitcher passed around, and Gregg said, 'Anyone else have anything to report?'

TWENTY-ONE

T hursday was just more work day of the same painstaking retrieval and analysis, except for one exciting realization. By Monday, I would have enough of the green salt to make a shipment. Best of all, the concentration had now reached seventy percent.

By the time I finished the last quality check, it was seven o'clock and time to call it quits. This steady diet of ten hours and more of work every day was exhausting but I was feeling very energetic as I hopped into my car for Knoxville. The weight of my purpose to deliver the news to Frannie grew a little heavier with every mile of the drive. I hoped I'd handle it well.

The only comfort I had to give her when it was time for me to leave was the last chocolate bar from my treasure chest. It sounded like an excellent idea when I grabbed it but now it felt pathetic.

When she answered my knock on the door, she smiled wide and said, 'Oh, if you're here, it must be good news.'

Her upbeat words felt like a hard kick in my shins. I wanted to turn and run but forced my feet across the threshold.

'I can order something from room service. Would you like some coffee, some tea? Can't get anything stronger because of the silly rules in this hick town. But, oh, have you had dinner? I could order something for you. What would you like?' Frannie said as she bounced between me and the telephone on a little table in the sitting area.

'Frannie, can you get an outside line on that phone?' I asked, thinking it might be a better way for Joe to keep in touch with his sister.

'Oh, no. I can get the front desk or any room in the building but you have to go to the lobby to talk to anybody who's not in the hotel. When will I get to see Marvin?'

I winced at her question. 'That's why I'm here – to talk about Marvin.'

'Oh my. Is he angry with me? Or does he think I'm a spy after all?'

'No, Frannie, not at all. Marvin is not upset with you in any way.'

'Is he sick? Is he hurt?'

I sat down on the edge of the bed and patted a spot beside me. 'Come, sit down, Frannie.'

She sunk onto the mattress, her eyes already welling with tears. 'Oh, please, tell me he's all right.'

My throat tightened with every word I spoke. 'Oh, Frannie, I wish I could.'

She threw her face in her hands and sobbed. 'I don't want to hear any more but I know I have to. How bad is it? When can I see him?'

'I'm so sorry,' I said, choking back my tears. 'You can't see him, Frannie. Marvin won't be going home after the war.'

'No, no, no, no,' she said jumping to her feet. 'Not Marvin. Marvin was going to be safe. He didn't sign up to fight. He's not going to the front. He's doing important work to end the war using his brain, not a gun. He's stateside. He's safe,' Frannie babbled, with her hands flying wildly in the air.

I rose and wrapped an arm around her shoulders and gently sat her back on the bed. Sitting down next to her, I quieted her hands between mine. 'Hush, baby, hush,' I whispered.

'How could this happen?' she wailed. 'Was he in an accident? Did something blow up in the lab? Did he get run over by one of those awful buses?'

'Remember the day we moved you out of that shack in the woods?'

Frannie nodded.

'We did that after we found Marvin's body.'

'Where did you find him?'

'In the woods. We thought he was on his way out to your shack and left the path before he got there.'

'And you didn't tell me?'

'We thought it was the right thing to do at the time, Frannie. We knew it would upset you and probably frighten you. And we needed to have you calm to get you to safety. That seemed like the most important thing to do.'

'Wait a minute. Safety? I'm confused. I thought he had an accident. Oh no, was he mauled by a wild animal? By a bear? I hear animals rustling in the forest when I go back and forth to the hutments. It made me nervous but I never really thought they would attack me.'

Would it be kinder to let her think that? Maybe. But I couldn't lie to her. 'It wasn't an accident. And it wasn't wild animals, Frannie. Marvin was murdered.'

She stared at me with her mouth slack and her eyes glazed. I waited for her to recover from that stark news.

She opened and shut her mouth a few times before she spoke. 'Is his body still in the woods?'

'No, Frannie. He has been moved to the morgue.'

'I want to see him. I want to see him now.'

'No, you don't, Frannie.'

'Yes, I do. I have to. After all he did for me, I need to say goodbye.'

'First of all,' I reminded her, 'if you set foot on the reservation, you will be arrested.'

'I don't care. If I can see him first, I don't care.' A hard look darted across her face and she added, 'You'd be surprised at what I can handle.'

I wondered what ugly truth in her past was hidden behind those cold words. 'Frannie, please trust me. You do not want to see him. Not now. You don't want that sight stuck in your mind. The image of his body when I found him haunts me. It pops up in my thoughts when I least expect it. It intrudes on my dreams. Believe me, it was awful. It was a dreadful experience for me and I've only known him a short time. You won't be able to live with it.'

'What did they do to him?'

'You don't want to know, Frannie, really you don't.'

'Either you tell me or I will take a bus with the other workers going in tomorrow morning and see him for myself.'

I couldn't look her in the eyes as I choked out a description of his bound body, broken fingers and fractured legs.

'But how did he die? What killed him?' she asked.

I closed my eyes, took a deep breath and said, 'A rope – a length of it was cinched around his neck.'

Her hand flew to her mouth and her sobbing began anew. She fell into my arms with all the drama of an actress in one of those B movies she loved. In a couple of minutes, her shoulders stopped heaving and she sniffled as she pulled away. 'It was all my fault, wasn't it?'

'No, Frannie. You did not cause that. Marvin only did what he felt he had to do.'

'But it was because of me. They tortured him to find me, didn't they?'

'That's what we're assuming.'

Her eyelids floated down and for a second, she looked as serene as a madonna. When she opened them again, she said, 'That makes it all my fault, Libby. If I hadn't been such a sucker, he wouldn't have been killed. It was Hansrote, wasn't it?'

'We do think it was all at his instigation but we're certain others were involved.'

'Tell me exactly what happened and how you were able to find Marvin.'

I explained about the man in the suit and the place that others lay in wait and the marks left along the trail.

'The man in the suit was Hansrote,' she said with conviction.

'Maybe.'

'Maybe? Just maybe?'

'Okay, probably. It probably was Hansrote,' I admitted.

'I'm going to kill him. I'm going to get a gun and kill him.'

'Frannie, you don't mean that. We're working to get information on him so that we can have him arrested. You don't want to throw your life away like that.'

'But how can I ever face my family again? My Aunt Sophie? My heavens, she'll probably never speak to me again. Maybe I'll just shoot him and then shoot myself.'

'Stop, Frannie. Stop that right now. Killing Hansrote will not bring Marvin back. If it would, I'd do it myself. We have leads to follow and we're going to follow them. We need you to stay calm, quiet and in your room. Not only is the army looking for you but so are the spies. We need you to stay safe – you have to be alive to tell the authorities what happened so we can put Hansrote away forever.'

'Death penalty,' she said, rising to her feet and pacing the room. 'That's what he should get. But before they kill him, they ought to tie him to a tree and break every bone in his godforsaken body.'

'He could be executed, Frannie, but we don't know right now. First we need to find the evidence. I have to get back but I really want you to think about Hansrote and remember everything about him that you can. Write it all down so you won't forget. We will not give up until he gets his reckoning. I promise you that.'

Frannie flopped back on the bed as if her anger had run its course and the only thing left was fatigue. 'I just want to die.'

'You can't, not now. Not until we get justice for Marvin.' I almost asked her if she wanted to call Marvin's parents to inform them about his death but then I realized that was next to impossible. She's have to leave the hotel to do that and that was too risky. Handing her the chocolate bar, I said, 'Here, it's not much, but it's yours.'

'I couldn't eat anything right now. I just want to go to sleep.'

'Okay, Frannie. I'll just leave it here on your dresser for later. I really have to go.'

She sat up and clutched my upper arm. 'Please, please, don't leave yet. Wait until I fall asleep, please?'

I really needed to get home and climb into bed, too, but the desperate pleading in her eyes made my needs feel insignificant. 'Okay, Frannie. Get dressed for bed and I won't leave till then.'

When she returned from the bathroom, I tucked her in like a little child and gave her a kiss on the forehead.

'Thank you, Libby. Thank you for everything.'

'Hush, go to sleep now,' I said as I sat down in the chair by the telephone table.

Frannie flipped and flopped from one side of the bed to the other. I despaired that she would never drift off. Then she made a deep moan and her breathing slowed. I sat watching the rise and fall of her chest for a few minutes then tiptoed out of the room.

I felt hollow and numb. Telling her was almost as bad as finding Marvin tied to that tree. I trudged to the car and set off for Oak Ridge. I had promises to keep and feared the challenge might prove to be too much for me.

TWENTY-TWO

O n Friday morning, I woke with the realization that this night I might unlock the door to an important piece of evidence I needed to snare Hansrote and secure justice for Marvin and Frannie. My thoughts drifted to Marvin and the fact that I was far too late for him. For a moment, I felt the weight of disconsolation descend down on my shoulders. I reminded myself that although I could not bring him back to life, I could avenge his death and complete his mission to save his cousin. I just needed a little bit of help from Mabel. I was confident I could get it. I understood southern girls; I was one by birth. I knew the right buttons to push.

At lunch time, I told Gregg that when I was in town that night, I'd call Marvin's mother.

'I don't think that's a good idea, Libby. Not right now.'

'But that's why we made the list with contact information, so our loved ones could be informed,' I objected.

'Think about it for a minute. First of all, they'll wonder why Frannie didn't call. And if you tell them he was murdered and Frannie is in hiding, don't you think they'll demand to know more? You can't tell them everything – not yet – and I doubt they'd sit quietly and say nothing to anyone. And if you blame his death on an accident, they'll want to talk with Frannie and make arrangements.'

'This seems so wrong, Gregg. It makes the whole idea of our list seem stupid.'

'We just need more answers first, Libby. If we can solve the problem with Frannie and Hansrote, then Frannie can tell them. She's family. If she tells them, they have to keep quiet because of the security situation, they are more likely to listen to her.'

I sighed. I knew he was right but I didn't like it one little bit.

After work that day, I parked by the curb in front of Mabel's building and took the elevator to the fourth floor. As I said I would do, I stood and listened for a moment. Seeing no one in the hallway, I pressed my ear to the door. I heard some sound of movement but no voices. I knocked.

A few footsteps came in my direction and the door opened wide. The woman standing in front of me was not a raving beauty but she was attractive enough to turn more than a few heads. Her auburn tresses were styled just like Rita Hayworth's and she was blessed with the thick, wavy hair that pulled off that look well, although her nose was a bit too large, her lips too thin and her eyes too dull to fulfill the complete image. On her left ring finger, she wore a wedding set.

I stretched my hand towards her and said, 'How do you do, Mabel. I'm Libby Clark and my friend, Jessie Early, told me to look you up while I was in town. She thought we'd enjoy each other's company.'

'Jessie sent you? What a surprise! I thought she'd given me the brush off when she didn't answer my letter. Come in, come in. Coffee? Or would you like something stronger?'

'Coffee would be perfect.' I looked around the living room and saw that however despicable Hansrote might be, he wasn't stingy with Mabel. The furniture was of good quality and the sofa felt quite comfortable.

Quicker than I thought possible, she returned and said, 'The percolator's on. I keep it fixed and ready in case of visitors. So alls I have to do is turn on the stove.' She plopped in an easy chair and said, 'So how is old Jessie? I miss the girl.'

I certainly didn't want to tell her that Jessie's mother wouldn't approve of her visiting someone with a tarnished reputation. 'Oh my, that girl is so busy – all day long. Most of us have to work ten hours or more every day and each day they tell us to work harder.'

'Tell me about it. I was so relieved to find a way to get by without slaving away out there. And don't tell me I was doing my bit to help win the war because I stopped believing that line a long time ago. Do you work with Jessie?'

'No, I—'

'Oh, so you met her in the dorm?'

'No, actually, she sought me out when she thought I might be at the reservation. We are from the same farming community in Virginia. We went to school together.'

'Are you that girl she was talking about right before I quit my job? The one she swore up and down had to be a scientist?'

'That's me.'

'I declare. Of course, you're not a scientist, are you?'

'Yes, in fact, I am.'

'Are you pulling my leg?'

'No, Mabel,' I said with a laugh. 'Cross my heart and hope to die.'

'Well, well, well. And you took time to visit me? Let me get the coffee and then you can tell me how you went from being a farm girl to a career woman – sounds like something out of a Joan Crawford movie.'

When she returned from the kitchen, I said, 'Jessie didn't mention that you were married.'

'Oh this thing?' she said, pointing to her ring finger. 'This is just camouflage. When I go out with my soldier boy, I don't wear it. C'mon, didn't Jessie tell you? I'm what they call a kept woman and I'm enjoying every minute of it.' She sat down with a smug, haughty look on her face as if daring me to criticize.

'Pfft,' I said with a flash of my hand as I attempted to make her think I approved of her behavior. 'Jessie told me that but when I saw the wedding band and diamond on your finger, I thought she was wrong. But I will say this: I think every woman should be able to live her life the way she wants to and if this is what you want, then go for it.'

'It is and thank you very much. You have a refreshing and very modern attitude, Libby. I like that – Jessie was right. Now, where were we? Oh, yes, you were going to tell me how you went from gathering eggs in the hen house to doing fancy things in a laboratory.'

'Right,' I said with a smile. I told her about losing my father and brother and going to live with my dad's sister up north. I left out the ugly parts of the transition.

'But your mama was still alive. Why didn't you stay with her?'

'She was awful sickly,' I lied. 'She had to go into a sanitarium.'

'TB?' she asked.

I nodded.

She came over to the sofa, sat beside me and put an arm around my shoulders. 'That pretty much made you an orphan, didn't it, poor thing?'

'I did feel that way at times,' I admitted. 'But my Aunt Dorothy took very good care of me and made sure I got an excellent education. I often wonder what would have become of me without her.' I had a question on the tip of my tongue that froze there when I heard a scratching noise on the front door. I immediately went rigid.

'Did that durned cat scare you? He belongs to one of my neighbors and always is trying to get in. I think he smells the tuna cans in my trash. Nothing I like better for lunch than a tuna fish sandwich.'

The visit was going well but somehow I needed to steer the conversation to her lover and subtle didn't seem the right method to use with Mabel. 'So who is this man who has set you up in this fine apartment?' I asked.

'Why do you want to know?' she said with a grin. 'I'm sure not going to let you steal him away.'

'Please,' I said, 'the last thing I want is a man in my life telling me what to do and when to do it. Don't get me wrong, I think you have a good set-up here but it's just not for me. It sure seems to beat being married, though, and having to wait on a husband hand and foot every night and all weekend.'

'My feelings exactly,' Mabel said and laughed. 'Anyway, he's a scientist – a hotshot scientist to hear him talk. Being a scientist yourself, maybe you know him. His name is Hansrote, Dr Edwin Hansrote.'

'I've heard the name,' I said, 'but I don't know him. What's he like?'

'As you can see looking around here, he's not a skinflint. He stocked me up with liquor, stockings, roast beef, sugar, and cigarettes and this past Wednesday, he showed up with chocolate. I can't complain.'

'Does he come around a lot?'

'That's the best part. Usually, I can expect him on Wednesday evenings. He comes over, I go for a walk while he makes a phone call and then I let him have what he's paying for and he goes home. He said if he ever needs to come by at any other time, he'll give me a call. One night a week is not too much of a sacrifice to live like this. It's almost like there isn't a war going on.'

'Who does he call on Wednesday nights?'

'I don't know. I asked once and he told me that it was top-secret stuff that no one could overhear at the risk that it would get back to the enemy. Then he said, "If you want to keep this apartment, don't ask that question again."' Mabel shrugged. 'So I don't.'

'Still, he must think you're special to go to all this trouble.'

'I'm not blind about the man. Honestly, I wouldn't be surprised if he had another girl or two in some other apartment building – or even in this one. I wouldn't know. He was playing up to every girl at K-25, it seemed like. A lot of them were too prissy to even listen to what he had to say. But I recognized a good thing when I saw it. Those Dumb Doras can just keep slaving away.'

So there could be other Mabels scattered about town. He must have realized how risky it was to use Frannie to go through the switchboard. He must have been planning an alternative long before she listened in to his conversation. If she hadn't done that, would he just have disappeared from her life or would something deadly have happened to her?

'Yoo hoo, Libby. Did you hear a word I said?'

'Sorry, Mabel. You reminded me of a scientist who's been getting too familiar,' I lied. 'I'm trying to get him to leave me alone. I sort of got lost worrying on that.'

'No matter,' she said. 'I was just wondering if you could come back for a visit sometime soon and bring Jessie.'

'I know I can but I can't really speak for Jessie.'

'Oh sure you can. We'll make it Sunday – oh no wait, my soldier is coming by for dinner then. Let's say Tuesday evening. I'll fix a nice roast beef for dinner. Just tell Jessie that – she won't be able to resist the idea of a home-cooked meal.'

'Jessie's on night shift this coming week. We'll have to set something up later. Do you mind if I drop by the next time I'm in town?'

'I look forward to it,' Mabel said, 'just so long as it's not on a Wednesday night.'

'I really have got to get back home. My kitty is bound to be hungry and tomorrow morning will come far too early as it is.'

I drove home thinking about my new dilemma. If I told Jessie I needed her help, she'd probably be willing to give it. But how much would I have to tell her? And how much risk would I be taking if I confided in her? I knew I was walking on the edge of disaster. If everything with Frannie blew up in my face, I could be charged as a conspirator. In the face of that, the risk of confiding in Jessie seemed small in comparison.

TWENTY-THREE

Teddy stopped me on my way out of the lab Saturday evening. He wanted to take me to dinner and a movie but I resisted. It had been an exhausting week and all I wanted to do was get into my pajamas, eat a peanut butter and jelly sandwich and read myself to sleep.

When I saw Jessie slumped on the steps to my flattop, I sunk into a deep well of disappointment. I needed to talk to her about Mabel but I certainly didn't want to do it tonight – I didn't want to see anyone.

I got out of the car and Jessie looked up at me. Her face stretched long, her brow furrowed and she was as pale as the moon. Something was wrong. 'Jessie, what happened?'

She held up the telltale yellow of a telegram. 'I never got a telegram before and I never want to get another one.'

'Oh, dear, who died?'

'No one died – well, that's not right. Someone did but I don't care about him and you don't either. It's just the how of it and the who of it. It's just a mess.'

She must have understood what she was talking about but it wasn't making any sense to me. 'Come on in, Jessie. I'll fix a pot of tea.'

Jessie followed me into the house and I put the kettle on the stove right away. When I returned to the living room, she was just standing there with a peculiar look on her face.

'Sit down, Jessie. Sit down and tell me what's got you so upset.'

On the way to the chair, Jessie said, 'I talked to Mama today and she had serious news.'

'Not about my mother, I hope.'

'More than that, Libby. There's war news, too.'

'About D-Day?'

'Yes. Company A was in the first wave of the invasion – they might have been the very first. At least that's what Mama heard at Green's Drug Store.'

'Company A?'

'Oh that's right, you were already gone. You remember the Bedford County National Guard.'

'Yes, it's hard to forget – they never missed a parade.'

Jessie smiled but it quickly faded away. 'They sure didn't. But those boys became Company A in the 116th Infantry division.'

'And they were the first on the beach?'

'That's what Mama heard. There were a lot of upset ladies there wondering about their sons, their husbands, their brothers. They're all sure that the casualties had to be high in that first assault.'

'Did you know anybody in the company?'

'Yes. And you do, too. At least when they were boys. You remember the Stevens twins from the farm up the road.'

'The family with more kids than we could count?'

'Yes. There were fourteen of them. Both of the twins were assigned to Company A. And remember Ray Nance?'

'His folks grew tobacco mostly, right?'

'Yes, indeed. And there's Taylor Fellers – he's the captain, he's a bit older than us.'

'Can't say I remember him at all,' I admitted.

'Well, anyway, there's a lot more. That's just all the boys Mama mentioned.'

'Are they okay?'

'Nobody knows and Mama says the whole of Bedford is on edge waitin' for word. Like Mrs Nance told Mama, it's the not-knowin' that's tearin' up their insides.'

'Let me know if you hear any news but sometimes it can take a month or more to get word on the dead and wounded.'

'I thought I'd call Mama in a couple of days even though it will probably be too soon to hear any more but then considering what else has happened, you'll probably hear before I do.'

'Me? How would I? I'm not in close contact with anyone there any longer.'

'I imagine you'll be changing that soon whether you want to or not.'

'What are you talking about, Jessie?'

Jessie threw her hands over her face. When she took them down, her eyes darted back and forth but she wouldn't look straight at me. 'I don't know how to tell you. I don't know what to say. I don't know how to start. I never got a telegram before and I hope I never do.'

'That bad? Let me read the telegram,' I said.

She handed it over. I read: 'Urgent STOP Call me today STOP Love, Mama STOP.' That certainly wasn't much help. 'Did you call her?' I asked.

'Oh, yes, I did and I almost wish I hadn't. She wanted me to talk to you.'

'Another message from my mother pleading for my help immediately?'

'No, it wasn't from her but it was about her. But it's too late for you to help her get rid of Ernest. She's already taken care of it.'

'Really? Well, good for her.'

'No, Libby. Not good. She didn't kick him out, she done him in.'

'What? My mother? She killed him? There has to be a mistake.'

'There's a mistake all right and your mother made it. Mama said that Annabelle loaded the shotgun and fired it into the back of Ernest's head while he was sleeping.'

'How do you know my mother shot him? Ernest has made a lot of enemies over the years. Any one of a dozen people could have shot him and felt justified doing it.'

Jessie sighed. 'Annabelle called the sheriff. She told him that she shot her husband. She sat by the body with the shotgun draped across her legs while she waited for him to arrive.'

'Was she arrested?'

'Yes. She's in jail now.'

The harder I tried to absorb this news, the less real it seemed. My mother was not a woman of action – not by any means. And why couldn't she wait until I could get there to resolve the situation legally? 'What else did your mama say?'

Jessie let out another big sigh. 'I hate telling you about this, Libby. But . . .'

'I need to know.'

'Mama had given your mother the message that you were coming as soon as you could. Mama thought she was relieved and ready to wait until you got there. So when Mama went to visit your mother in the jail, she asked her, "Why, Annabelle?

Why couldn't you wait for Libby? Why now after all these
years?" Your mother said it was on accounta Ernie. Ernest
punched him in the face and knocked out a couple of teeth.
Then he locked him in the tool shed and told him he would
stay there till mornin'. Your mother tried to get Ernest to give
her the keys after it turned dark. She told Mama that Ernie was
terrified of spiders and he'd probably die of fright if he stayed
out there overnight. Ernest refused and when he went to bed,
he stuck the key to the shed under his pillow so she couldn't
get it. She told Mama she had to get that key and that the last
time she asked for it, Ernest said, "Over my dead body," and so
she obliged him. She said she had to do it for her boy.'

I bit back a surge of bitterness. When Ernest had turned my
world into a place of misery, she hadn't raised a finger but now,
for her son – it was as if his life was important and mine didn't
matter. I was torn between conflicting emotions. On the one
hand, she was my mother and I could not turn my back. But
the hurt little girl buried in my core wanted her to sit in that
cell, miserable and alone, until she rotted away.

'What are you going to do, Libby?'

'I don't know. I have to have time to think – time to accept.
At the moment, it all seems so preposterous that it can't be true.
How, in heaven's name, did murder strike her as a solution?
And how – wait – what about Ernie? Did your mama say anything
about Ernie?'

'Oh yes. How could I forget to tell you that? Annabelle let
Ernie out of the shed and sent him over to our house. Ernie is
staying with Mama for a bit until you can get there. I told her
maybe you wouldn't want to come and she said that you had to.'

'How is he?'

'Mama said he's fine, considering. He's not talking much and
seems to be lost in a fog. She expects he'll snap out of it once
the newness wears off. She also said that the only thing he wants
to know is when you're coming. He said that your mother told
him you had to come now.'

'I do have to, don't I? I don't want to go but I must. I
hope my Aunt Dorothy can come, too. I'll need her both for
advice and moral support when I go back to the farm. I should
have dropped everything and gone back the day you gave me

the message from my mother. But I didn't and now we'll all
have to live with the consequences.'

'Do you need me to come with you?' Jessie asked.

'I'm not certain how quickly I can get leave and find my way
there. Hopefully, when I do I will have my aunt by my side.
But, thank you, for offering. I appreciate that a lot. But it's
Saturday night. Go out, have fun and don't worry about me.'

'But I do worry about you, Libby. I worry a lot. I don't know
what it is, but I've sensed that you've been pulling a two-horse
plow all by your lonesome since I found you here. Then when
I gave you the message from your mother, you talked about a
matter of life and death. I have a feeling it has something to do
with that creepy Dr Hansrote, but I don't think it's just his
tomcattin' around. It seems like it would have to be more than
that. I don't know what it is, but I will be glad to help you in
any way I can.'

The room felt as if it started to spin, built up momentum
and then jerked to a stop. How did she come to that conclusion?
How am I giving myself away? I stared down at restless fingers
fidgeting in my lap.

Jessie crouched down beside me and took one of my hands in
hers. 'You can tell me, Libby. I will never betray you. We come
from the same earth. We've found ourselves here, far from home,
working in a place without a real name. How did that happen?
It's as if we were brought together for a purpose. Maybe this
problem is the reason why.'

I knew I should talk to the group before I said anything.
They would have a fit over me sharing the story with her.
Most of them, though, are city boys, they don't understand the
sense of community in farmland, how we are forced by nature
and disaster to rely on one another. I felt my roots running through
the dirt of southwestern Virginia, stretching long and entwining
with Jessie's. We had a kinship that ran generations deep. I told
her everything about Hansrote and Frannie and Marvin. I only
held back the group's name and composition. The whole time I
talked, Jessie's mouth hung open and her eyes never left my face.

We sat in silence for a while before Jessie spoke. 'That's why
you wanted to meet Mabel, isn't it?'

I nodded.

'We've got to warn Mabel.'

'No, we can't.'

'No? How can we not tell her?'

'Listen, Jessie, I need to gather information about Hansrote – the more the better. If she doesn't care that he is passing secrets to the other side, she might tell him. If she's appalled by the idea, she could cut him off completely and he could be on to someone else and we'd have to start all over.'

'It kinda doesn't seem fair, Libby.'

'No, it might not be, Jessie. We know she's helping him just by allowing him to have a private phone in her place and call some man named Raymond in Manhattan. It is possible that she knows exactly what he's doing – after all, she's already compromised her morals in one area. Who knows where she draws the line?'

'You're probably right. Is one of your group working in K-25? And could I help him in some way?'

'That's one of our problems, Jessie. None of us work there and none of us have clearance there.'

Jessie smiled. 'I do. I'll let you know if I see him doing anything suspicious.'

'Don't do anything, foolish,' I urged. 'One person is dead already and another is in hiding. This is serious.'

'I don't have your smarts or education, Libby, but I do have a lot of common sense. Don't worry about me.'

I watched Jessie descend the steps. When she reached the boardwalk, she turned around and gave me a wave and a smile. I waved back but I think my attempt at a smile fell far short of cheery. I didn't hold out hope that she could possibly catch Hansrote in anything compromising but she might ferret out a valuable tidbit. Now, I'd be leaving to attempt to set things straight in Virginia. In addition to everything else, I'd have Jessie to worry about, too.

TWENTY-FOUR

I almost put off calling my Aunt Dorothy until the next day but I was glad I hadn't. I felt a lot better once I reached her on the phone. She took charge of the situation and of me. Growing up, I sometimes resented her ability to grab one of my problems and wrestle it to the ground, but now I appreciated her strength and clear-headed, dynamic personality. Talking to her, I actually smiled for the first time since I'd received news of my mother's arrest the night before.

My aunt's initial reaction was much like my own – total disbelief. She, however, recovered from the shock a lot more quickly than I did. She grasped the current reality and ran with it. 'How quickly can you get away?' she asked.

'I'm not sure. I'll have to talk to Charlie to request leave.'

'I'll plan our departures for Monday morning then.'

'But, I haven't talked to him—'

'Merciful heavens, Libby. He can't exactly refuse to allow you to leave under the circumstances. If this does not qualify as a family emergency, I don't know what does. Call me back tomorrow after you speak to him. I'll try to have all the arrangements made by then.'

I felt as if I could breathe again. And my previously muddled thinking now grew crystal clear. I had a lot to do before Monday morning.

Before going to bed, I wrote a letter to my half-brother, assuring him that I would be there soon. I knew that there was a good chance I'd arrive before the mail did, still it seemed important to make this gesture. From the time I'd left home, a decade ago, I'd always sent him a note and a present for his birthday and at Christmas. That remembrance had kept alive a weak but constant connection and it seemed, from what Jessie's mama had said, to be an important one to him.

*   *   *

Early Sunday morning, I went over to Teddy's dormitory and spooked the boy at the front desk by walking inside. After shooing me out, he agreed to rouse Teddy Mullins, who stumbled through the doors a few minutes later appearing to need at least two more hours of sleep. I asked him to find Gregg and Joe and come over to my place for breakfast.

'Is something wrong?' he asked.

'My life just got extremely complicated.'

'What happened?'

'Honestly, Teddy, I don't want to go over this all again and again. Could you gather up Gregg and Joe and come to my place. I'll fix breakfast and let you all know at once.'

'You're worrying me, Libby.'

'Please, Teddy. Just get the others. The sooner you do, the sooner I will explain.' I turned and walked away as Teddy called out my name a few times before giving up.

By the time the three joined me, I had a fresh pot of coffee steaming on the stove, potatoes sizzling in one skillet, slices of spam frying in another and eggs sitting on the counter waiting for their moment on the heat. I answered the door, poured them all a cup of coffee and slid bread into the oven to toast.

I had insisted that they stay out of the kitchen and they did, but stood in the doorway, raising their voices to ask me one question after another. 'Five minutes. I'll sit down with you in five minutes and give you all the information you want.'

I called them in to the kitchen to fill their plates and carry them out. Gregg and Joe sat at the table while Teddy and I sat on the sofa with the plates on our lap. For a few minutes the questions were stilled as the three of them shoveled forkfuls into hungry mouths, mumbling barely coherent compliments as they chewed.

Gregg still had another egg and half his spam on his plate when he set down his fork and said, 'Libby, I am really loving this breakfast but why are we here? Did something happen to Frannie? Did Crenshaw threaten you again?'

'As far as I know Frannie is okay and Crenshaw has not given me any more trouble. I have a family problem, Gregg, and it is going to take me away from here for a while.'

'You can't leave now,' Joe said. 'You have to help us with the Frannie and Hansrote situation.'

'Can't it wait a bit?' Gregg asked.

Teddy, on the other hand, asked, 'What's wrong, Libby?'

My first instinct was to not answer the last question and simply address the first two but the obvious compassion and concern in Teddy's voice made me realize I needed to be totally forthcoming with them all. 'My mother is in jail.'

'Are you serious?' Gregg asked.

'Yes, I am.'

'What did she do? Or, I'm sorry, what do they think she did?' Joe asked.

'She's not denying it, Joe, so no apologies are necessary. She shot and killed my stepfather.'

'Why?' Teddy asked.

'Things had gotten very bad in their house. My stepfather was drinking to excess and becoming very nasty and physical when he did. He broke one of my mother's ribs recently and blackened her eyes a few times. My mother's asked for my help this past week. Mrs Early, who sent me the message thought she was going to wait until I could get there before she did anything. Then Ernest knocked out a couple of my little brother's teeth and locked him in an outbuilding. That's when my mother snapped her cap.'

'And it's Ernie you're worried about, isn't it?'

'There's little affection lost between my mother and I. If it was just that she was in jail charged with murder, I'm certain that I would feel compelled to go anyway, but I'd give it a lot more thought before deciding. My little brother, though, is only twelve years old – he can't cope on his own. I'm not sure what I'll do but I have to find a stable situation for him. And something needs to be done with the farm. I'll have to find a manager or sell the property. I just won't know what is possible and what is best until I get there.

'And I don't know. I'm probably partly to blame. She wanted me to come home and stay, to get rid of Ernest for her and remain there to run the farm. I don't think I could be happy with that life in general terms. And most particularly, I know with certainty that living with my mother is not my idea of living at all. I sent

back a message saying I would come as soon as I could to extri-
cate her from the mess she's made of her life – for little Ernie's
sake. But I did say I couldn't come right away and I would not
stay long term.'

'Well, then,' Joe said, 'we're just going to have to work harder
and smarter while you're gone to get the situation with Frannie
and Hansrote brought to a satisfactory resolution so you won't
have to worry about that, too.'

I smiled at them and said, 'Just keep this quiet. Don't spread
the tawdry news around, okay? I'm going to have to tell Charlie
but I really don't want to be the subject of gossip all over Y-12.
Now, where are we with our investigation? Have we made any
real progress at all?'

Gregg shook his head from side to side. 'Libby, I am beginning
to worry that this is a hopeless cause. Unless we can actually
hear what Hansrote is saying when he makes those phone calls,
how can we hope to unveil his treachery?'

'That's another reason I feel dreadful about leaving right now.
I think the only way we'll be able to do that is if Mabel will
help us. I am building a relationship with her and trying to
determine if she is as in the dark about Hansrote as she seems.
I can't move anything forward while I'm in Virginia.'

'Is there anything we can do in that regard?' Joe asked.

'Not that I know of,' I admitted. 'But if you thinking of any
approach while I'm gone, don't feel as if you need to check in
with me. I'll give you all the phone number at the farm in case
of an emergency but you do not need to consult me, just make
your own best decisions. Follow up any lead that can give you
more information about Hansrote, you never know where it will
take you. If one of you can drive me to the train station, you all
can have the use of the car while I'm not here.'

Joe said, 'I was thinking, Libby, if I told my sister what we're
trying to do, she might be able to feel out Henrietta on the issue
of espionage.'

'Risky move,' I said.

'That's what I said when he suggested it to me,' Gregg said.
'But he convinced me that it made sense.'

Joe said, 'I know she would be discrete and is definitely a
master of subtlety. She won't give us away but she can be more

useful if she knows the story. You see, Libby, she's doing anything that's suggested to her to help the war effort. She works for the war bond drive, she volunteers with the civil air patrol, she fills packages for shipping to soldiers and – much to my mother's horror – she actually tends her own victory garden. Mother told her that it's not seemly for someone of her background and breeding to muck about in the dirt. My sister is a true-blue American without an ounce of stuffiness, hesitation or doubt.'

'What if she asks about the work you do, about what's going on here that would make Hansrote's spying worthwhile?' I asked.

'That's easy,' Joe said. 'If I tell her that the government swore me to secrecy, she'll be satisfied with that. If she knew of my concerns about what the leaders of this country were up to, she'd be horrified that I'd dare question the righteousness of any of their actions.'

'Okay, Joe, that sounds safe enough. If the Mabel approach does not yield results, it would be good to have a better idea of how receptive Henrietta might be if confronted with her husband's espionage.'

'If she doesn't want to come down here to chastise him about his spying, maybe she'd be indignant over Mabel,' Teddy said. 'And there is one other thing we could do.'

'What's that?' Joe asked.

'We could search his house while he's at K-25. There's a window in the back that he has left open for days now. It would be easy to slip in and out without anyone being the wiser.'

'How do you know that and what do you think you'll find there, Teddy?' I asked.

'I've been keeping an eye on his house. I was worried the first time I walked past the rear of it, but no one seemed to notice when I cut through there so I kept going back. There has to be something inside his home. Maybe no direct proof, but a little note or official documents or who knows what – he can't be spying in a vacuum.'

'If you go inside his house, though, the risk of getting caught becomes much greater and the consequences of that grow more severe,' I cautioned.

'I thought about that, Libby,' Gregg said. 'We need to all be waiting nearby for him to go to work. A series of brief checks inside might be the best way to manage the risk. Two of us go in, one stays guard as a look-out. If we can find a spare key on our first reconnaissance that would decrease the suspicious nature of our activities on subsequent visits. Don't know if we'll find anything incriminating but I also feel that we need to try.'

'It's up to you,' I said. 'Use your best judgment. Wednesday night, he is supposed to be in Knoxville at Mabel's – that could be a good time to look as well. At this point, I think we have to take on a higher level of risk if we ever expect to resolve Frannie's problem. In that regard, I want to let you know I've made an independent and irreversible move. I'm fairly certain, given the tenor of our conversation, that you three will understand my on-the-spot decision but I'm not sure the others will accept it. I very well could get drummed out of the group.'

'What did you do, Libby?' Gregg asked.

'I told you about the old hometown friend who works in K-25. I believe she is trustworthy based on our childhood bond and my estimation of her character at this time and I also was confident that if she knew what was happening, she'd be better equipped to recognize suspicious behavior from Hansrote at work.'

'You told her?' Gregg asked.

'About us?' Joe added.

'Not about any of you but about the situation – everything about Hansrote, Frannie and Marvin.'

'I, for one, will endorse your decision, Libby,' Gregg said.

Joe and Teddy echoed his sentiment and Teddy added, 'Maybe we shouldn't mention it to the others until something develops.'

'That would be the simplest,' I said, 'but it has to be your decision, not mine.'

The men moved on to plan their first foray into Hansrote's home the next morning and we wrapped up our impromptu meeting. When they were gone, I dressed for the Episcopal service at the Chapel on the Hill, wondering the whole while what I would find when I did get back to Virginia, hoping I could resolve it quickly and get back to the work I loved.

TWENTY-FIVE

Afterchurch, I had a stroke of luck. Charlie was waiting with his family for the next service in the chapel when I emerged from the sanctuary. He agreed to grant me leave to return home, without any argument. His only condition was that I would call if I was not able to come back in a week. I certainly hoped to keep to that schedule but knew there were no guarantees.

I had a good laugh at Aunt Dorothy's expense when I called her after lunch. She seemed terribly put out that the train schedules did not run as she wished they did and that Knoxville was further south than she had estimated. Her plan to meet in Washington, D.C. was scrapped and we agreed to rendezvous at the Knoxville train station. She was scheduled to arrive there an hour before me.

The next morning, Teddy drove me to the train station and promised to find Jessie Early and let her know that I had gone to the farm. I waved to him as the train pulled away, my heart filled with yearning to stay and a guilty sense that I was abandoning him when he needed me the most.

I spent the trip alternating between enjoying the scenery, finishing my read of *A Tree Grows in Brooklyn* and reliving vignettes of my childhood. I wished I could hold tight to the good memories of my father when he was still alive and forget the agony of his death and the wretchedness of my life on the farm after he was gone. But, as usual, the contemplation pulled me back and forth – the bad times and the good times. Just like the ethical dilemma I had when I thought about the ultimate task of the gadget. I no longer resisted the obvious. I knew it was a bomb. Basic scientific principles indicated that it would be a weapon unlike any before. One that would fall on the just and unjust without regard to their value or their future, bringing destruction and suffering to all.

These thoughts left me feeling morose as I disembarked from the train but the sight of Aunt Dorothy's smile on the platform chased away the gloom of the past, the present and the future in a flurry of happiness over our reunion. And, of course, being Aunt Dorothy, she had the rest of the day planned. We left our luggage at the station and went for lunch. After that, we had an appointment with Wilford Coxe, attorney at law. Finally, we would go out to the farm.

Aunt Dorothy had arranged and Mr Coxe delivered. He had visited my mother in the jail that morning and obtained her signature on a document that awarded me unconditional power of attorney with the ability to take action regarding any of her property and the welfare of her son. When my aunt asked how Annabelle was doing, Mr Coxe said, 'She already looks as drained as many do after a much longer term incarceration but she is facing the future with more equanimity than I would. She expects to be convicted and be imprisoned for the rest of her life but understands that death in the electric chair is also an option. She's stalwart in her belief that she did the right thing because she was protecting her child and she would do it again. She told me, Miss Clark, that she made a mistake when she didn't stand up for you and she refused to repeat it with her second child.'

Her words collided with a numb spot in my heart and left me speechless. Could I trust this expression of regret? Or would that simply open me up to further pain and disappointment?

'If she means what she says, Mr Coxe, that is welcome news indeed. Isn't it, Libby?' Dorothy said.

I forced my mouth to move and form the proper words, 'Yes, it certainly is, sir, thank you for passing that along.'

Aunt Dorothy looked at her watch and said, 'We must be moving on, sir. I am sure we'll be calling on you again in a day or two but I arranged for transportation to the farm and it should be arriving at the station at any moment.'

As we walked down the street to pick up our luggage, Aunt Dorothy said, 'Agnes is coming to get us in her wagon. I hope you don't mind. She assured me that it's quite comfortable. Although it will take a bit longer, it will give you a better look at the changes in the countryside.'

'Agnes? Old man McLeod's daughter?' I asked. When my

aunt nodded, I said, 'You've kept in touch with each other after all these years?'

'Yes, we've had some lively arguments from time to time but when you're disagreeing through the mail nothing ever gets too heated. I suppose the fact that she never married either is part of our bond. She's never even considered another man after her sweetheart died at Blanc Mont Ridge during the Great War. Broke her heart permanently when she lost him. Any romance brewing in your life, Libby?'

'You never married so why do you always ask me about that? I wouldn't think it would interest you.'

My aunt chuckled. 'Everything about you interests me, child. You only had your dad for a short time but he was a good man and an excellent father. I imagine that would have imprinted strongly on your heart and because of that, I always imagined you'd marry one day. I just want to make sure you don't throw your life and your career away on a man who is not worthy of you.'

'I imagine you have set the standards of worthiness at the impossible to achieve level. I think you hold me in too high a regard.'

'Not at all, Libby. You simply do not value yourself as much as you should. Oh, there's Agnes.'

I looked across the pavement and the first thing I saw was an old straw hat being waved through the air. It was attached to a thin but muscular arm and angular body. None of the pillow softness of Aunt Dorothy was apparent in Agnes' physique. Farmers' wives around here tended to my aunt's plump shape after years in the kitchen cooking, baking, canning and jelly-making. Their only outdoor exercise consisting of gathering eggs, slopping hogs and milking cows. That was definitely not Agnes' lot in life. She worked every aspect of the business and, as a result, was as rangy as an old farmhand.

When we crossed the street, she gave me a hearty slap on the back. 'Well, Libby, old girl, you sure have grown up.' She squeezed an upper arm and said, 'But we'll have to toughen up your muscles a bit.'

'And why is that, Agnes?' my aunt asked in an acidic tone.

'Look at me, Dorothy. No woman can be as soft as you and

do the work required out here. I took over running a farm that had risen to its full potential. Libby here is fixing to take on one that has seen better days. No way to do that without real physical strength.'

'What makes you think Libby is staying here, Agnes?'

'Heavens, what else would she do? Her stepfather is dead. Her mother will never see the light of day again. And her little brother doesn't have any more sense than Annabelle and he's too young besides. Who else could run it? Libby has an obligation.'

'She also has an obligation to her country, Agnes. She is playing a vital part in ending the war. She can't just walk away from that.'

'Really? Just what does she do?' Agnes said and turned her eyes on me.

It seemed to me that it would be exceedingly unwise to jump into the argument. Certainly it was about me on the surface, but I sensed a deeper current, one that ran all the way back to their school days.

Aunt Dorothy snatched up the reins of the debate and allowed me to hold my peace. 'Libby is not going to throw her life away toiling in the sun and snow. She is far too intelligent and has far too much to offer the world than to stay cloistered down here in the sticks.'

'Ah, there we go again. Just like always. You think you are better than me. You think I wasted my life. And you think you're some paragon of virtue and womanhood. You think your life matters and mine doesn't.'

'I never said that, Agnes, and you know it.'

'Oh, you don't need to come right out and say it, Dorothy. I know, I know. Now where is that danged luggage?'

With both my aunt and her old friend mumbling under their breath, we retrieved our bags and climbed into Agnes' horse-drawn wagon. I sensed that my aunt wanted to make a big deal out of sitting in the back and leaving Agnes alone up front driving but the other woman beat her to the punch. 'Now, don't go arguing over who's going to ride shotgun because I prefer to sit alone centered on the seat when I'm driving the team, so you both are going to have to sit in the back.'

Aunty Dorothy harrumphed and I swallowed my amusement as we climbed up and settled into the front of two bench seats. It seemed as if these two women had formed a relationship based around the argument over the relative merits of their lives, perhaps as shields against the outside world where both of them were considered odd for never marrying.

Listening to occasional rumbles of discontent from my side and up ahead, I took in the scenery that I had not seen for a decade. The town seemed to have expanded out beyond the boundaries I had known and overall the area appeared a bit more prosperous than it had been during the Depression years. Not only did it take me back to my childhood, it also spoke to my current life. Between the reservation and Knoxville, the land and its people seemed very much the same.

TWENTY-SIX

When we reached my father's farm, the changes wrought in the last decade grew more pronounced. The white plank and board fencing cried for a coat of paint and some of the wood had slipped into rot. Piles of dried leaves from last fall, still filled the front yard. On the house itself, a couple of shutters hung crookedly and one was gone altogether. Honeysuckle had overrun one end of the broad front porch, where it seemed to swallow a rocker whole. After sitting empty for just a few days, the home already appeared abandoned.

As Agnes pulled the horses to a stop, she said, 'As I told you, Libby, you've got a lot of work ahead of you. I can send a man over to help out if you want. One of my farmhands has got a knack for carpentry work, he might prove useful.'

'Thank you, Miss McLeod.'

'Just make that Agnes, girl – you're a woman now. I'll send Andy over in the morning. And I've sent someone over every morning since your mama was arrested to tend to the livestock so they haven't been going without food and water but they have been cooped in. They'll all want to get out in the morning. Well, I'll leave you to it,' she said. Turning to Dorothy, she added, 'See you later, you old grouch.'

'Would you like to come in for some tea before you leave, old friend?'

'No, thank you. I've neglected my chores this afternoon and I've got to make sure Cook has gotten dinner started. The boys get hungry after a full day's work. I'll see y'all around,' she said as she climbed back into the driver's seat. She snapped the reins and she was off.

Aunt Dorothy and I watched as a low cloud of dust whirled around the wheels when she headed back up the drive. I felt as dispersed as that dirt – overwhelmed by the endless work here and anxious about the situation back at the city behind the fence.

We walked in through the kitchen door. The room was neat

and clean. The absence of dirty dishes and any mess from food preparation indicated that the last evening of Ernest's life had begun in typical fashion with my mother straightening up after preparing and serving the meal. What else happened before she shot her husband? Did the conflict build slowly or simply erupt like an untended pressure cooker?

In the living room, everything was neat and tidy except for the roll-top desk where papers were strewn all over the floor as if it had been upturned. Probably the result of a law enforcement search or maybe my mother's desperate hunt for a spare key to the shed before she decided that shooting him was the only answer.

We walked upstairs and set down our bags in the hallway. We approached the door to the master bedroom and paused to look into each other's eyes as if gathering strength to face what we would find. Dark blood and clumps of hair and tissues dotted the headboard. The blankets crumpled at the floor by the footboard were spattered with dark blotches of red. The pillows and sheet on the mattress were dark and crusty.

I shuddered. I had no regard for Ernest Floyd but to see his life's blood spilled by an act of violence still hit me hard. How did my mother feel when she saw it? Did the memory of it still haunt her? Or was she able to dismiss the thought of it, just as she seemed to erase me, once it and I were out of her sight?

'We will have to clean this up tomorrow morning,' Aunt Dorothy said. 'I'd like to bring little Ernie back here to stay with us until we've resolved his future but we can't while the evidence of his father's violent death remains in this house. The mattress will definitely have to go. We need someone with a truck to haul it away.'

I nodded and backed out into the hall. I showed my aunt the room that once was Ernie's nursery. Now it was filled with boyish things: a rock collection, a squirrel skull, a snake skin, a yo-yo and a slingshot. I was delighted to see a shelf of boy's adventure books: the Hardy Boys, the Rover Boys, the Submarine Boys and, a stack of comic books. Most importantly, for our immediate needs, there was a full-sized bed.

'Wonderful,' my aunt proclaimed. 'I can stay here until your mother's bedroom is fit for habitation again.'

I approached the door to the room that was once mine. I

hesitated with my hand on the knob not knowing what I would find. When I pushed it open, I felt as if I were stepping back in time – I was twelve years old again. Nothing had changed. My Raggedy Ann doll was still propped up on my pillows. My bookcase overflowed with childhood favorites: Nancy Drew, The Bobbsey Twins, Five Little Peppers and more.

I ran my finger across my dresser. There was not a speck of dust anywhere. Had my mother freshened up the room once she asked me to return or had she kept it this way all these years? If the latter was true, what did that say about her? And about me?

I was ready for bed when the phone intruded. Gregg was on the other end wanting to make sure I'd arrived safely and to offer an update on the first foray into Hansrote's home. 'We found a notebook,' he said. 'It appears that it was written in some sort of code. Teddy started transcribing it but since we needed to get into the lab, there wasn't time to do much.'

'What did it look like to you?'

'I went in there in a suspicious frame of mind and the notes made an impression that they were some type of record for information given and payment received but we haven't had time to analyze it today. I think we don't have enough data to get the full picture of what was there. When we have more, maybe it will be clearer. We're going back as soon as we can. But we're giving it a close look tonight and will try to get more tomorrow morning.'

'Did you find a spare key?'

I could hear Gregg's grin in his voice. 'Yes. We just hope he doesn't notice it's missing tonight. Joe came into town with me to get a copy made at the hardware store. He also plans to call his sister. Listen, I know you said we don't have to report to you but do you mind if we call? I think we'd all feel better if we keep you informed. You might notice something we're missing. But, if you don't want to be disturbed or interrupted . . .'

'You absolutely will not disturb me. And if you call after dark, I can't be doing farm chores or taking care of legal problems at that hour so you wouldn't have to worry about interrupting anything.'

'Great. We'll call when we can. But we'll manage here. You don't have to worry about us.'

'Don't be careless, please. You don't know where the next volley might originate.'

TWENTY-SEVEN

I woke up at dawn the next morning, amazed that my old habit reasserted itself when I returned to the farm. I dressed and went out in the yard with stealth in hopes of not disturbing Aunt Dorothy's sleep.

First, I went to the chicken coop where the hens were in a tizzy. It wasn't just their days of confinement, there was a black snake in one nest surrounded by shattered shells. I shooed the chickens outside and went to the barn to retrieve an axe and a shovel, grumbling about rural life on the way.

When the snake rose up at my approach, I raised the axe and slammed it through him and into the wall. His head fell into the straw and after a few squirms, both pieces went limp. I regretted killing him but knew if I merely removed him, he'd return now that he'd found this easy feast making the hens neurotic and eggs non-existent.

I used the shovel to scoop up his bloodied remains, the mess of jaw-pulverized eggs and the bedding in the nest. After throwing all that into the weeds along a field, I filled the bin with a fresh armload of straw. I went to the barn and saw that our once large herd of dairy cattle now numbered three. Soon after Ernest married my mother, we'd had to terminate them all when tuberculosis swept through the valley. An unbidden smile crossed my lips as I realized getting the new ones had to have been my mother's idea. She was useless in caring for them but there was nothing she loved more than a fresh glass of milk, still warm from the udder. I got down the stool and a pail and pulled on each set of teats one by one, then herded them out into the pasture before carrying the bounty into the kitchen.

When I got there, my Aunt Dorothy, still in her robe and slippers, was busy fixing breakfast. 'You had so many eggs in the refrigerator, I decided to scramble a few. Don't know what you're going to do with them all,' she said.

'Hoard them for now,' I said. 'Not sure the hens will be laying again any time soon. I just killed a snake in the hen house.'

'A snake? You killed it?' Dorothy said with a grimace.

'Oh, please, don't tell me you never had to do in a snake?'

'Ages ago, before I left the farm. But I was a child then. I can't imagine doing it now.'

'Trust me,' I said, 'it all comes back. You never lose the knack for some things. If I find another one, I let you do the honors and you'll see.'

'No, thank you,' Dorothy said, furrowing her brow.

'I still have to slop the pigs but that can wait until after breakfast. I'll clean up and be back as quick as I can.'

I shuddered at my first glimpse of the door to the left of the stairs. I was not looking forward to the task of cleaning the master bedroom. I was not all that squeamish and I'd certainly seen some gruesome sights in my life; but, somehow, knowing my mother had pulled the trigger and created that bloody scene, made the thought very unnerving.

Back in the kitchen, sitting at the table, I was amazed. 'Aunt Dorothy, I didn't know you knew how to make biscuits,' I said.

'Oh, fiddlesticks and nonsense, my child. As you said, there are some things in life you never forget how to do.'

'Sure are good,' I said after taking a bite. 'What's the plan for today?'

'While you take care of the pigs, I'll get started in the bedroom. I don't know if we'll get the cleaning finished before we have to meet the attorney and go to the jail to see Annabelle.'

'We're going to visit my mother with an attorney?'

'That's simply for easy access, dear. You will have time to speak to her alone if you want.'

'I don't know, Aunt Dorothy.'

'You have a couple of hours to decide. Go on, finish tending to the stock. I'll clean up the kitchen and then move upstairs.'

While I was out tending to that chore, I noticed that the barn was in need of repairs as well. I'd have to make a top-to-bottom inspection and decide what was the most critical. At one end, I could look up and see through a hole in the tin roof – that was probably on the top of the list of items needing to be patched or repaired. Running a close second was one of the doors to the

outside that hung by a single hinge and another one that had
signs of rot along the bottom six inches of wood. Even if I wanted
to stay, the state of this place was apt to send me running away
as quickly as possible.

I returned to the house and passed the bloodied linens piled
in the hallway with an equally stained braided rug balanced on
top of them. In the bedroom, the headboard now gleamed
without a speck of blood in sight. The mattress was another
matter.

'You're just in time to help me move this mattress,' Dorothy
said.

'Move it where?' I asked.

'We have to get it out of the house,' she said.

I wasn't sure how the two of us would manage that but I was
willing to try. A lot of pulling and tugging later and we'd gotten
it off the bed frame and onto the floor. We pushed it over to the
door and then struggled to get it up on its side so it would fit
through the opening. Our arms didn't seem long enough or strong
enough to get it up and hold it up. 'Face it, Aunt Dorothy. We're
going to need some help.'

'Oh, don't give up yet. We'll manage if we keep trying.'

'Your face is flushed and you're out of breath. You'll keel over
if you keep this up.'

'Libby, don't be a quitter.'

I sighed and picked up my end again and tried to shove. We
both dropped it when we heard footsteps on the stairs. I know
it was ghoulish but my first thought was that Ernest, with his
bloodied face, was marching up the stairs. By the look on my
aunt's face, she had some equally dreadful thought.

'Hello! Hello! Miss Clark! Miss McLeod sent us over to give
you a hand.'

We popped our heads out of the door and both said, 'Thank
heavens.'

'Interesting choice of words, ladies. I was just telling the little
woman this morning that she should count her blessings because
I was heaven-sent. Only an angel could put up with all her griping.
I'm Andy,' he said and pointed down a few steps and said, 'and
that's Larry. What seems to be the problem here? Y'all look
tuckered out.'

Waving my arm behind me, I said, 'We're trying to get this thing out of the house.'

'A mattress. Well, shoot, that's just too much for a couple of ladies. Me and Larry will make short work of it.'

The two men picked it up and carried it downstairs as if it were as light as a pillow. 'You need this hauled off? We drove the truck over and I know where you can dump it.'

'Why, certainly, sir. That is most kind,' Dorothy said.

'You gonna be wanting a new mattress?' he asked.

'Yes, but I hadn't thought that far yet.'

'Go into town to Peoples, see Mike Reynolds and tell him Andy sent ya. He opened up the furniture store about eight or nine years ago and he believes in customer service. He'll get it delivered out here, bring it upstairs for you and put it in place.'

'Thank you, Mr . . .?'

'Andy. Just call me Andy. If folks called me anything more formal, I'd feel like I'd need to work in my go-to-meetin' clothes. We'll go get rid of this thing and come back and see if you need help with anything else. Miss McLeod said we could stay here as long as you need us.'

My aunt pulled out a tip from her purse and tried to hand it to Andy. But he backed away.

'No, ma'am,' he said. 'Miss McLeod is paying us. No need for payment for helping a friend of the family.'

'But I feel as if I'm taking advantage of you,' Dorothy said.

'No, ma'am, not at all. You get in the mood to bake some pies, Larry and I wouldn't be able to turn them down.'

'I'll have to find that mood, Andy,' Dorothy said with a smile. 'We have to leave shortly to go into town. If you could fix the bottom step on the porch and the broken railing today, that would be wonderful.'

'We can do that and maybe clean up the leaves and twigs out of your front yard, too.'

On the drive into town, Aunt Dorothy, the social worker, marveled that after all these years, the spirit of neighborliness still flourished in the rural population. 'I wish I could generate more of that feeling in the urban areas. Certainly the war has united us in a common cause but when it's over, can we transfer that drive and determination to other areas of our lives?'

TWENTY-EIGHT

My mother has never been an outdoors person and, as a result, she usually sported winter white skin all year round – I used to call her Snow White when I was little. Nonetheless, the sight of her this morning was still a shock. Her face looked wan and pasty with a texture that looked as if a touch would cause it to crumble like pie crust dough. When the three of us walked into the room reserved for attorney-client meetings, her eyes remained riveted on me even when Aunt Dorothy and Mr Coxe greeted her. 'Libby,' she said in a whisper that reverberated with remorse and redemption.

When I uttered my curt, 'Mother,' I saw the hope in her eyes replaced with pain. And I felt guilty and hated myself for feeling that way.

Mr Coxe sat in the chair directly across the table from her and Aunt Dorothy and I slid into the seats on either side. 'Mrs Floyd,' Coxe began, 'you have given your daughter control of all your property and your son. She will make all the final decisions and has no obligation to comply with your wishes but this is your opportunity to make them known to her.'

Annabelle swallowed, the dryness of her mouth made clacking noises before she spoke. 'Libby, I am so sorry—'

'Mother, what do you want?' I snapped.

Annabelle closed her eyes and straightened her spine. Looking straight at the attorney she said, 'I would like my daughter to take over the running of the farm and to raise her little brother there.'

Dorothy interrupted. 'Annabelle, please don't pretend as if Libby is not here. Talk to her, for heaven's sake.'

Annabelle clenched her jaw and pivoted her head in my direction. 'Libby, would you be willing to stay here and raise your brother?'

'No.'

'Will you sell the farm?'

'I haven't decided. I think Ernie should be part of that decision
– and, of course, Aunt Dorothy since she owns half of it.'

'What about Ernie? If you sell the farm, what will happen to
him? Will you take him back to Tennessee?'

'With the long hours I'm working, Mother, I do not think that
I could provide him with adequate supervision.'

Annabelle jerked her attention over to Dorothy. 'Will you take
him up north with you?'

'As Libby said, nothing has been decided yet,' Dorothy
answered.

'But he loves it here. It's his home. He has friends. He has
his roots here. He's only twelve years old.'

'I adjusted just fine, Mother,' I said. 'And, if you recall, I was
twelve years old, too. It didn't bother you then.'

Annabelle's face twisted, her eyes welled and a sob escaped
her throat before she dropped her head into her crossed forearms
on the table. Mr Coxe pulled out a handkerchief and pressed it
into one of her hands.

I felt far less merciful. 'Let's not get dramatic, Mother. It has
never been a good response to your problems and yet, you revert
to it again and again.'

She raised her tear-stained face to mine. 'Did living up north
give you a cold Yankee heart?'

'No. Having a heartless mother did that. The Yankees have
nothing on you,' I said.

The attorney spoke again. 'This confrontation is not doing
my client any good. I need to have her in a good frame of
mind to work on her defense. Perhaps you two should leave
now.'

'No,' Annabelle said. 'I deserve this and much, much more. I
should have been there for Libby. I should have thrown Ernest
out the first time he bullied her. But I didn't and now I have to
pay the price. I knew Ernest was not half the man Libby's father
was but I was frightened by the future. I have seen the error of
my ways. At last, I understand that I need to stand up for myself
and my children. That's why I shot Ernest. That's why I aimed
to kill. I should have done it a long time ago. And that's why I
need to take anything that Libby wants to say to me. I was a
miserable mother and an equally miserable wife to my first

husband. I betrayed the memory and legacy of John Clark by placing his family farm in the hands of a man like Ernest Floyd. I will never stop regretting it.'

I sat in stunned silence, my thoughts and emotions in turmoil. My early childhood affection and love for this woman battled the feelings of betrayal and resentment that came in my adolescence. My stubborn desire to hold her responsible fought with my urge to just let it all go.

My Aunt Dorothy was more resilient. She reached out a hand and laid it on my mother's arm. 'Annabelle, I know my brother forgives you.'

A bitter laugh erupted from my mother's throat that seemed to surprise her. 'Of course, he does Dorothy. He always did. He knew I was weak and helpless. I think a large measure of the attraction he felt toward me was his desire to protect me from the world. Once when he was frustrated with me, he said, "Good God, woman, is my spine the only one available for you to use."' She blew out a huge sigh and then turned back to me. 'Libby, do *you* forgive me? Can you *ever* forgive me?'

I looked down at the table at my hands folded neatly on its surface. I listened to the sounds of scraping chairs and footsteps as my aunt and the attorney rose and left the room. When the door shut behind them, I raised my face. 'Mother, I'm sorry but I don't think I'm ready. Not yet.'

'Oh, Libby. Maybe one day? I know I don't deserve it but I so hope you can forgive me before I die.'

The flow of my tears now matched hers. 'I hope so, too, Mother. I do. I really do.'

She reached across the table and squeezed one of my hands. 'I do love you, Libby, and I always will.' After speaking the words I'd waited too long to hear, she stood and followed the guard out of the room.

I just sat there, still feeling her hand on mine, lost in a jungle where misery and anger swallowed one another whole.

A hand fell on my shoulder and a male voice said, 'Miss, it's time to go now.'

I looked up at a guard's face and nodded. Then, I rose and walked out to the hall.

*　　*　　*

134 Diane Fanning

That evening after supper, Aunt Dorothy and I sat together at the kitchen table drinking tea as we talked. I probed her with questions about the progress she was making in organizing and running the new school of social work at Bryn Mawr, the well-being of her cook, Mrs Schmidt as well as neighborhood gossip.

We were interrupted by the telephone. When I answered, Teddy was on the line. 'Teddy! So nice to hear your voice,' I said, and realized at that moment, how much I really did appreciate him.

'I'm glad you think so, Libby. I volunteered – no, I'll be honest – I begged to be the one to call you. But Gregg and Joe are standing nearby in case you have any questions for them. And, boy, is it good to hear your voice. Are things going well over there? Did you see your mother?'

'Yes and yes. It's difficult to see your own mother locked up but she finally said some things that I wish she said years ago. But the past is that way – when you ignore something, it doesn't go away, it just puts its sticky fingers all over the present. But I'm sure if all three of you thought I needed to be called, it wasn't because you all wanted to see how I was doing. So what's on your mind, Teddy?'

'We went back into Hansrote's house tonight while he was in town visiting Mabel. I think we passed him on the highway when we drove in to call you. We took turns transcribing and got down all of the notations he'd made in that little book.'

'And what does it look like?'

'It's tricky, Libby. It does look like he is keeping some sort of record of what he's sent to Raymond and of funds deposited somewhere. Joe thinks it's a Swiss bank account but we don't know that. We found some of his local bank books but what we are seeing in the notebook doesn't match up with any funds put in those two accounts. We also found a new phone number by Raymond's name on a slip of paper. We jotted that down, too.'

'Great work, Teddy. Is Hansrote going to know you were there?'

'We made sure everything was back exactly as we found it. And we strolled out of the house like old friends in case anyone was watching.'

'Ah, good. See, you all don't need me. You're making great progress.'

'We do need you. We're like a ship without a captain, a company without a commander, a—'

'Enough, enough,' I said as I laughed. 'You made your point. I'll be back as soon as I can. Be careful. All of you.'

I was grinning when I sat back down with Aunt Dorothy. 'Now, where were we?'

'Oh no, you don't,' Dorothy said. 'You're not getting off the hook that easy, not with that Cheshire Cat grin on your face. Is that the young man you've not been telling me about?'

'We don't have a relationship – not that kind.'

'Oh really? Then what did I hear in the tone of your voice when you were talking to him and why are you blushing now?'

She knew me too well. I should have never thought that I could slide this one past her since she was the keeper of all the secrets of my heart throughout grade school and into college. 'I admit it. He is a possible. He really likes me. I could maybe see it developing into something serious but we're not there yet.'

'I'll accept that at face value but what else is going on? What are you not saying, Libby? And don't say nothing. I could tell by the worried little furrows that danced across your brow when you were on the phone. Something back in Tennessee is bothering you, isn't it? Can you tell me what it is?'

Although I shared a lot about my life down south with my aunt in letters and phone calls, I didn't dare mention anything about Hansrote's treason, Frannie's fugitive status or Marvin's murder in communications going through the censors. Now, I let it all spew out in a cleansing rush that shocked and dismayed Aunt Dorothy. As I expected, she instantly grasped the gravity and sensitivity of the situation. She pulled out a piece of paper and pencil to make a list of what needed to be done to get me back to my work as quickly as possible.

We pulled all the information about the farm out of the roll-top desk and stacked it on the table. Considering Ernest's lack of business acumen, the farm seemed to be thriving and turning a profit – not as flourishing as it was when my father was in charge but better than average. That meant there was ready money to hire a manager and a dependable hand. Aunt Dorothy volunteered to invest some of her personal funds into replenishing the herd and making needed repairs to the property.

The big question remaining was what to do with Ernie. He certainly couldn't stay out here on his own even with a farm manager at hand. My aunt wasn't sure if she was up to raising a boy in her home but she was willing to try if that was what Ernie wanted. However, we both suspected that he'd want to stay in the area.

When we finished for that night, we had a long list of things to do and an even lengthier list of questions that needed answers. But, we did have a plan of action. If all went as it should, I could leave on Monday and Aunt Dorothy, who was not teaching any classes this summer, could stay a while longer to get everything running smoothly.

TWENTY-NINE

The next morning, Peoples delivered the new mattress and the men who brought it in were willing to move the bed over to another wall. I found the lovely barn-raising quilt my grandmother made along with several other decorative pieces to put in the room. We wanted it to look as different as possible for Ernie's sake. We placed the contents of the dressers and the closet upstairs in the attic storage area. Finally, we moved my Aunt Dorothy's things out of Ernie's room and settled her into the master bedroom.

We drove off in the countryside, stopping at farms here and there to talk to my father's old friends about men who could be trusted and were suitable to run the farm with an absentee landowner. When we finished our rounds, we had a short but promising list of prospects. The last stop of our outing was at Mrs Early's house to pick up Ernie.

We sat down for coffee and coffee cake as Jessie's mom plied me with questions about her daughter, what she was doing and what was going on in that strange place we called home. There were, of course, a lot of them that I couldn't answer but that didn't stop the rapid-fire flow. Mrs Early simply wanted to know every little thing I could tell her.

Abruptly, she changed the subject. 'Ernie really does not want to move to Tennessee or Pennsylvania. He says he wants to stay right here. He thinks he should be able to live in the house on his own, but as you all know, that's not possible. But, Libby, he could stay here. He's a good kid – I can't believe I'm saying that about a child of that worthless Ernest Floyd but it's the God's truth. He's a hard worker, wants to learn as much as he can and has already been a big help to Henry. Come harvest time, he'll be a godsend.

'I reckon I'll need some guardianship papers for school and the doctor and such, but me and Henry would be glad to take him in until Annabelle gets out of jail – or if she doesn't until he really is old enough to care for himself and the farm on his own. Now, I'm not telling you what to do, Libby. I'm making an offer that I think would make Ernie happy. He has a knack for farming and we'd be proud to raise him as one of our own.'

I certainly could not have found better parental surrogates but still there was much more information to gather before we reached a decision about Ernie's future. 'Thank you, Mrs Early. It's nice to have that option. I tend to think you're right but we'll need a bit more time to think it all through.'

'I think this is all a cryin' shame. Did the lawyer tell you what her chances were for not guilty?'

'We've talked but I've not gotten an answer to that yet.'

'I imagine if it was up to the womenfolk around these parts, Annabelle wouldn't have been arrested, she would have gotten a medal.'

At first, Ernie seemed thrilled to be going to the house and staying with me, even though we warned him that I'd only be around for a few days. When he walked up on the front porch, however, his smiling face turned somber. He set down his suitcase and stared at the door. We gave him time, not wanting to rush him. After a couple of minutes, Aunt Dorothy said, 'If you've changed your mind about staying here Ernie . . .'

'No. No. Just a minute, please.'

He shuddered, grabbed the bag and opened the front door. He didn't pause there but rushed up the steps and dropped the suitcase on the landing. I followed and found him standing outside the doorway of the master bedroom with his eyes closed. He took a deep breath and walked inside.

His head turned as he absorbed the changes. He looked back at me with a weak smile and said, 'Thank you, Libby.' Leaving there, he picked up the piece of luggage and walked into his sanctuary. 'I need to be alone for a while,' he said before shutting the door.

I didn't really want to leave him alone – it seemed harsh, even though it was his decision. Reluctantly, I went back downstairs.

'He's going to be all right,' my aunt said. 'He's made of tougher fiber than his mother and more determined stock than his father. Little Ernie is going to do fine. I suspect that one day, he'll be running this farm much as your father did with the same spectacular success.'

'I hope you're right. What about his lunch? It's way past time.'

'He told me at the Early house that he'd like peanut butter and jelly. I'll fix one for him and carry it up with a glass of milk. For supper, he wants meat loaf, mashed potatoes and he thinks there is some corn on the cob ready in your mother's victory garden.'

'My mother has a victory garden?'

'Yes, Ernie surprised me with that tidbit of information. He says Annabelle started the spring after Pearl Harbor and kept with it even though Ernest told her it was a stupid waste of time. Sounds to me like her rebellion against her husband's control has been brewing for a couple of years now.'

'I'll go find the patch, pick the corn and see what else is growing out there while you take care of Ernie.' The garden plot was surrounded by a fence to keep out any renegade cows or pigs. Everything was laid out in precise, neat rows. Seed packets, faded and ragged from the weather, adorned sticks planted at the end of rows. I picked four ears in case Ernie wanted two, selected the two ripest tomatoes and noted that green beans and cucumbers were ready for harvesting, too.

At supper that evening, Ernie acted like a normal kid. He babbled on about the coming school year and pleaded with me to wake him up at dawn to help with the chores. He was excited when I told him about the snake and asked me to show him where I dumped it. I worried about what he was burying inside and whether one day, it would explode outwards in blind fury.

When I came in from milking the cows, on Thursday morning, I heard the ring of the telephone as soon as I set foot on the porch. I hurried in and grabbed the receiver, hoping it hadn't woken Aunt Dorothy. 'Hello. Floyd residence.'

'Libby?'

'Yes . . .?'

'This is Jessie.'

'Oh good heavens, what is wrong?'

'Well, nothing's wrong – not really, but . . .'

'It's just so early, it sounded as if—' I said.

'Oh, Libby, I think it's important. I'm not calling from behind the gates. I'm in Knoxville. I've been so scared since I found it.'

'What? What are you talking about?' I listened with mounting anxiety as Jessie explained Hansrote's movements on Tuesday night and what she did on Wednesday night.

THIRTY

The night before last, Jessie had seen Dr Hansrote on the floor of the lab. It was odd because she'd never seen him in there that late before. She had been on her way back from the restroom when she spotted him coming out of one scientist's office and entering a different one. In his second stop, he walked out with a folder. It struck her as a bit suspicious but then, she didn't know if the scientists made a habit of going in and out of each other's spaces all the time.

It crossed her mind several times and every time it did, she grew more concerned. She decided that if she saw him that night, she would have to figure out what he was doing. For hours, she looked up at the sound of every footstep but all were false alarms. Finally, after a mid-shift break, she spotted him crossing the floor and going into an engineering office. She scurried in that direction.

When Hansrote emerged with a folder in his hand, she stumbled and intentionally fell into it. She felt the rush of success when she saw the papers flying everywhere.

'Watch where you're going, girl,' he snapped.

'Oh, Dr Hansrote, I am so sorry. I am so clumsy, sorry, sorry, sorry.' She dropped to her knees gathering up papers, mixing them up as she did. When he wasn't looking, she stuffed one sheet into her coveralls.

The whole time, he was sputtering, 'I've got it. I've got it. Get back to work. You've caused enough damage already.'

After making sure the piece of paper she'd hidden was secure, she rose to her feet and said again, 'I'm so sorry, Dr Hansrote.'

'Please, just get out of my sight.'

'Yes sir,' she said as she curtsied and rushed away. The heat in her face made her feel like she would explode. She trembled so much inside that it transferred out to her fingers. She struggled to even her breath – in and out, slow and sure.

Running into the restroom, she pulled out the piece of paper and stared at it. It was some sort of technical diagram, that much she knew, but for what, she had no idea. She pulled open her coverall and tucked it away in her underwear, to make sure it couldn't fall out while she worked.

At the end of her shift, she headed over in dawn's light to the pay phone at the Town Center. She started to dial and then realized she shouldn't use a phone on the reservation to tell Libby about what she found. She changed clothes, grabbed breakfast in the cafeteria and hopped the first ramshackle bus into Knoxville. She carried the page from the file, folded in her purse. She was terrified that she'd be stopped and searched at the gate on the way out. Once she passed that danger point, the bag seemed to grow hotter in her hand with every mile of the drive. By the time she disembarked, her palms were sweating and she had beads of perspiration across her upper lip.

It was too early for the drug store to open so she walked the streets looking for another option. She found an outside phone booth at a gas station, slid in and shut the door. 'The phone rang so many times I was about to hang up but then you answered,' Jessie said.

'Describe what's on the paper, please,' I asked. By now, my heart was pounding. What she had found might be just what we needed to implicate Hansrote in espionage. If it was, it was also something that could get Jessie in a lot of trouble.

'It shows tubes. I think like the ones I'm cleaning shift after shift—and where to connect to something else. I can't make any sense of it, really. Do you think it will help?'

'It very well might, Jessie. But you can't be carrying this around . . .'

'I'll stick it in my jeweler box when I get back to the dorm.'

'No. If Hansrote reviews that file and discovers something is missing, he might remember you. If he does, he could point a finger at you just as he did at Frannie. At that point, your room would be searched. You need to find Teddy, Joe or Gregg and turn it over to one of them. But make sure you don't do it standing in front of Y-12. Walk a bit away from the place – there are too many guards there. And make sure no one is listening into your conversation. Can you do that?'

'Yes. I'll be glad to get rid of this thing. I'll keep an eye out for Dr Hansrote and see what else he does.'

'But don't try that trick again. He'll never be fooled by it a second time,' I warned.

Returning to Oak Ridge as soon as possible was now imperative, I just hoped that Monday would be soon enough. I needed to see that paper and decide what to do with it. And should I take it to Crenshaw? Or is there someone else better suited to handle this situation?

THIRTY-ONE

I felt that I galloped through the rest of Thursday. We talked to two potential farm managers and both of them met Aunt Dorothy's approval and seemed capable of doing a good job. I relied on my aunt's judgment about character because she was used to hiring people, but it was all new to me. We had three others scheduled to come by Friday morning and then we'd have to decide.

We talked with Ernie and once we got him past the expectation of living in the house, he decided that he wanted to go to Tennessee with me. When he realized that although that might be a possibility in the future, it wouldn't work now, he said that he would rather stay near the farm and his friends at the Early place rather than move away with Aunt Dorothy. He did have the graciousness to apologize for rejecting her offer – better manners than I'd expected from a twelve-year-old.

Wilford Coxe stopped by that afternoon and I talked to him about my mother's future. He admitted that he would consider it a victory if he could save her from the death penalty. 'With a life sentence, she could be out in thirty years.'

'She'll be almost eighty by then. She may never get out of prison except in a coffin.'

'We can only hope and pray she lives to see freedom again. I wish I could do more. Normally, in a case like this I would try to get an acquittal with a self-defense plea, but your mother admitted that she intentionally shot him in the back while he was sleeping. I will do my best during the penalty phase to itemize the abuse she suffered and little Ernie experienced. That might keep her from the electric chair and maybe we'll get lucky and get a second-degree murder conviction, but don't count on it.'

The harsh reality of the sentence rocked me. Yes, my mother did something wrong but she did it for all the right reasons. If only she shot him when he was coming at her. Then again, she probably was not capable of looking him in the eye and pulling the trigger. More's the pity.

'One day,' Aunt Dorothy said, 'brutish behavior by men like Ernest Floyd will not be tolerated – not by the police, not by anyone.'

'I hope you're right, Miss Clark,' Mr Coxe said with a sigh. 'This is not the first case I've seen where the law sanctions a miscarriage of justice. Now, what have you decided about little Ernie? Your mother gave you unconditional control over him and the farm. If she ever gets out of prison she couldn't get either back unless you agreed. I would suggest that no matter where you place Ernie, you maintain as many options as possible to reverse your decision.'

I explained our plans and he promised to have the paperwork ready by the end of the day. He was completely in sympathy with getting me back to work even without knowing any of the details of what I'd left behind. He suggested meeting me in the evening at the Early place and wrapping up that detail as soon as possible.

After that meeting and with the agreement that Ernie could stay on the farm as long as I or Aunt Dorothy were in residence, we returned home. I was feeling good about our progress and the future. Then, the telephone rang.

The man at the other end of the line was unrecognizable at first from his breathlessness and the gasps separating each word. 'Libby . . . they're . . . gone!'

'Joe?' I asked.

'Yes.'

'Where are you?'

'Knoxville . . . phone booth.'

'Who's gone?'

'Gregg . . . and . . . Frannie. They're gone, Libby. They took them.'

'Gone? Gregg? Frannie?'

'Yes.'

'Who took them?'

'I don't really know but . . .'

'You don't know? Do you think Hansrote was one of them?'

'I don't think so. If he was, there is something really peculiar going on.'

'Start from the beginning and tell me what happened.'

THIRTY-TWO

G regg and Joe had taken Libby's car into Knoxville for Gregg to visit with Frannie and Joe to call his sister. After Joe finished an interesting conversation about Hansrote's wife, he returned to the hotel. The two men chatted with Frannie, played some gin rummy and then Joe went out to get some magazines and toothpaste for her before they left.

Joe stood on the sidewalk opposite the hotel waiting to cross the street, when he saw four men go into the front entrance of the hotel – two civilians and two soldiers looking very official. He felt the unwelcome electric charge warning of danger and wanted to flee immediately. Sneaking into the lobby and up to the front desk, he leaned behind a post that blocked him from their view. One of the men asked about any new guests. The clerk mentioned a couple of names and room numbers including one for Mr and Mrs Gregg Abbott. Joe slipped out the front door and, running as fast as he could, circled to the back of the building and pounded up the service stairs two at a time to Frannie's floor. Joe felt defeated when he saw that the suits and uniforms were outside of Frannie's door by the time he got there.

Joe hid in the stairwell, peering through the small window as they went inside. He heard muffled voices and then saw an MP emerge with one hand clasped on Gregg's elbow and the other flat against the center of his back. Another uniformed military policeman came out of the room holding on to Frannie whose wide eyes and twitching face made her look like a cornered rabbit. Behind them was one of the men in civilian clothes who stepped in front of them to press the down button for the elevator and held it open until everyone was inside. Joe waited for the second man to enter the hallway through the now opened door of Frannie's room. Joe then eased open the entry to the stairs a crack and heard the sounds of opening drawers and overturned items and assumed the room was being searched.

Heading down the stairway to the parking lot, he stared out

at three other MPs roaming through the spaces between the vehicles. He held his breath every time one of them got near Libby's old Buick but after a while it became apparent that they were seeking a car but had no description to back up their hunt. After going up and down the aisles for a while, they went around to the front of the hotel with Joe following them at a distance. He saw them go inside and then emerge only a moment later. They looked up and down the street as if waiting for someone.

'I decided it would be safer to wait until nightfall to approach your car,' Joe told Libby. 'The delay was making me crazy but I knew I couldn't risk getting picked up because I needed to remain free to warn you about what happened. So I looked for a phone booth – the drug store was closed for the day. I was afraid that by the time I reached you, someone would have paid you a visit at the farm and taken you away, too. It's growing darker by the minute now so I probably should hurry back to warn Teddy. You came to my mind first but Crenshaw knows his name, too. I better go see him.'

'I think I need to go see Crenshaw as soon as possible,' I said. 'I'm not sure if I can make the train tomorrow morning or not. Check at the station before you go back home. See when the train from here will arrive tomorrow and tell Teddy to come pick me up then. Tell him if I'm not on the train tomorrow, to call me. I'm going to get there as soon as I can.'

'What if I can't find Teddy to give him the message and he doesn't know to be there waiting for you?'

'If you can't find him, you meet me tomorrow, okay? I won't ask you to go with me but I'll need to know if I need to ask Crenshaw about him, too.'

'And what if I don't get back?' Joe asked.

'Then I'll find another way to return to the reservation. If there is no one waiting for me, I'll have to get back without going through a gate. God speed, Joe. I'll see you as soon as I can.'

When I hung up, Aunt Dorothy said, 'I'm not sure what's going on, dear, and don't know if you can tell me. But it is apparent from hearing your end of the conversation that your immediate return is required.'

I went through the latest development with her and then we

discussed the open issues about the farm and my mother's case. 'I feel so torn. I don't want to leave with all these loose ends still hanging but everything back there seems so terribly urgent right now.'

'Don't you give it another thought. I'm grateful that you were able to come here at all. I'll have you on the train in the morning. Please call me as soon as it is possible. I know it's not easy but I don't want to make any irrevocable decisions without your opinion on matters first and I will worry about you between every call.'

I promised her to keep in close touch and hoped it would remain possible. I didn't want to draw any more attention to the fact that it was just as likely that I would be rounded up as soon as I arrived. I'd worry about that if it happened.

THIRTY-THREE

My departure from Bedford before dawn the next morning was more emotional than I had anticipated. Not only did my aunt surprise me with the tears pooling in her eyes, but little Ernie insisted on coming with us to the train station where he broke down and sobbed. I promised to visit as soon as I could but he was inconsolable. It was odd considering that we'd been so disconnected for so long but I guess I was all he had left.

My internal tension wound tighter with every click of the track. I was anxious to arrive and dreading my destination at the same time. At every stop on the journey I studied each platform on the hunt for anyone who might be coming to take me away. I kept telling myself that I was over-reacting but I could not relax. When we finally chugged into Knoxville that evening, I was numb, exhausted and ready to accept any ending to the tense day.

Seeing Teddy and Joe both standing outside of the train station was a deep, emotional release that caused tears to dampen my cheeks. I brushed them away and waved like an excited child until they spotted me in the compartment window. When I came down the steps to the platform, two pairs of hands reached for my suitcase – I didn't notice who won the battle. Regardless, it was sitting on the platform as if abandoned as we chattered and embraced one another in relief.

They wouldn't let me drop them off at the dorm but insisted on accompanying me back to my house. Once there, they searched in every closet and cupboard and under the two twin beds. Before they left, Teddy and I made plans to visit Crenshaw before going to work in the morning. Joe made me promise to jamb a wooden chair under the doorknob before he left. I laughed at him but when I was all alone, fear tickled the back of my throat. I didn't hesitate to implement his primitive security suggestion and hoped it was as laughable as I initially thought.

*   *   *

I walked out of my flattop before sunrise Saturday morning and found both Teddy and Joe waiting on the boardwalk in front of my house. I smiled at both of them. 'Good morning, Teddy. Joe, I don't think you want to expose your identity to Crenshaw unless you have no other recourse.'

'I thought I'd make the offer,' he said. 'If you think it's unwise, I'll just go most of the way with you and stand by to make sure you get out of his place without an armed escort.'

'Good thinking. But keep hidden. If we come out unfettered, we could use your help to get the rest of the group together. If not, you can raise the alarm about us, too.'

We talked for part of the way about our frustration with the investigation and then switched over to news from the European front. It still sounded very positive but we all three knew that the government had a tendency to share only the good news and keep the setbacks to themselves for as long as they possibly could. Joe stopped a block away at a treed lot and Teddy and I approached Crenshaw's house and knocked on the front door.

Crenshaw answered and gave us a sour look. 'What now?'

'Another chemist in the Y-12 laboratories is missing. He never returned to his dorm room last night,' I said.

'Did you find his body?' Crenshaw sneered.

'No, sir. We are just concerned. After what happened to Marvin . . .'

'We understand now why your little scientist friend died,' Crenshaw said. 'At least we know it was one of two reasons. Either he was involved in a spy ring and that got him killed or he decided to turn in his treasonous cousin and he was murdered for that reason. Are you two involved in this? Were you complicit in harboring a spy? Is Gregg Abbott one of your secret little group?'

'Marvin was not a spy,' Teddy said. 'He was a hard worker and doing everything he could to contribute to winning this war. The man is dead. How dare you disparage him when he can't be here to defend himself?'

I worried Teddy's response was a bit too forceful, that his defensive reaction just might get us taken away, too. I jumped in trying to soft-pedal the message. 'Sir, I think it is unlikely that Marvin is a spy. He was very lacking in self-confidence, he's always been very reluctant to confront anyone, and he agonized over doing the right thing at all times.'

'So, tell me, Miss Clark,' Crenshaw said, 'how do you know that those aren't the ideal characteristics of a spy? I suppose next you'll tell me that Frannie Snowden is an unimpeachable patriot, too.'

To buy a little time to think, I said the only thing that came to mind, 'Who?'

'You're telling me you don't know and never heard of Frannie Snowden, Marvin's cousin?'

'Oh, that Frannie,' I said. 'Yes, Marvin spoke of her but I don't remember him mentioning her surname.'

'And just what did he say about her?'

'It wasn't very flattering, sir. He said she was rather simple. Naïve and gullible.'

'Like a persuasive person could readily convince her of the rightness of providing information to the enemy?'

Oh, dear. 'No, sir, I didn't say that at all.'

Crenshaw's ice-cold blue eyes seemed to pierce the skin of my face with a sharp, unrelenting stare. He kept his eyes on me even as he directed his comments to both of us. 'My advice to you, Miss Clark and Mr Mullins, that you steer clear of any involvement in the disappearance of Mr Abbott. I can assure you that he is very much alive. Put him out of your mind or pay the price. You are this close,' he said holding his thumb and forefinger a quarter-inch apart, 'to being charged as an accessory or with involvement in a treasonous conspiracy. Now leave my home before I change my mind and have you both arrested.'

Part of me wanted to yell at him and tell him how wrong he was. Teddy obviously sensed my escalating anger and placed a calming hand on my forearm. 'Libby, we really need to get to work. We're going to be late if we don't leave now.'

I accepted the wisdom of Teddy's unspoken words, spun around and left the residence without another word. I had to survive this encounter to fight another day. Now the stakes were higher, it wasn't just Frannie in the crosshairs; Gregg's life was on the line, too.

In Y-12 that day, Teddy and I contacted as many members of

the group as we could locate to arrange a meeting that night at eight about Gregg and Frannie's arrests. I blamed travel fatigue and left work at six to try to find Jessie before it was time to go to Joe's.

I drove to the dorms to plead with Jessie to help me with Mabel. As I entered the lobby, I caught Jessie on her way out. 'Can I walk with you wherever you're going?' I asked.

'I was going out to find you,' Jessie said. 'Now you're here, come on up to my room.'

'I really wanted to speak to you in private.'

Jessie laughed. 'The floor is not wild like it was the other night. And my roommate is out with some fella. Nobody will bother us. If they do, I'll shoo 'em away.'

'I wanted to ask you to go to dinner with me at Mabel's place Sunday night.'

'Mama would tan my hide, Libby. You know she would.'

'You know how important this is.' I updated her on Gregg and Frannie's arrest to explain the current urgency.

Jessie sighed. 'Okay, I will go with you to dinner at Mabel's – just don't you dare tell Mama.'

'I wouldn't dream of it. Just follow my lead on turning the conversation in the right direction. I know you don't want to believe Mabel is capable of helping a spy and if you're right, maybe she'll tell us something that will clear her of any complicity.'

Before I left her room, I answered all her questions about her mama and family, the local gossip back home and the new status of Ernie in her home. She was hoping for good news about my mother but there I had to disappoint her.

When it seemed all had arrived at Joe's, grabbed a seat and satiated their thirst, I said, 'In the absence of Gregg, I'll call the meeting to order. Before I begin with my report, I'd like to know what you think of the document Jessie swiped from Hansrote.'

Joe said, 'I think we all agree that it is a schematic for a portion of a gaseous diffusion set-up.'

'Good. As soon as it seems appropriate to pass along to someone in a position of authority, I will. Now, for my report. Teddy, please jump in if you have anything to add as I tell them

about our conversation with Crenshaw.' I related that morning's
meeting and answered a few questions about it. Then, I informed
them that I would be going to Mabel's for dinner the next night
and Jessie Early, a friend from my childhood home was going
to be with me.

'The fact that you're not going alone makes all of us feel a
lot better, Libby,' Dennis said. 'But how are you going to find
out anything with her along?'

'I sketched out the bare bones to her because I needed her
cooperation.'

'You what?' Tom said. 'You should have talked to us about
that first.'

'There wasn't time. I had to play it by ear. Just like Gregg
and I gave Joe the go-ahead to be a bit more forthcoming with
his sister. Sometimes action is required without prior consensus.'

'I don't like it,' Tom said.

It struck me at that moment that Gary was not serving as
Tom's yes-man tonight. In fact, he wasn't even there. 'Where's
Gary?' I asked.

Tom shrugged.

'I talked to him myself,' Joe said. 'He told me he'd be here.'

I sat there wondering if Gary's absence had anything to do
with Gregg and Frannie's arrest. It was such an awful accusation
to make against one of our own that I couldn't bear to voice it.
An unsettling silence had spread through the room.

Tom broke the barrier. 'It can't be.'

'So I guess everyone is thinking what I'm thinking,' Dennis
interjected.

'Please tell me it's not true,' I added.

Rudy looked around the table with a furrowed brow. 'What
are you talking about? Let me in on it, please.'

'I'm not sure I can speak for everyone else here, Rudy,' Dennis
said. 'But I'll stick my nose out and tell you what I'm thinking.
I'm wondering if Gary's not here because he squealed about
Frannie's hiding place.'

'Gary's never had an independent thought in his life,' Tom
said. 'He follows my lead on everything. He even wants my
opinion before he asks a girl out to the movies.'

'Maybe he's rebelling, Tom,' I said. 'Maybe he finally got

tired of being controlled by you and this is his way of lashing out.'

'Please!' Tom said. 'He's not a girl. He doesn't have little emotional snits at some perceived slight.'

'Really, Tom? Why don't you share a bit more from your vast store of wisdom about women and their motivations?'

'Oh, jeepers. There you go again. Making a big deal out of nothing. See I told you – you females are all alike.'

Teddy shot to his feet. 'You want to settle this outside, Tom.'

Long and lanky Dennis slowly rose from his chair. He was taller than any of the others and knew how to use his deep voice to the most intimidating effect when the situation required it. 'Let's all just take it down a peg. We don't need to be scrapping among ourselves. We've got enough problems. Do I need to remind you that we have one member dead, one member arrested and a damsel in distress whom, thus far, we have failed to rescue? On top of all that, the two of us who are known to Crenshaw have been threatened and one more of our number is AWOL under suspicious circumstances. Tom, I see you getting ready to object but you really can't deny the suspicious nature of his absence – could be harmless, but right now, we don't know.'

'Okay, okay,' Tom said. 'When I leave here, I'll find him. No matter how long it takes, I will find him. And if he doesn't have an acceptable answer, I'll punch the taste right out of his mouth.'

'Just don't jump to premature conclusions,' I urged him.

'Don't worry, Libby. I know him well. If he's the rat, I'll know by his reaction. There won't be any doubt about it.'

I certainly didn't want to condone any act of violence – there was enough of that going on overseas – but still I couldn't bring myself to criticize Tom for his justifiable anger that one of our group may have betrayed us all.

THIRTY-FOUR

Sunday, my supposed day of rest, should have been a day to lay in bed and stare at the ceiling for a while. After getting up to start the coffee brewing, I usually jumped back under the covers and played with G.G. until he remembered it was breakfast time and demanded I fill his bowl. Not today.

I had barely turned the burner on before a never-ending stream of men started flowing through my front door. Tom was the first to arrive.

'I looked everywhere I could think of last night and couldn't find him anywhere. This morning, I went by his room. Stanley said that his roommate left for Joe's Saturday evening and he hadn't seen him since then.'

As Tom left, he passed Teddy and Joe coming up the steps to my flattop. The two of them told me that they retraced the path Gary most likely would have followed from the dorm to Joe's and found no sign of him anywhere even though they'd looked into every nook and cranny they could find.

Dennis was the next to knock on the door. 'I got a little lucky in the cafeteria,' he said.

'You found Gary?' I asked.

'No, not a lot lucky, just a little. I found a group of Calutron girls who knew him and we talked. One of them told me that she'd seen Gary the night before, heading in the direction of Joe's. They chatted for a few minutes but she hasn't seen or heard from him since. But surprisingly, I walked out of there with a date for the movies Wednesday night.'

'You all are so outnumbered by women in this place, how could that possibly be a surprise?'

'Because of the girl. This is not another Calutron girl with a chopped-off bob, this is a real woman with long, long, beautiful hair. She works in the administration building so she doesn't have to worry about hair pins being pulled out of her head by magnets. You don't find heads of hair like that around here very often.'

'I'm so happy for you, Dennis,' I said trying to keep the sarcasm out of my tone of voice. 'Where are you going now?'

'Gary's got a buddy in the army here. I'll go talk to him.'

Another rap on the door sent Dennis on his way as Rudy walked inside. 'I've been standing outside the Chapel on the Hill for a few hours watching people come and go as services cycled through the denominations at the sanctuary but never saw Gary at any of them so far. The Episcopal service is underway now. I'll go back up there and keep watching.'

After a short pause in the traffic, Tom returned to my place. 'I walked through every public room in the dormitory building and then I walked all of the halls. Anytime I saw any residents up and about, I asked them if they'd seen Gary. No one I talked to has seen him after he left for Joe's last night. Has anyone been to the hospital or to the police asking about him?'

'Not to my knowledge, Tom. I think the hospital is an excellent idea but the police? I'm not so sure if we want to get them involved yet.'

'You're probably right. I'll go see if he's sick or injured at the hospital. We can save the police as a last resort.'

I watched Tom bounce down the steps to the boardwalk, hoping he would find Gary totally incapacitated for medical reasons. I really didn't want something to be seriously wrong with Gary but it was preferable to other possibilities – either that he was picked up by the men who got Frannie and Gregg or that he had committed an infraction against our increasingly paranoid little band of Walking Molecules.

I ate a peaceful lunch amazed that I hadn't been interrupted with my mouth full. I cleaned up the kitchen but before I could sit back down, the influx began anew. Every one of them arrived separately or in groups of two within the space of ten minutes. Before I knew it multiple conversations were in full swing and I could barely hear myself think.

When the uproar settled down we came to a general consensus that I needed to talk to Crenshaw about yet another missing scientist. All agreed, though, that I should put off going to see him until I'd had dinner at Mabel's. It was possible that I could get information there to help prove our suspicions of Hansrote and I should not risk being detained by Crenshaw until I did that. Teddy, Joe and I planned another early-morning rendezvous.

I shooed them all out, got changed and at five that evening picked up Jessie for the ride into Knoxville. Before we went into Mabel's apartment, I reminded her to try not to sound judgmental or act shocked at anything Mabel did or said.

'Oh, Libby, I might be an old-fashioned country girl but I did get that lesson on flies, honey and vinegar.'

I could only hope that would be enough to do the trick. I felt the rising tide of desperation, worried that every minute in Crenshaw's hands the situation for Gregg and Frannie grew direr. At the same time, I was anxious about that situation back home. I needed to find the time to call Aunt Dorothy.

When Jessie and I arrived at Mabel's, our hostess could not have been more gracious. She was clearly excited about seeing me again but her reaction to Jessie's presence at her apartment was more exuberant than I had anticipated. Fresh flowers adorned the dining table which was set with fine china, heavy silverware and crystal goblets. The meal was fit for a queen. The main course was a standing rib roast – I hadn't seen one of those since before the war – served with asparagus, mashed potatoes and a smooth, rich brown gravy. 'I had no idea you were such a good cook,' Jessie said as the three of us cleared the table.

'A lot of a girl's talents go to waste on the reservation,' Mabel said. 'How is anyone supposed to land a husband without being able to prepare a good home-cooked meal?'

'Is that what you want, Mabel?' I asked.

'Doesn't everyone?'

'How does Dr Hansrote figure into that equation?' I pressed.

'He said, he's leaving his wife,' Mabel replied. 'But when he added it might not be until after the war, I reminded him that after the war, there would be a lot of eligible young men around and I might be pickier then than I am now. That's when he promised me that it would be soon.'

'You believe him?' Jessie asked.

'I certainly do,' Mabel said. 'Look around. He gives me everything I could want. It might be his wife's money that he's spending on me now but he's developed a new invention that will enable him to make a fortune of his own.'

'Really? What kind of invention?' I asked.

'I don't know. He said he can't reveal anything about it to me just yet because he promised his investors to keep quiet. He said that everything should be in place by the end of the year.'

'Mabel, I don't want to burst your bubble,' Jessie began, 'but I worry about you. Men sometimes lie about things like that. How do you know he isn't?'

'Because he loves me,' Mabel said. 'You can mock that if you want but I believe it with all my heart.'

'Do you love him?' Jessie asked.

'He's nice enough,' Mabel said. 'I could learn to love him.'

Her willingness to marry a man she did not love spoke volumes about her internal yearnings. I knew that a direct appeal to Mabel would not be effective. She saw Hansrote as the man who would rescue her from any fear of poverty or spinsterhood or anything else she felt was lacking in her life. She had idealized her vision of him and saw him as a savior of sorts. And who would betray the one person whom she believed could save her from a life of misery? I tried one more question in hopes of penetrating her tunnel vision about Hansrote. 'What if you found out he was not the man you thought he was?' I asked.

'Yeah,' Jessie added, 'what if he was secretly another Jack the Ripper? Or what if he was one of Al Capone's boys? Or a Nazi spy?'

Mabel fumbled the plate she was rinsing in the sink. It shattered as it struck the porcelain. As she cleaned up the broken pieces, she laughed and said, 'For heaven's sake, Jessie. What an imagination you have. He's none of those. Except for being an ace scientist with a big brain, he's just an ordinary guy with ordinary needs.'

I thought Jessie's comments were a bit too much but maybe she understood that was the approach that needed to be taken with Mabel. They seemed to unsettle Mabel but I wasn't sure why. It was possible that she was hiding something but just as likely was that Jessie had planted a seed of doubt.

'Humph. Well, you can never be too careful, Mabel,' Jessie added. 'Everybody back home thought the world of Brother Blackthorne until they found out he was gambling away the church bank account. When the church elders asked him about the missing money, he disappeared into thin air, leaving behind a wife and six kids. The organ player disappeared at the same time. You just never know.'

'Dr Hansrote is no backwoods preacher man, Jessie. He's a sophisticated man of the world. He doesn't run from problems or complications, he resolves them to his benefit. Oh my, I'm getting a headache – it's pounding right fierce. Let's leave this mess for now. I have a nice bottle of wine chilling. Go sit down in the living room, I'll bring three glasses and we can forget about men and just gossip about the girls we know,' Mabel said.

Jessie and I sat next to each other on the sofa. We gave each other quizzical looks but knew if we spoke, Mabel would over-hear us. Jessie shrugged when I mouthed, 'What do you think?'

Mabel entered the room carrying a tray and handed us each a glass before sitting down with hers. The first sensation of the wine hitting my tongue was absolutely delightful but when I swallowed, it left a bitter aftertaste as if it had aged in an oaken barrel a wee bit too long.

Jessie chugged a big swallow and screwed up her face. 'This is sour,' she complained.

'Oh, Jessie, don't tell me you have never had wine before,' Mabel asked.

'Sure, every year my grandma makes blackberry wine. I've had a glass at the end of harvest since I was a little kid – of course, it was diluted with a lot water back then but still . . .'

'Blackberry wine?' Mabel sneered. 'That sticky sweet stuff? Oh, Jessie, good wine is an acquired taste. You need to cultivate it if you ever want to escape the backwoods. Bottoms up, girl. If you still don't want another glass, I'll be surprised.'

Mabel's idea of gaining appreciation for good wine was a bit bizarre, but Jessie drained the glass in a quick swallow. I continued sipping mine trying to be polite by ignoring the distasteful echo it left in my mouth.

I wasn't paying much attention as Jessie and Mabel chatted about the girls they both knew at K-25 until Jessie's words suddenly seemed to slur. At first, I thought she was simply unac-customed to alcohol and that one glass quickly consumed was having a disproportionate effect on her. But when I tried to say something about that, my own words tangled up in my mouth and came out in nonsensical order.

At first, I was confused. Then, the realization hit me: the bitter aftertaste was not the wine at all. It was something Mabel put into it. I stumbled to my feet and tried to pull Jessie up to hers. She went totally limp and hung like a dead weight in my hand. The room spun in lopsided circles. I heard Mabel laugh – or was that Jessie? It sounded like two voices. Then, there were none.

THIRTY-FIVE

My eyes opened and I slammed them shut – the brightness of daylight hurt. My whole head throbbed like a just-skinned knee and it felt as if a snake was alternately coiling and relaxing in my stomach. I struggled to think but my brain felt swaddled in dark, rumbling clouds.

I heard bickering voices at some distance but although the tone was clear, the words were indistinct. I realized I could not move my arms or legs, my buttocks were numb and my shoulders ached. By instinct, I knew that I needed to remain quiet and conceal my dawning consciousness from the arguers.

Hansrote had to be one of them. Mabel was the most likely candidate for the other but I had to admit that it could just as easily have been Jessie. That acknowledgement was hard to accept. Mabel barely knew me. My history with Jessie made the possibility that she cooperated with Hansrote a clear case of betrayal. Could I have misjudged her that much? Then, I remembered her wooziness before I lost consciousness and almost let go of those unwelcome suspicions. But wait. Was it all an act?

With the passing minutes, my thoughts grew more nimble and I was able to organize the facts that I knew and the conclusions they shaped. No real surprise that Mabel was involved in my current predicament – Hansrote had manipulated her by recognizing her points of vulnerability and exploiting them. But, Jessie? Had she betrayed me? She'd slugged down that wine very quickly. Was that her inexperience or was that a ploy to ease my mind? Was she really slurring her words or did they only sound that way to me? Had it all been planned in advance?

The voices still seemed to be off in another room so I risked opening my eyes and making a scan of my immediate surroundings. The light burned in my eyes and made the pounding in my head more intense but I kept them open until I'd assessed as much as I could. I was still in the living room, tied to a dining room chair. I flexed muscles to ascertain any weakness in the knots that bound me but found none. The rope that held me in place fit my imagined image of the one used to throttle Marvin.

The daylight drifting through the windows brought me to the realization that it must be the next morning. I wondered how long it would be until my band of merry scientists noticed my absence at work and deduced the possibility that I might be held against my will in Mabel's apartment. And Jessie, where would she be now? She wasn't restrained in this room with me. What was she doing? Going about her life as usual? Fleeing the reservation? Or had she escaped from the apartment and, at this moment, was bringing help. I imagine it all depended on whether or not she'd betrayed me and whether or not she thought I'd leave this place alive.

I heard approaching voices and the words and identities were now apparent. Hansrote said, 'She should be awake by now. Go get a pot of cold water and throw it in her face.'

'But it'll get all over the carpet and everything, Eddie.'

'Stop calling me that. I hate it. Edwin is my name – I'm not some street corner thug.'

'But Eddi– Eddi– Edwin . . .'

'Just do what I tell you. By the time this is all over, we'll have more than water on the carpet and we'll have to replace it anyway.'

I kept my eyes shut and my body limp to buy a moment more of time. I listened for the water to stop pouring. I didn't want to risk water on the ropes, it could make them constrict tighter.

The tap shut off and I blinked and shuddered. 'What? What?' I mumbled.

Hansrote kicked the leg of the chair, bouncing it back a bit. I shook my head and looked at him as if I couldn't focus clearly.

'Are you going pull yourself together, girlie, or do you need a bucket of cold water in your face?'

'Water? No. Please. I can't seem to move,' I said.

'That's because we tied you up nice and tight and you're going to stay that way until you tell me what I want to know.'

'Where's Jessie?'

'Don't you remember? She got out of here as quick as a little scaredy bunny. She doesn't care, Clark. You're all alone here.'

I swiveled my head to the far right and faked surprise. 'Mabel? Mabel? I thought we were becoming friends. You helped him?'

Mabel flushed and said, 'I told you. We're getting married. Do you think I'd let you hurt my future husband?'

'Does he know you don't love him?' I taunted. 'Does he know you're only after his money?'

'That's not true, Edwin. She's lying.'

'Leave the room,' he said to Mabel. 'You're too much of a distraction.'

Turned as I was toward Mabel, I didn't see the blow coming but I felt it connect. The punch to my left cheek made my teeth rattle and sent the whole chair with me in it to the floor. I twisted my head just in time to keep my nose from taking the direct impact of the fall.

Hansrote jerked the chair upright, making everything in my head clang. 'Keep your focus on me, Clark.'

Once my eyes stopped rolling around in their orbits, I turned a hard gaze on him and sneered. 'Oh, are you just a lonely little boy desperate for attention?'

He kicked me in the chin so hard I feared it would break but the resulting pain felt more like a severe bruise than a fracture. 'Don't be a smart aleck, Clark. It just annoys me. And when I'm annoyed I tend to lash out.'

I knew somehow I had to get out of the restraints or he could easily beat me senseless or worse. Belligerence was not going to get me what I wanted. 'I am sorry, Dr Hansrote. The pain in my shoulders, shooting down my arms is preventing me from thinking clearly. If you could, please, loosen the ties a little. I'll tell you whatever you want to know.'

Hansrote threw his head back and laughed. 'I'm not a stupid little boy like those chemists you spend time with. You're probably thinking that anything you can do to drag things out will give your acolytes time to come to the rescue. Think again, Clark.' He lifted his wrist and looked at his watch. 'Just about now, one of your little science pals should be arriving back at Oak Ridge. He's chock full of surprises for your other little disciples.' He folded his arms across his chest and leaned backward as he studied me. When I said nothing, he continued. 'You're not going to ask? I am so disappointed. I thought you were a scientist with a curious scientific mind. Well, well, well. You're just another boring dame.'

I blinked but said nothing.

'We picked up one of your pals just as he was arriving for one of your secret meetings,' he said, leaning in and putting his face up close to mine. 'My, you are a mess. Tsk. Tsk. You would never make it in espionage, Clark – you are so transparent.'

'That's what happened to Gary? You got him?' I asked, wishing I hadn't spoken.

'Oh, yes, indeed,' Hansrote chortled. 'Two federal agents – at least, that's what that little sheep thought – told him the horrible truth. He was stunned to learn that you were manipulating all of them, that the real spy ring was you, Frannie and Jessie. He firmly believes that the document Jessie turned over to them for safekeeping was something she stole to give to the enemy but decided she needed to use it to continue her duplicity and cover-up. And wipe that disbelief off of your face. Yes, he believed it. Every word. I know because I showed up when they'd finished with him and he apologized to me – me! Yes, he did. I let him go and told him he'd better warn his friends before they were all dragged down into the muck with you. Now, simply tell me where I can find Frannie Snowden and once I am able to verify that you are telling me the truth, your ordeal will end.'

I knew now that he had no intention of allowing me to leave that apartment alive. I also knew he'd have no chance of getting past the military guards to harm Frannie, so telling him where she was bore no risk. 'Crenshaw has her,' I said.

'Liar!' he screamed and kicked the chair backwards.

My legs and arms instinctively jerked in an attempt to break the fall but bound as they were, they were useless. The back of my head bounced on the floor. Now my vision was blurred but my hearing was still fine and I listened as he stomped out of the room.

He returned, grabbed the back of the chair and thrust it upwards where it jiggled around on its legs before settling down into place. When it did, I knew why he had left the room. He was holding a heavy rolling pin in one hand, tapping it against the other. 'I talked to Crenshaw yesterday afternoon. He told me that he is still searching for that girl. So tell me the truth or I'll be forced to use this.'

'Crenshaw is lying to you. Don't take it personally – he lies to everybody.'

I saw the rolling pin swing through the air. It collided with my rib cage on my right side. This time it knocked my chair over to the left and excruciating stabs of pain seared through my body where the implement struck me and made black swirls float before my eyes. Every inhalation made me want to scream. I tried not to make a sound but whimpers escaped despite my best efforts.

When he righted the chair again, the movement made me scream. I could no longer hold up my head. It slumped lifeless, with my chin resting on my chest. I tried to will myself to hold it erect but my internal strength could not overpower the intensity of the pain.

'Now, tell me where Frannie Snowden is or the next time I'll crack your skull with this thing.'

'Mabel, help me. He's going to kill me!' I shouted with little hope that she'd respond.

Much to my surprise, Mabel rushed into the room. 'Eddie, you said you were going to rough her up. You didn't—'

Her words were cut off by the pounding of multiple fists on the door to the apartment. Mabel's mouth dropped open as she froze in place and stared at the door.

Hansrote waved the rolling pin in front of my face and whispered, 'One sound and I'll kill you before they know what happened.'

The pounding now made a sound that resonated with more force and caused the door to bulge. Someone was trying to break it down. Hansrote tossed the rolling pin aside and ran for a table against the far wall. He pulled open a drawer and grabbed a pistol. Hansrote ran to my side and held the barrel to my head.

'He's got a gun,' I shouted and the door gave way.

Hansrote swung the pistol in the direction of the doorway and pulled the trigger. Charlie's face crumpled in anguish as he fell to the floor. Joe and Teddy stood right behind him. Hansrote held the gun high, pointed at the two of them. I jerked my body with all the strength I could find crashing the chair over and into his legs. I screamed again as my body collided with the floor.

THIRTY-SIX

My head was swimming and I couldn't focus. I heard someone cry out in pain. I didn't think it was me but I couldn't be sure. I remained lying on my side in a forced fetal-type position and realized someone was behind me untying the ropes holding my arms. I blinked my eyes hard and saw a prone Hansrote on the floor, writhing in pain, as Teddy kicked him in the side. Mabel stood over the two of them, bouncing the rolling pin in the palm of one hand.

Across the room by the door, Charlie was still on the floor but now he was sitting up and, somehow, he had Hansrote's gun in his hand. Joe moved from behind me and knelt down as he worked on the knots binding my legs to the chair.

He stood with rope dangling from both fists. 'Okay, Teddy, ease up. I can't tie up Hansrote while you're still kicking him.'

Teddy landed one last thump into the man's side, then pulled back one arm while Joe grabbed the other. They tied the first knot so tight, I could see the rope embed into the flesh of Hansrote's lower arms.

Teddy kneeled down by my face and gently laid a hand on my shoulder. 'Libby, can you sit up?'

'I don't know.'

'I'll help you. Just tell me if I touch a spot I shouldn't,' Teddy said as he eased an arm under my lower shoulder.

'Wait,' I hissed. 'The rolling pin.' When I saw the puzzled look on his face, I knew I must not be speaking distinctly. I wanted to move my arms but my joints felt like rust-hardened hinges. 'Closer.'

Teddy slid out his arm and put an ear to my lips. I worked hard to enunciate. 'Don't trust Mabel. Get rolling pin.'

His forehead crinkled and his eyes squinted in response. Then, his face brightened as understanding of my meaning registered. He gave me a grin and a nod before bouncing to his feet. 'Hey, Mabel, hand that thing to me. I'll put it away for you.'

Mabel clutched the rolling pin to her chest and said, 'No.'

Without a moment's hesitation, Teddy gave her a shove backwards, snatching the kitchen tool as Mabel stumbled, lost her balance and took a pratfall. 'I'm sorry. I know I'm not supposed to push girls around, but for you, I'll make an exception. And don't get up,' Teddy snapped.

All our attention turned toward the bedroom at the sound of banging and muffled cries. Charlie swung the gun in Mabel's direction. Teddy held the rolling pin over Hansrote's head. 'What is that? Who is in the other room?' Teddy asked.

Hansrote laughed.

Mabel answered. 'It's Jessie.'

Teddy started towards the sound when Hansrote shouted, 'She's armed.'

Mabel said, 'She is not.'

Hansrote laughed again. 'What's behind the door, Teddy? The tiger or the lady?'

Teddy handed the rolling pin to Joe, grabbed the gun from Charlie and raced into the other room. Hinges creaked and the noises grew louder and then stilled. 'Oh, Jessie. Oh, you poor thing.'

'Help me! Help me! Help me!'

'Calm down, girl. That's why we're here. Let me get you untied.'

'Libby? Libby? Where's Libby?'

'She's okay. She's in the other room.'

'Is she alive?'

'Yes, Jessie. Please stop squirming. Thata girl.'

'Is she hurt?'

'Yes, but she's going to be okay.'

'I have to see her.'

'Okay, hold on. One more knot.'

I heard her limping gait before I saw her. Just as her feet came into view, I noticed the blood seeping through Charlie's shirt. My arm still felt too heavy to lift. I left it lying limp on the floor and pointed my index finger towards the injured man and said, 'Charlie' as loudly as I could.

Joe and Teddy turned in his direction while Jessie fell to the floor beside me. 'Oh poor Libby,' she moaned.

Jessie's face was bruised and swollen. One of her front teeth was missing and her hair was clotted with blood. 'I couldn't look worse than you,' I said.

Jessie, a possessor of perpetual sunshine, giggled. 'I imagine I do look a fright. See, Mama was right. I shouldn't be spendin' time with girls like Mabel.'

On the other side of the room, Joe barked into a telephone. 'We need an ambulance and officers. There's been a shooting.'

THIRTY-SEVEN

Moments later, the apartment supervisor appeared in the doorway, stared at the door frame, and said, 'What seems to be the problem here?'

Everyone started talking at once but Hansrote's authoritative voice stood out from the rest. 'My name is on the lease for this apartment. These people broke in and attacked me.'

The manager stepped toward Hansrote. 'I am sorry, sir. We've never had this kind of trouble here before. I assure you that we will handle all repairs and cleaning and—'

Joe stepped between the two men, placed his palm on the chest of the newly arrived man, and said, 'Stop right there. The police are on the way.'

The supervisor looked ready to challenge Joe's authority to stop him in his own building until he caught sight of Charlie, leaning against the wall who, once again, was in possession of Hansrote's gun. 'Okay. Don't want any trouble here. I'll just go back downstairs and escort the officers up when they arrive.' With his elbows bent up and his palms facing the room, he backed out. Once he was out of sight, the sound of his running footsteps echoed through the hall and down the stairs.

'Call Crenshaw right away,' Charlie said. 'Everything could get very messy before this is all sorted out. You never know which way locals will see things when it comes to dealing with us.'

Teddy placed the call. 'This is Teddy Mullins calling from Knoxville. We need Crenshaw and we need him now. A scientist has been shot and another has been wounded.' After a pause, he said, 'I don't care what kind of meeting he is in, Nichols. There are, let me see, five scientists here and we are all apt to be arrested when the local law enforcement gets here – if we're all still alive.' Teddy turned to the room and said, 'Nichols is informing Crenshaw of the situation but not making any promises.' His attention was drawn back to the phone. 'Yes. Yes?

Yes, Libby Clark is here, too. Yes, she is injured.' Putting his hand over the mouthpiece, he said, 'Well, Libby, Crenshaw is only interested in you. Not sure if he wants to rescue you or lock you up.'

I wanted to sit up but the pain was too strong. I wanted to ask a question but all that came out was a moan. It felt as if every move was driving a knife into my lungs.

A moment later, Teddy said, 'Okay,' and disconnected the call.

'What? What?' Joe asked.

'I was just told to make sure no further harm is done to Miss Clark or I'd be scrubbing pots in the desert next week.'

'You're not military. He can't send you anywhere,' Joe objected.

'I bet if he was mad enough, he could get me conscripted against my will. Besides, I have my own personal reasons for not letting any more harm befall Libby, don't you?' Teddy said.

'Yes, indeed. Is there anything we can do to make Libby more comfortable?'

Laying on my side on the floor, I did the only thing I could without raising an angry red cloud of pain. I squeezed Jessie's hand.

'Libby hears you – she just squeezed my hand. I don't think she should be moved at all until the ambulance arrives. Yeah, she just squeezed my hand again. So she agrees. But Joe, grab the seat cushion off of that easy chair and put it behind her. If she falls back, I don't want her hitting the hard floor.'

'Charlie?' I forced through my lips in a whisper.

'Yes,' Jessie said, 'Charlie's hanging in there – aren't you Charlie?'

'Yes, ma'am. I'd probably keel over if I tried to stand but I'm doing fine right here.'

'I hear a siren,' Joe said, rushing to the windows. 'An ambulance just pulled up in front of the building and there are two running patrolmen just crossing the street. Now, they're coming inside.'

Pounding feet echoed in the stairwell like a herd of stampeding cattle. I could see through the broken doorway as two uniformed officers entered with drawn guns and slitted eyes.

Charlie stretched out an arm with the gun held upside down with the tips of his fingers on the grip. 'This is the gun that injured me.'

An officer stepped forward and took it from him and Charlie pointed to the bound Hansrote and added, 'That is the man who shot me.'

'He's lying,' Hansrote shouted. 'Ask the manager. This is my apartment. They came in and attacked me. Tell them, Mabel. We're the victims here.'

I couldn't see Mabel's face but the delay in her response told me that she was reassessing the situation and figuring the odds of escaping the trap with Hansrote if she readjusted her position again. In defiance of Joe and Teddy, she rose to her feet and said, 'Yes, officer. These crazy people broke in here – you see the door. They forced their way in and attacked us. All I want to do is get out of here alive. Thank God, you've come to our rescue.'

From the doorway, the apartment manager said, 'That's the truth. That woman lives here. The tied-up man's name is on the lease. You need to let them go and arrest these young hoodlums.'

I had to admit that was a first. I'd been called a lot of things in my life but never a hoodlum. The involuntary chuckle that escaped made the pain swirl and throb in my chest.

The one officer who had control of the weapon that fired the shot into Charlie kept his distance from all of us as if afraid we'd jump him for it. The other approached Hansrote, kneeled on the floor and untied his knots, grumbling about the tightness as he did. He talked under his breath to Hansrote, who mumbled responses to him. I couldn't understand what was being said but it sounded almost conspiratorial. And that was not good.

Suddenly a shout, 'What are you doing? Give me back my gun.' And another shot fired. The officer slumped from his knees down to all fours, then fell flat on his face. Hansrote was on his feet, gun in hand. He swung the weapon toward the other officer and ordered him to drop the pistol in his hand as well as his half-drawn service revolver and put his hands on top of his head.

'Everybody, keep back,' Hansrote ordered.

Mabel took two steps forward. 'Oh, Eddie, I knew you'd get us out of this mess.'

Hansrote pointed the gun at her and said, 'You, too, stop it right there.'

'But, Eddie . . .'

'Take another step and I'll shoot you, too, girl.' He kicked the pieces of rope towards her. 'You want to help, Mabel – go tie up that policeman.'

'Oh Eddie, you won't regret taking me with you,' Mabel said.

'Shut up and do what I tell you. I need a hostage. Sounds like Clark here is the only one the brass care about. Get her to her feet.' When no one moved, Hansrote shouted at Jessie. 'You, stupid girl, you heard what I said. Get Clark on her feet. Move it.'

With the barrel of the gun pointing at her forehead, Jessie just sat there on the floor beside me. She folded her arms across her chest and sat up straight while glaring at Hansrote.

Hansrote fired another shot that pierced the wood floor inches from Jessie's knees. Jessie flinched at the noise but stayed in place. Unbelievably, she smiled at him. 'You can shoot me if you want but you can't force me to help you,' she said.

'Mabel, are you finished over there yet?' Hansrote demanded.

'Yes, Eddie, he's all tied up.'

'Then get over here, dammit. Get that Clark woman up on her feet. I need to get out of here.'

Mabel grabbed one of my wrists and jerked upward. Everything went black streaked with red. I thought I'd pass out but I struggled to hold onto my consciousness, then my knees gave out. As I fell, Mabel pushed my body toward the sofa where I landed with a soft plop. Breathing was difficult. Each inhalation and exhalation sent stabs of pain jolting through my ribcage. But if I held my breath the agony was even worse.

'I'll be your hostage,' Jessie said. 'Let the medics outside the door come in and take her to the hospital and I'm all yours.'

Hansrote laughed. 'No one cares what happens to you, stupid girl. All they care about is that nosy little smart aleck Clark. You can come with her, though – you can be her crutch. Get her to her feet,' he said swinging the barrel in my direction.

A scuffling noise in the hallway drew his attention away from me. 'What's going on out there? Mabel, go check.'

A moment later, the barrels of an Enfield Rifle and a Thompson submachine gun swung into the doorway. Crenshaw appeared behind the soldiers and boomed out a command, 'Drop the damn gun, Hansrote. You're outnumbered, outgunned and out of time.'

THIRTY-EIGHT

Time seemed to freeze in place for a moment, then Hansrote stepped backwards and trained his weapon on Crenshaw's head.

'Go ahead and pull the trigger, Hansrote. The split second you do, my men will open fire and you will die without knowing if you even hit your target.'

Hansrote laughed. 'Ah, Lieutenant Colonel Crenshaw, relax. You might get a promotion out of this. Just remember, you may be able to stop me but you can't stop us all. We're everywhere. Some of us are in it for the money, others are involved because of deeply-held principles – they are the really dangerous ones. You'll never break them.' He did not change his aim but swiveled his head slightly away. 'Joe?'

'Yes,' Joe said.

'Say goodbye to Henrietta for me,' Hansrote said before putting the barrel to his head.

I heard yells of 'no', and the sharp retort of one more gunshot. Hansrote's blood and brain matter spattered on the wall behind him and his body crumpled down to the floor. Jessie sobbed and Mabel shrieked, 'Don't you leave me alone, Eddie. Don't you dare!'

The sounds reverberated in a now silent room. Crenshaw broke the spell by barking orders. 'Corporal, secure that woman,' he said pointing at Mabel. 'Medics, get in here and care for the wounded.'

It seemed as if everyone started moving at once. I drifted in and out of consciousness – at first, from the intensity of the pain; later on a cloud of morphine.

The first real awareness I had of anything around me was the feeling of someone's hand wrapped around mine and the sight of a brown head resting on the mattress beside me. I looked at my physical surroundings. I was no longer in the apartment. Everything was white and spartan. Was I in a hospital?

The head rose, the eyes blinked – it was Teddy. 'Libby! It's so good to see you open your eyes. I was so worried. Do you feel okay?'

'I feel confused and foggy,' I said in a voice that didn't quite sound like mine.

'Do you need anything? Should I call the nurse?'

'Water. Just some water please.'

Teddy grabbed the pitcher on the nightstand and poured a glass. I swallowed as much as I could but held on to the glass. 'Okay. How's Charlie?'

'He's just down the hall. The surgery went well. If nothing bad happens, he'll go home in a couple of days.'

'What about Jessie?'

'She's been treated and released. She's seeing the dentist tomorrow because a couple of her teeth were knocked out.'

'And wasn't a police officer shot?'

'Yeah . . .'

'Well, is he okay?'

'No. No. He didn't make it. He died right there in the apartment.'

'Did they arrest Mabel?'

'Yes. Crenshaw's men did. She's being questioned about the others.'

'How did you all know to come looking for me?'

'Gary.'

'You found Gary? Is he okay?'

'Sort of. We'll have to decide what to do with him.'

'What do you mean? What happened?'

'Well, Monday morning, he showed up at Y-12. He sent a message into our lab for Tom saying there'd been a tragedy in his family. When Tom came back in, he was furious.'

'Why? Was there a death in his family?'

'No. That family tragedy business was just his way to get Tom to come outside. Gary told his story to him and Tom came inside and told Joe and then they both went to Charlie. Charlie got me out of my lab.'

'You still haven't said why Tom was so angry.'

'That's because of what Gary said. He said that just a block away from Joe's, he was approached by a federal agent who took him to an office building in Knoxville. The agent asked him about our group and Frannie's location. He said that he told them nothing.'

'So what's the problem? Even if he had, his information was outdated. Crenshaw had already picked up Gregg and Frannie.'

'True but Gary didn't know that he was in on the latest development. And it didn't end there. Another federal agent came in and knocked him around a bit – he's got a black eye and his glasses are now held together with tape. He still told them nothing except that the person they needed to arrest was Hansrote because he was a spy. The next thing he knew, he woke up in a dark room somewhere else. That's when Gary went off the rails.'

'What happened?'

'Gary is sitting out in the hall waiting for permission to come in to talk to you. Might be best if he tells you the rest.'

'Why should I talk to him if he thinks I'm a spy?' I asked.

'He's been sitting out there all night and all morning because he now realizes he's been manipulated and used and he wants to apologize and explain himself.'

'All right. Send him in.'

Teddy stepped to the door and said Gary's name.

Gary entered, his head hanging low. When he looked up, he appeared ready to cry. 'I'm sorry, Libby. So sorry. I'm sorry I doubted you. I'm sorry I thought the worst of you. I'm so sorry.'

'Why don't you tell me what happened after you woke up in that dark room.'

THIRTY-NINE

G ary woke up with no idea of where he was or what he was doing there. His face hurt and his arm throbbed. He cringed when the door flew open.

A man rushed in and said, 'Oh my God, here you are! We've been looking everywhere for you.'

'Who are you?' Gary asked.

'I'm a federal agent,' he said.

Gary shrunk away from him. 'Get away from me. Leave me alone.'

'Hey, hey, calm down. You got something against federal agents?'

'Considering two of them tricked me and beat me up, not very much.'

'Those two men were not federal agents. They are working for the spy ring.'

'For Hansrote?'

'Oh no. The real spy ring framed Hansrote because he was trying to find the evidence to expose them. They killed your friend, Marvin, too, because he betrayed them.'

'Who are the real spies?' Gary asked.

'A bunch of crazed women who are dedicated to making sure the Nazis win the war.'

'Do I know them?'

'I'm sure you know one of them – she's a lady scientist named Libby Clark.'

'No,' he said. 'That's not possible.'

'I know you don't want to believe it, Gary, but it's true. That woman has fooled a lot of people. Frannie Snowden and some other girl working at K-25 are working with her. That Clark woman is the one who got you and your group involved in framing Hansrote, isn't she?'

'I–I–I,' Gary stammered.

'Yes. She's a tricky one. Teddy Mullins thought he was in love with her. Now he knows the truth, too. He's devastated.'

'Teddy believes she's a spy?'

'Teddy knows it. We need to find that Clark woman right away before she hurts anyone else. We think she's planning on eliminating another enemy today. God help anyone who gets in her way. Now, let me check out the damages. You have a real shiner coming up on your right eye. I'll get some tape and put your glasses back together so you can see until you get a new pair. Your right arm might be broken. You need to have it checked out in a hospital.'

The pain and swelling in Gary's arm made him accept that he needed to have his arm set and the building agony of that injury, and the man's concern about it, amplified Gary's willingness to believe everything he said. 'Can we go now? I'm in a lot of pain.'

'Do you know where Snowden is?'

Gary told him what he thought to be true at the time of his abduction, that Frannie was staying at the Andrew Johnson Hotel.

The agent said, 'I'll have her picked up right away. But you need to stay right here for your own safety until Clark and Snowden are arrested.'

Gary paced the empty room, cradling his right arm in his left, while the pain and impatience escalated. He debated running out and finding a drugstore so he could at least get some aspirin – or even a local who could sell him a couple of shots of splo, anything to numb some of the pain. He tried the door but found it bolted and resumed his endless walk from one side of the room to the other.

When the pain drove him off his feet, he tried to distract himself from his physical ailments by thinking about the problem of Libby Clark. What the agent alleged seemed impossible on the surface. But the poison of his lies seeped into Gary's thoughts and colored his interpretation of past actions and comments made by Libby. By the time the agent returned, Gary was totally convinced of the truth of the man's allegations.

The agent was scowling when he returned. 'Frannie's gone, buster. Did you call her and warn her I was coming?'

'No sir. Why would I do that?' Gary denied. 'Look. Look around this room – do you see anything, anything at all? Do you see a telephone? How could I?'

The man crouched down in front of Gary and leaned into his space. 'Where else does Clark go when she comes to town?'

'I don't know all the places Libby goes besides the hotel but I do know she has visited a woman named Mabel who is romantically involved with Dr Hansrote.'

'Oh my. We think Hansrote is Clark's next target. If Mabel gets in the way, Clark will probably kill her, too.'

'I've got to get something done about my arm,' Gary pleaded.

'It's a risk, but if you're willing to take it . . .?'

'Anything to dull this pain,' he said, choking back the tears that threatened to break loose.

Daylight was seeping into the streets as the agent escorted Gary downstairs and into his car. There was enough light for the shabbiness of the neighborhood to show everywhere, adding to Gary's unease.

The man drove him to the hospital entrance and said, 'Don't mention me. I don't exist. You fell and heard your arm snap, okay?'

Gary nodded.

'And keep your eyes open for Snowden and Clark. No one followed us over here but you never know when they'll track you down through their secret networks. They'll know you've been injured and with that information, the hospital would be a logical place for them to look for you.'

Gary was paranoid before that last comment. Now, sitting in the curtained treatment area, his adrenaline spiked with every approaching footstep. As soon as he had a new cast, he got out of the hospital as quickly as he could.

He behaved like someone in a cheesy old movie as he walked to the bus stop constantly looking back over his shoulder for anyone who might be following him. He approached the group of workers waiting at the stop for transport out to the reservation. At first he thought it would be best to hide among that small crowd but after he caught a couple of people looking at him, he peeled away and stood off to the side where he could watch them all. As his eyes darted back and forth in response to each movement any one of them made, it didn't cross his mind that the way he isolated himself made him stand out like a movie marquee.

FORTY

When he finished his story, I simply stared at him for a moment, still finding it hard to comprehend that anyone who knew me at all could possibly believe all those lies. Under the pressure of my gaze, Gary hung his head and shuffled his feet.

'How could you fall for that?' I said. 'You're a scientist, Gary. Where was the proof to give it credibility? What were you thinking?'

'I don't know, Libby. I'm just so sorry,' he whined. 'I didn't realize how stupid I'd been until after I talked to Tom.'

'Gullibility is a weakness in anyone, Gary, but in a scientist, it's a total tragedy. The only excuse I can make for you is the pain. I realize it's hard to think in times like that. You really need to build up your ability to respond better in a crisis situation.'

'Libby, honestly, it sounds like you want me to be someone I am not,' Gary said. 'And it might all be irrelevant now. Tom told me to resign my position and go back home. He said if I don't, he will first get me thrown out of the group and then he'll have me fired.'

A wave of pity washed over me. Certainly, Gary had been an annoying person to have around in the best of times but now that he'd been brought low, I had no desire to kick him. 'Don't do anything rash, Gary. Give this all some time. Let me get Tom and the rest of the group together and we'll talk it all out. Okay?'

Gary sighed and his shoulders slumped down even further. 'Sure,' he mumbled. 'Like Tom said, I need to apologize and then get my miserable self out of your sight. I hope you're better soon and again I'm sorry.' He shuffled out the doorway and back into the hall.

Although I was angry at how easily Gary accepted the lies about me, I felt sorry for him and appreciated his remorse and willingness to apologize.

Teddy, however, had no empathy. 'He needs to be dropped from the Walking Molecules immediately.'

'Teddy, he was manipulated by a master.'

'No excuse. All for one. One for all. He violated the trust of the entire group.'

'It's not all that black and white, Teddy,' I said, wondering whether his rigid attitude was a character flaw or simply a response to his fear for my safety and the close call all of us had in Mabel's apartment.

'We'll discuss it when we are all able to get together for a meeting. Right now, I have something more immediate on my mind. I want to go see Charlie.'

'Let me ask the nurse if you can get out of bed first.'

'You go ahead. By the time she gets here, I'll have gone down the hall and found Charlie.'

'Libby, you have been through a horrible ordeal. You have to think of your health and well-being first right now.'

'Well, I can't and I won't. Either you are going to help me or you are going to make things more difficult for me. Your choice. Decide. I'm not lying in bed and waiting for your decision.' I swung my legs out from under the covers.

He reached out to stop me but I shrugged him away and said, 'Don't you dare touch me unless you want to help me get up and go down the hall.'

Teddy sighed. 'You are stubborn. But my mother raised me to appreciate that quality in a woman. C'mon. Lean on me.' He slipped an arm around my waist and I put one around his shoulders.

As we hobbled down the hall past the nurse's station, one of the angels in white shouted, 'Stop, Miss Clark. Stop! You need to be in bed. Young man, what are you doing? She should not be out of her room.'

'Ma'am,' Teddy said, 'this is what she needs to do right now and I recommend that you let her do it.'

'I'm calling the doctor.'

'Good,' I said. 'I'll be glad to see him when I get back to my room.'

I walked into Charlie's room shocked at how pale and helpless he looked all bandaged up and tucked in. He turned his head in my direction and his face lit up.

'Libby! You're awake. You're walking.'

'Sort of, Charlie. I think without Teddy's assistance, I would have had to crawl down the hall. Come to think of it, down on all fours I might have been able to slip past that nurse without her noticing.' It was so good to see him smile and hear him talk. So good to see him alive.

'Oh, Libby. I wish you'd come to me sooner. I understand why you didn't but—'

'Can't undo the past, Charlie. What happened, happened. I'm here first of all to see with my own eyes that you survived. Secondly, I was hoping you might know more about what's going on back at the reservation than we do.'

'I am alive. Or experiencing a reasonable facsimile. And yes, I probably know a bit more. Crenshaw paid me a visit. Gregg and Frannie have both been released. Mabel, who proved in the apartment she's a crafty individual with a keen survival instinct, is reinforcing my opinion in her behavior with Crenshaw. She is revealing everything to the military. She knew a lot more about what Hansrote was doing than she let on to you. She knew he worked for Snowden and she told the military as much. She gave him the names of all the people involved in Marvin's murder and Gary's abduction. Crenshaw told me they'd picked up all but one of them.'

'Who were they? Who is evading capture?'

'Crenshaw wouldn't answer either of those questions but assured me that they wouldn't rest until every single person was apprehended. The big problem is Raymond. His phone line leads to an empty apartment.'

'Teddy, did you all give Crenshaw that new phone number?'

'Yes, Joe got our notes we copied from Hansrote's notebook out of the hiding place and gave them to him.'

'That's what Crenshaw said they used, Libby,' Charlie said. 'They also verified it when they found the original in Hansrote's cemesto. Military and federal investigators went to the Manhattan address for that phone number and there was nothing in the room but a telephone sitting on the floor next to the wall. Not a piece of furniture, not a scrap of trash and the whole place had been wiped down and no fingerprints were found anywhere. They did find a lot of prints in Mabel's apartment but they've all been identified as belonging to Mabel, Hansrote, the men Mabel named as cohorts and that one soldier Mabel saw on the side along with your and Jessie's prints. In all likelihood, Raymond was never there.'

'So he's free to recruit more people and steal more information from our facility and probably, the others as well. Just knowing that is enough to make us paranoid about all the people working by our sides, and everyone we meet at a dance or at the market,' I said.

'It certainly would be better if they'd been able to remove the threat but, at least, all of you have solidified a group you can trust,' Charlie said.

'To a degree,' Teddy said. 'Gary's actions proved that we had a weakness in our unity.'

'Yes, Teddy,' I snapped back. 'It is a pity that we are all human and subject to the weakness of not being perfect. Who knows how any of us would react in a similar situation?'

'But, Libby, no matter how forgiving you may be, can you honestly say that you will ever trust Gary again? Or if anything goes awry in the future, would you automatically suspect him first, above all the others?'

Charlie jumped into our spat. 'With or without Gary, I would be thrilled to be part of your group.'

I imagine the look on my face appeared a lot like the one I saw on Teddy's face. It was certainly never a possibility I'd considered. 'You realize that Crenshaw – and probably all the military, as well as the police and administration officials – consider us nothing but nuisances and troublemakers?'

Charlie laughed and then grimaced with pain. 'Haven't laughed since I left the lab. I didn't realize how much it would hurt. I know you all have reason to distrust me but I learned through the situation earlier this year that what you were doing is more important than the rules you've broken. I would be proud to be among your number. I know you can't answer now but I only ask that the group consider me.'

Teddy looked at me and I nodded. 'We can do that, Charlie. Don't know the reaction we'll get but we'll ask.'

The doctor chose that moment to enter the room with a nurse pushing a wheelchair. 'Miss Clark, if you could please have a seat and we'll get you back to your room and talk about your recovery.'

I thought about objecting – on principle, if for no other reason – but I realized I was very tired and the idea of walking back down the hall seemed overwhelming. I walked to the wheelchair and surrendered.

FORTY-ONE

Although Charlie was still in hospital because of a secondary infection in his wound, the rest of us were back. The Walking Molecules' first meeting since our fatal encounter with Hansrote was called to order in the back room of Joe's. A celebratory ambience filled the air as we clinked beer steins and toasted that we didn't lose another member in the experience.

Initially we focused on the roundup of the individuals responsible for the murder of Marvin. We were all frustrated about not knowing the names of those who were already locked up but even more so about the one who was known to still be at large. Who was that person? And were we all in danger from that individual? We all felt, for our own protection, Crenshaw had an obligation to reveal that identity to us. Teddy and I agreed to go see him in the morning.

We then turned to the subject of Gary. He was pointedly not invited to this gathering and it was clear from the onset that my willingness to give him another chance to prove himself was not shared by the majority.

Tom, once Gary's closest friend, was now the most adamant. 'I will never feel as if I can talk freely again in this group if Gary continues to be part of it. I think that most of you, if you are honest, will admit that you, too, will feel a bit constrained in his presence.'

Joe jumped in with his agreement. 'Trust is the most important component. Without it, we have nothing. He did not trust us – most particularly, he did not trust Libby – and that attitude made him betray us all. This group loses all its value if he remains a part of it.'

When it came to a vote, only Dennis and I voted for Gary to remain. Under pressure from all of us, though, Tom promised not to do anything to cause our former member to lose his job and be sent home in disgrace. Gregg agreed to deliver the mixed bag of news to Gary the next morning.

The really contentious issue was Charlie. Joe was enthusiastic about the prospect. 'He took a bullet for us – for all of us. If for no other reason, he deserves to come on board.'

'A management guy?' Tom groused. 'Really? How can we possibly trust him? Don't forget when we were hunting down the killer of Irene Nance, he didn't stand up for Libby or any of us.'

'Tom, don't you believe in redemption?' Dennis asked. 'If, as Teddy and Libby are telling us, he has realized the mistake he made in the past and now has our backs, how can we not welcome him into the fold – the prodigal son and all that.'

'Oh, please, Dennis, not more of your holy-roller malarkey. Redemption? Phooey? He just wants to be on the winning side and he'll stab us in the back when it's in his best interest.'

'I don't think that's fair, Tom,' Teddy said.

'Why not?' Rudy asked. 'The world right now is full of spies and double agents. And people like Gary who crumble under pressure. How could it be unfair to protect ourselves from them?'

At that question, everyone seemed to start talking at once. The clamor of their voices was deafening. Gregg rose to his feet and pounded his beer stein on the table to get everyone's attention. 'Arguing without any real input from Charlie will not get us anywhere. I propose that we table this discussion until we can bring the man himself in to answer our questions.'

'But then,' Rudy said, 'he'll know who we all are.'

'Because of his involvement with the demise of Hansrote, he knows most of us and from being down the hall from me in the hospital, I'm sure he could have been informed about any number of you who paid me a visit if he had any nefarious purpose. I really think that is a moot point,' I said.

'And, of course,' Joe added, 'if we did find him acceptable after our interview, he would still have to pass the Dossett Tunnel test before we voted on his approval.'

'All in favor of my proposal to bring Charlie to a meeting to talk to us after he's released from the hospital, raise your hands.'

Everyone's arm went in the air and a few expressed surprise

that Tom had raised his. Tom said, 'Even if he is our worst enemy, it would be better to assess him face-to-face so I say "yes" bring him in.'

With that resolved, we finished up the last pitcher and called it a night. I decided that once we got through the Charlie decision, I'd bring up Jessie. I knew there would be a lot of objections because she wasn't a scientist, but in my opinion she'd earned a place at the table. Besides, it would be nice for me to have another woman in the group.

FORTY-TWO

Teddy and I walked together back to his dorm. He wanted to escort me to my home but I brushed him off. I knew if he did, I'd feel obligated to invite him inside for a cup of tea or something and I just wanted to be alone with my thoughts for what little remained of the evening.

When I return home, G.G. usually rushed to greet me to beg for attention, affection and food. But tonight, nothing. I called him and got no response. I finally found him under my easy chair but no matter how much I coaxed him, he wouldn't come out. I went into the kitchen, put on the tea kettle and opened a can of tuna – he still wouldn't emerge from his hiding place. Cats are weird.

I got down a cup and a tea bag and was pouring the boiling water over it when I heard a sound behind me. I turned and there was Frannie Snowden. I was surprised to see her but was even more amazed to see a pistol in her hand pointing straight at me.

'You betrayed me,' she said.

'Frannie, what are you talking about?'

'It took me a while to figure it out but I realized while I was still locked up that it had to be you who told Crenshaw that I was in the hotel.'

'No,' I objected. 'As a matter of fact, we found out—'

'Shut up! I don't want to hear any more of your lies.'

I didn't know what to say. The woman standing in the doorway of my kitchen was not the same Frannie Snowden that I had met in the shack. Had she snapped under the stress of the situation or was she simply one of those dark personalities that Dr Cleckley wrote about – an individual who wore a mask to hide their true nature from the world?

Frannie continued, 'I know you sicced Crenshaw on me in the hotel and I know after he let me go, you sent him after me again.'

'What are you talking about?'

'Oh, don't play innocent with me. He's looking for me right now. I can't find any of the others so he probably has them. I went to the train station and tried to buy a ticket out of this godforsaken place. Just in time, I saw the suits and uniforms closing in on me and managed to give them the slip. I sure hope they found that woman I left tied up in the ladies' room stall. Her clothes and hat made it possible for me to escape. I gagged her, too, 'cause she wouldn't shut up. I sure hope she could breathe.'

'You don't know?'

'She was making whistling noises through her nose so I had to cover that up, too. But I think she could still get some air into her lungs.' Frannie shrugged. 'Be a shame if she couldn't.'

'How long ago did you leave her there?'

'Oh, hours and hours ago. If she couldn't breathe, she's long gone now. But back to my problem with you. I trusted you because I thought you were Marvin's friend, and because of that, I thought you believed every word of the story I fed him – I thought you'd keep your promise to him to take care of me. But now I know better,' she said.

'I was Marvin's friend,' I insisted. 'It is why I was willing to meet you. It was why I was willing to help you. It was why I was so determined to find his killer. I don't understand you, Frannie Snowden. I don't know what has happened to you. You are not the younger cousin Marvin adored and wanted to protect. Who are you?'

'Oh, you like that Dumb Dora? You like someone you can boss around and laugh at behind her back?' Her face went through a dramatic transformation: the eyes grew wider, the lips ever so pouty, her posture softened – yet still the gun aimed straight at me. In a sweet, sweet voice she said, 'Is this who you want, ma'am?'

I realized my chin had dropped open. I blinked, closed my lips and said, 'Are you telling me that you've been playing Marvin since you were a child?'

Her laugh was a cackle. 'How else do you think I always got my way? I was never as smart as Marvin but I was far, far more clever. He was as easy to manipulate as my parents were who always thought I was perfect and believed it was all the others who were the problem. I'd say I won because right now I have control of your life. One little twitch of my finger and your life is over. Now who's the Dumb Dora?'

I had no idea of how to end this stand-off. I knew she could pull the trigger before I could reach her. My only hope was finding out why she hadn't done that right away and use it to my advantage. She wanted me for something. She needed me for some reason. As long as I didn't kill that plan, she wouldn't kill me. 'What do you want me to do, Frannie?'

'That's better. But don't think your change in attitude is going to make me relax – I'm on to your tricks. Right now, what I want is a cup of cocoa. Can you do that?'

I turned toward the kitchen cabinets and reached for a knob.

'Stop. Don't move. Tell me exactly what you are doing before you do it. Every little move, every little twitch.'

'Okay, I want to open the cabinet door and see if I have enough sugar left to make your cocoa.'

'Okay, but fling it open and take two steps back and wait until I tell you to make another move.'

I followed her directions and watched as she changed her angle of sight to look inside. 'All right. Pull out the sugar and check it.'

I picked up the box and set it on the counter. 'Yes, I have enough.'

'Fine. Make my cocoa.'

I picked up a saucepan, turned and took a step toward the refrigerator. A gunshot rang in my ears and I froze in place, looking down at the hole in the floor two paces in front of me.

'Next time, I'll aim closer or maybe shoot to kill. Describe every move you make.'

I exhaled and tried to steady my breathing. 'Frannie, I need to go to the refrigerator to get the pitcher of milk.'

'No, go back and stand by the counter.' She walked backwards and, keeping the gun pointed at me, pulled out the milk, walked sideways to the stove and set it down. She stepped back a safe distance and then wiggled the gun at me. 'Go, do it.'

Step by step, I talked my way through the process. 'I am setting the saucepan on the counter. I am pouring the milk into the saucepan. I am lighting the burner on the stove. I am placing the saucepan on the burner. I need to walk over a few steps to get a cup.'

'Fling open the right cabinet door and step back just like before,' she said.

I continued describing the movements I was making – it was both mind-numbing and terrifying. I kept looking for an opportunity to disarm her but never saw one. With the cocoa made, I carried it into the living room and set it on the little table by my easy chair. Then as ordered, I sat down on the floor cross-legged.

'Ahhh,' she said after her first sip. 'You may be a dishonest liar and an unfaithful friend but you certainly make a good cup of cocoa.'

I sensed she wanted me to respond to her negative assessment of my character but I refrained and simply said, 'I am so glad you like it.'

'I bet you are. Probably because you know I could kill you if I didn't.' She cackled again and took another noisy slurp out of the cup. 'Well, I bet you are wondering what's next, aren't you?'

Again, I was speechless. I couldn't deny what she said but at the same time, I didn't want to encourage her to toy with me.

She giggled. 'You're kind of cute when you're distressed, confused and lost, Libby Clark. You ought to use that facial expression more often – it works on those men like you wouldn't believe.' She sat in my chair, looking as serene as a well-loved queen perched on her throne. She hummed under her breath as she sipped the rest of her cocoa until the cup was empty. She upended it for a moment and then without warning threw it in my direction. I ducked just in time to prevent it from hitting me in the head. I sprang to my feet and another shot rang out. G.G. darted out from under the chair and ran into the bedroom as if demons rode his tail. I was relieved to see that Frannie did not appear to notice him as she lurched to her feet. 'On your knees!' she bellowed. 'What did I tell you about moving?'

I dropped and hung my head trying to still the pounding in my chest.

'Tell me! What did I tell you about moving?'

'I cannot move unless I tell you what I am doing first.'

'Exactly. Now sit cross-legged and don't you dare move again until I tell you.'

I folded my legs beneath me and lowered down, explaining each little action before doing it.

'Here's what I can't figure out. Getting Marvin to believe my story was easy. I needed him when I had to hide from Hansrote and the military. And Hannah? That was child's play – literally. She's been doing my bidding as long as I can remember. She took the blame for anything I broke or destroyed. She supported every lie I told. She was my first puppet ever. They were both only stopgap measures to keep me secure until I could eliminate Hansrote. But you? I was worried when Marvin brought you into the picture. Oh, so smart, Marvin said. Brilliant, he said. Getting you involved was the first black mark against Marvin. But then, you didn't measure up to your billing. You were like putty in my hands. I can't believe how stupid you are.

'You got it all wrong from the beginning, girl. Hansrote wasn't in charge. I recruited Hansrote – I knew a greedy little man when I saw one. Seducing him was easy and I thought I had him tied tight. But then he went behind my back and hooked up with that tart Mabel. He decided he didn't need me around any longer. I told him to drop her or else I would tell Raymond that he was a double-agent. He didn't want the money to stop flowing and he didn't want to give up his plaything. So he turned me in to Crenshaw and then told Raymond that I was the problem and that he should be in charge. When one of my men reported that Hansrote had talked to Marvin that was black mark number two and I knew Marvin had now become a big risk to my survival. Marvin and Hansrote both had to go.

'I set up Hansrote for a fall to keep him occupied while I made my plans but eliminated Marvin first – he was easy since I knew when he'd be in the woods. Hansrote was a little trickier and after you moved me out of the shack against my will, I couldn't get to him. And honestly, I hoped you and your merry little band would take care of him for me. I didn't care if he was locked up for the duration of the war or dead – I just wanted him out of the way. But your little group of scientists was incompetent. You just couldn't get it right. Then, you turned on me. I don't know what gave me away. But, I've got to give you your due, you finally caught on and went to Crenshaw. I can't say that I blame you. But I'm not going to forgive you either.'

My head was spinning at her revelations. I could not believe I'd fallen into her trap. And it was worse than she portrayed because I never once suspected her until she stood before me with a gun. I have no idea what her plans were for me but I knew they had to be foiled or my survival was a debatable point.

'I'd like a little sleep before we leave but I can't trust you at all,' Frannie said.

I wondered what she meant – where was I going to go? And what did she expect me to do?

'I'll just have to have some coffee then. And what about some sandwiches for the road? We'll both get hungry before it's safe to stop. Don't just stare at me – up. Up, up! In the kitchen. And get busy,' she said motioning with her gun.

I narrated my progress every step of the way. As I filled the percolator with water, I fought an urge to throw it in her face but she looked too eager to shoot and too close to miss.

'Hurry up! Hurry up! Go open the pantry after you set the pot down on the burner. Open it up and step back.'

She ordered me into a position where she could keep an eye on me and look at the contents of jars and cans at the same time. 'I am amazed at how much you have crammed in here. Where did you get it all? Is that jelly?' She pulled out a jar and held it up so the light shone through the glass infusing the jam with a jewel-like glow. 'And you have peanut butter, too. Okay. Let's fix some sandwiches.' She set the two jars on the counter and asked, 'Where's your bread?'

'In the refrigerator,' I said.

'Well, don't just stand there, get it. I can see you thinking, but don't get any funny ideas. I prefer you alive but I can manage if you're not.'

When I said I was pulling out the drawer to get a butter knife, all I could think about were the sharp knives in the same drawer. Could I grab one and thrust faster than she could pull the trigger? Could I slip one in my clothes to use later? Before I had it all the way open, she ordered me to back away.

She pulled open the drawer, looked inside and back-handed me with her gun hand. I staggered back. 'Now look what you made me do. We're going to have to clean the blood off your face before we go.'

She slapped a butter knife down on the counter beside the bread and slid the drawer shut. 'You still think I'm slow-witted, don't you? You seem to forget that you owe me. You betrayed me. And you promised your good friend Marvin to protect me. And first chance you get, Libby Clark, you go for a knife? Poor Marvin! He trusted you. But before he died, I told him that you were the real spy, that you forced me to do your bidding. I told him that you had ordered his execution. He died thinking you betrayed him but still he wouldn't give up any of the others. Stupid boy.'

That broke my heart. I could only hope she was lying. To die abandoned by friends while a family member watched with pleasure was too much to contemplate. I blinked my eyes to fight back threatening tears while I spread the peanut butter and jelly on the bread. I had to stay focused on Frannie. Sooner or later, she would do something that gave me an opportunity and I needed to be ready to act without any hesitation.

We left my flattop with a sack of sandwiches, a thermos of coffee, two canteens filled with water and a rolled up blanket. I took a seat behind the wheel of the car and Frannie settled in right behind me. 'The gun is now pointed to the base of your skull. When we approach the gate, I will hide but I will be aiming straight for your spine – might not kill you but you'll never walk again if I shoot. If you do anything suspicious and they decide to search the car, I'll shoot you first and take my chances on getting away in the confusion. Is that clear?'

After I nodded, she added, 'If you cooperate, I will let you go when I get to safety. Think about that – just one small piece of your life helping me beats being eternally dead or permanently crippled and helpless. Those are your alternatives. Let's go.'

If I believed her, I'd have a shred of hope to clutch to my heart, but I didn't. I suppose it was possible that she might decide that it was simpler to dump me on the side of the road in the middle of nowhere. But I suspected she would use me until she felt I was too much of an obstacle. Then, she very well might drop me somewhere but I would no longer be breathing when she did.

As I started driving down the road to the gate, she said, 'If the guard asks where you're going, tell him the train station.'

'But passenger trains don't run at this time of night.'

'Tell him you're meeting a soldier. Troop transport doesn't always follow a pre-set schedule.'

'I'll try.'

'You better do more than try, Libby Clark, you'd better succeed. Your life depends on it.'

As I approached the gate, a yawning sentry approached, looked at my identification and waved me on. No questions. No interest in the blanket lumped behind my seat. Nothing. When we were a couple of miles outside of the reservation she clambered over from the back to the front. I was terrified that I'd hit a pothole and accidentally set off her trigger finger but she settled into the seat next to me without incident. I drove into the night with Frannie directing me to Highway 40. Three hours later, we were just outside of Nashville when she ordered me to stop at a truck stop to fill up.

'Smile at the nice man who pumps the gas,' she said slapping a ten dollar bill in my lap. When he finishes, pull up to the restaurant. We'll go into the bathroom and then I'm getting a cup of coffee. Before you ask, no, you cannot have a cup. I can't trust you not to throw it in my face. And don't forget, the gun will be on you every moment. So smile, smile, smile like we're two girlfriends on a road trip. You got it?'

I nodded. And, of course, I smiled. The expression felt phony on my face but hopefully anyone else who saw it would consider that a matter of character. The fantasy of some stranger coming to my rescue was a hope but a ridiculous one. I'd be dead before he could affect my escape. It was all up to me.

Walking into the truck stop, Frannie acted slightly intoxicated and chummy giving her the opportunity to lean against me and keep me aware of the gun poking in my side. The only attention we received from the late night crowd were leers and catcalls, not exactly the stepping stones to my salvation.

In the restroom she bullied me into the same stall with her and made me stand with my back in a corner with my hands on top of my head. When she flushed, she said, 'Your turn. And be grateful. I could make you use a cup in the car.'

She stood directly in front of me with the barrel pointing at my head. The close quarters created possibilities that weren't feasible when she was able to keep some distance from me. Even with my underpants down around my knees, I knew this might be my most opportune moment to act. I thought it through, assessed my chances, and took a leap of faith.

My right hand grabbed the pistol pushing it downward as I launched up from the toilet, aiming the top of my skull at the tip of her chin. As I made contact, a shot fired sending splinters of tile flying in the air and Frannie doubled over at impact.

My fingers wanted to pull back from the heat of the barrel but I held on, wresting control of the gun away from my tormentor. I grabbed the back of her head and shoved it down towards the toilet. I heard a distinct crack as her face smacked the porcelain rim. I pressed my hand against the back of her head forcing her face into the water, flipped the latch on the door and ran out of the bathroom out into the restaurant, now holding the grip on the pistol.

Once again, I was looking down the barrel of a firearm. This time, the weapon was a shotgun and the guy at the other end was wearing a grease-stained apron tied around his waist and a killer look in his eye.

'Drop the gun, lady. Drop it now.'

I spread my fingers wide allowing it to fall to the floor.

'Kick it over here. Easy now.'

I did what he wanted and then he asked, 'What's going on in there, lady?'

'That other woman kidnapped me from my home at gunpoint. That's her pistol.'

Frannie burst out of the bathroom. 'Oh, thank heaven. Thank heaven! I thought she was going to kill me. Oh please, don't let her hurt me anymore.'

The man with the shotgun swung toward Frannie for a moment then back to me. 'She doesn't look like no kidnapper to me. She looks like you've beaten her up pretty bad.' He called over his shoulder, 'Frank, give 'em another call and make sure they're sending an ambulance, too.'

'Sir,' I said, 'you are making a mistake,' I said. 'That woman is dangerous.'

Frannie interrupted, 'I don't need an ambulance. I just want to get away from that woman. She stuffed me in the trunk of my car and now she has my keys. I've never been so frightened in all my life.' Frannie exhaled a sob and continued, 'I am terrified of her. Please, please, I'm shaking just standing next to her.'

The armed man looked back and forth between us. 'We already called the law. I'd be inclined to let you leave, ma'am,' he said nodding at Frannie, 'but the sheriff's office is just down the road so it won't take them long to get here. I'm going to let them figure this all out.'

As if on cue, Frannie started shaking all over and looked ready to collapse.

The man shouted, 'Frank, get over here and help her to a booth and fix her a cup of coffee or whatever she wants. You,' he said staring at me, 'don't you move an inch.'

From where I stood, I could see Frank gently ease Frannie into a booth as she awarded him with her most simpering smile. Frank patted the back of her hand and was back in a moment with a steaming cup of coffee and a slice of pie. I could only hope the officers who arrived would listen to me.

Soon, I heard a siren pulling close, tires crunching the gravel as it came to a stop. The car door slammed and another vehicle arrived – this one at a faster speed, throwing little rocks into the side of the other as it screeched to a halt.

Two deputies walked in the door. The older one's pot belly proceeded him. The younger had a trim, fit appearance but his left hand was missing the middle three fingers, explaining why he was here and not in the armed services.

The older man asked, 'Clay, we'll take over now. Lower the shotgun. What's the trouble here?'

'It seems like this here woman,' he said gesturing toward me, 'kidnapped that woman over there in the booth and then beat her up in the ladies' room. Here's the gun I took from this one.'

As the deputies looked over to the booth, Frannie smiled sweetly and lowered her eyes. The older man, looking at me, ordered the younger, 'Snap the bracelets on that one.'

'Sir,' I objected. 'You are making a big mistake. That woman is wanted by the military for a crime she committed. You need to call Lieutenant Colonel Crenshaw at the Clinton Engineer Works near Knoxville.'

He snorted in response and added, 'I know we're in a war and all, lady, but the military has no say so in civilian affairs. Since neither of you are in uniform, I'll be calling the shots here. And I'm going to be taking you in to the jail for a nice conversation.'

I didn't know what I could say in my defense. I certainly couldn't share information about the facility or our work and if I said she was a spy, it would raise even more questions.

Turning to Frannie, he said, 'Ma'am, we have an ambulance on the way to tend to your injuries.'

'Sir, I just need to get out of here. My mother is sickly – in fact, she's on her deathbed. I was rushing home in hopes of saying goodbye.' She exhaled a jagged breath and patted her eyes with a paper napkin. 'Please just let me go, please let me see her before she's gone. I promise, I'll come back after the funeral and sign any papers you want, just please let me see Mama.'

I rolled my eyes – not that anyone noticed.

'Yes, ma'am, you certainly may. Just don't forget to stop by on your way back and take care of the paperwork. We can hold her until you do. We'll just need your name and contact information.'

'I'm Libby Clark and I do need my keys to drive the car. Can you get them from that woman, please?'

'What? She is not! I'm Libby Clark. Do not let her leave here, you are making a big mistake.'

The younger deputy jerked on my cuffs and growled into my ear, 'Where are the keys, lady?'

I refused to answer and he ran his hands up and down my body until he found the right pocket and pulled them out. He tossed them to the other man who handed them to Frannie.

She started to leave but turned back and said, 'Deputy, sir, you'd best do as she says and call Lieutenant Colonel Crenshaw. Let him know you captured Frannie Snowden. He'll probably give you a commendation.'

'She's lying, sir. She's very good at that,' I protested.

The deputy holding onto my handcuffs, twitched them again, sending sharp shooting pain into my shoulders. 'Shut up, lady.'

Frank left the cash register to escort Frannie outside. When he came back in, he was holding Frannie's purse dangling from his fingerprints. Handing it to the older deputy, he said, 'Miss Clark said that this belongs to that woman.'

The deputy held it up. 'Do you recognize this?'

'Yes, I do. It belongs to Frannie Snowden who is driving off in my car right now.'

He opened up the handbag and peered inside before pulling

out a big bundle of cash. 'Oh, yes, this pocketbook with all this money inside of it, belongs to the woman we let go and out of the goodness of her heart she left it all for you.'

'I've never seen that money before,' I said.

'Uh, deputy,' Frank interrupted, 'Miss Clark told me that the Snowden woman stole all her traveling money, so I pulled a few bills out of that wad and gave it to her so she could get to her mama's.'

'Sounds like justice to me, Frank. Don't worry about it.' He held the handbag upside down over the surface, dumping the contents in a messy pile on the table. 'Looks like a serious amount of cash,' he said as he picked up the bundle, sorted it into stacks of one hundred, fifty, twenty and ten dollar bills. He counted off one stack at a time. 'Merciful heavens, lady, you've got nearly ten thousand dollars in here. You planning on leaving the country or something?'

'I am not Frannie Snowden. I have never had that much money in my life.'

'Right, and that little lady you beat up, she doesn't look like the type to be carrying around that much pin money. And what else do we have in here?' he said continuing his search of Frannie's purse. 'Oh look! An identification badge for Frannie Snowden. You can stop your denials now, Miss Snowden. We know who you are. And we're taking you in. We'll call the army when we get back to the station and see what that Lieutenant Colonel has to say about you. I imagine he'll tell me you've been a very bad girl.'

I almost admired Frannie's ability. The dumb girl camouflage was immaculate cover for a clever, nasty woman. From the wad in her purse, it's obvious she was involved in espionage out of greed. And yet, she was willing to toss away all that money to make me look guilty and give her time to get away before the army arrived. I was certain that she would – her head start would ensure that. If Frannie stayed on Route 40, she'd be past Memphis and into Arkansas before Crenshaw could get here. And if she didn't stick to that highway, heaven only knows where she could go. There was no sense arguing any longer. I could only hope that Crenshaw made the trip personally before my restrained arms were jerked out of their sockets.

FORTY-THREE

A t the sheriff's office, I was led to the older officer's room, whom I saw from the sign on his door was Deputy Chief Arlo Steubens. The younger man shoved me down in a wooden chair as Steubens picked up the phone. After he was transferred multiple times, he was finally connected to Crenshaw. 'Hello, sir. This is Deputy Chief Steubens from the Wilson County Sheriff's Department. I understand you are looking for one Frannie Snowden.'

'This is Libby Clark, Crenshaw! They let Frannie get away!' I shouted.

'What? Oh, that's just the Snowden woman who keeps screaming about her innocence.' He put his hand over the receiver and said, 'You don't shut up, I'll get the deputy to gag you.' Speaking again in the phone, he said, 'Yes, sir. Seems like the Snowden woman kidnapped Libby Clark and beat her up in the ladies' room.'

After a pause, Steubens continued, 'I'm sorry, sir. I let Miss Clark depart. She was in a mighty big hurry to get to her sick mama.'

Listening to the conversation at the other end, I could see Steubens puff and get red-faced. 'I'm not in the military, sir. And you can't order me about. I had no way of knowing you needed to speak to Miss Clark and I will not cease my questioning of Snowden. She has been arrested for an assault in my jurisdiction and it's my responsibility. You want to come up here, she'll still be here. But don't try to tell me how to do my job.' He slammed the phone down and turned to me. 'Well, he's a prickly so-and-so. I sure wouldn't want to be in your shoes.' To the deputy he added, 'Get her out of here.'

The deputy led me rapidly down a flight of stairs where my stumbling resulted in being dragged for a couple of steps before I could get my feet back under me. The deputy pushed through an entryway into a tiny room with bars on the front and sweaty concrete blocks on the other three sides. A metal platform jutted out from a side wall with a piece of plywood on top of it. I surmised that was my bed and stretched out on it, too tired to do anything but fall asleep.

I was jarred awake by Steubens hitting the platform several times with his billy club, making my ears ring as the sound echoed in the small space.

'Sit up!' he ordered. 'Why did you attack that woman?'

'She was holding me captive and I was trying to escape.'

'Stop lying!' he said whacking the club against the wall beside my head.

I felt bile surging into my throat. The combination of fear and lack of sleep was churning up my stomach. I swallowed quickly to get it under control.

'Now, answer my question. The truth this time.'

'What do you want me to say?' I asked.

'I want you to tell me the truth.'

I sighed. 'Frannie Snowden was holding me captive and I was trying to escape from her when I was stopped by that man with a shotgun.'

'We'll see how you feel an hour from now when everyone else is being served breakfast and you don't even get a glass of water.'

I didn't stop to think about what he said. I simply laid back on my ersatz bed and fell back asleep. I was woken by the clatter of a wheeled cart rolling down the hallway. My stomach rumbled and my tongue adhered to the roof of my mouth as the trolley went by without stopping at my cell. I reclined again but didn't have time to drift. Steubens was back, banging on the metal bars of my cell this time.

'Wake up, lady. Getting hungry? Thirsty? Sorry, but until you tell me the truth, you get nothing. Now, once again: why did you attack that woman?'

Unless I was willing to confess to sins I did not commit – and he hadn't pushed me that far yet – I had nothing to say. I closed my eyes and turned my back to him. I heard the jangle of keys and the wrenching of metal as the door swung back. I felt a hard jab go into my side and flinched.

He grabbed my uppermost arm and jerked me to my feet. He

thrust his face into mine and screamed, 'I want an answer and I want it now.'

'She was holding me captive at gunpoint . . .'

He shoved me back on the platform with enough force that the back of my head hit the concrete wall, which, in turn, reawakened my nausea.

Just then, I heard Crenshaw's voice from a distance. I thought, at first, that I was imagining it. When I realized that the sound was heading in my general direction, I jumped up, grabbed the bars and shouted, 'Lieutenant Colonel! Crenshaw! Down here.'

In no time, Crenshaw was at my cell with a swarm of uniforms at his back. 'Miss Clark? What are you doing in here?'

'Ask him,' I said, nodding toward Steubens.

'Well, sir,' Crenshaw barked. 'What is your excuse for this travesty?'

Steuben's mouth hung open for a moment, then he shut it and said, 'That's Libby Clark?'

'It most certainly is. Get her out of there immediately. And where is Frannie Snowden?'

'I thought she was Libby Clark.'

'I don't want your excuses. I want answers. Where is she?'

Steubens looked too sick to respond. The younger deputy stepped up and said, 'She's gone, sir.'

'Gone? You let a spy escape. You locked up an important scientist and let that secret agent escape? Where did she go?'

'She headed west on Highway 40, sir.'

'You idiots! If Miss Clark were going to see her mother, she would have gone east. Are you working for the enemy here?'

Steubens finally perked up enough to respond. 'No sir. This is a big misunderstanding. We're all patriots here, sir.'

'You don't act like patriots.'

As much as Steubens aggravated me, I came to his defense. 'Sir, Frannie tricked them. As you and I know too well, she is very good at that. She engineered Marvin's murder and she'd been deceiving him since before she was old enough to start school.' Crenshaw spun around and addressed one of his men. 'Go out to your jeep and send out an alert with a description of Snowden and of Miss Clark's car. And spread the net in all directions. She could have doubled-back or turned off the highway anywhere. Come with me, Miss Clark, one of my men will take you by the emergency room to have you checked out before taking you back home.'

Crenshaw stepped up to Steubens nearly stopping on top of his feet. His finger flashed out and poked the deputy chief in the chest. 'I'll deal with you later.'

The younger deputy stepped up and said, 'Sir, we had no way of knowing.'

'You, too,' Crenshaw snapped. 'I will deal with you as well. And with anyone else who laid a hand on Miss Clark.'

I had to admit, I certainly appreciated that exchange. I stifled the grin that threatened to spread across my face.

FORTY-FOUR

I didn't think I needed to visit the emergency room, but Corporal Grant, who was given the responsibility for my transport, had his orders and that was one of them. The doctor looked me over and found no broken bones to set and no injuries needing stitches. He seemed a bit disappointed but got some consolation counting up the bruises and lacerations. I didn't remember the exact number, but they were numerous. He did say he was moderately worried about a concussion because of the injury to my skull. I ran my fingers over the tender, protruding goose egg on the back of my head – no wonder I felt off-kilter.

The doctor walked out of the examination area with me to speak to the corporal. He ran through a list of the warning signs of concussion and Grant said he would keep a close eye on me.

For a little while on the drive back, the corporal and I tried a little chit-chat but it didn't last long. He was from Chicago and all I'd seen of that city was the train station and the sights visible from the tracks. He'd never been to Virginia or Pennsylvania in his life and, in fact, had never been south of the Illinois state capital in Springfield before he joined the army. To make things worse, he hated chemistry, physics and math and I knew nothing about his work before the war, automotive repair. I did promise, though, to save him a dance the next time we gathered to make it a night in the cafeteria.

I drifted off and woke up when I realized the car wasn't moving. 'Where are we?'

'At a diner, Miss Clark. After I couldn't wake you up, I thought it might be a good idea to stop for breakfast and make sure you got something to eat and a hot cup of coffee.'

'I'd love some coffee but even if you pour a gallon of the stuff in me, I won't be able to stay awake.'

'Ma'am, the doctor said you had to stay awake.'

'Then before we leave, you best wire up an electric circuit in my seat so you can give me a charge from time to time. At best,

I had one and a half hours of sleep in that nasty cell and the day before started more than twenty-four hours ago – and it hasn't exactly been one filled with lazy bliss.'

'Ma'am, I have my orders.'

'They're not orders,' I snapped. 'The doctor said that. Not Crenshaw.' When I saw the chagrin on his face, I backed off. 'Sorry, Corporal. I'm exhausted and it's making me testy. Let's go in.'

I was so tired that I didn't know if I had the energy to chew but the aroma of toast and sizzling bacon roused me. Three sunny-side up eggs, a side of sausage, a few slices of bacon, a helping of home fries and four biscuits lathered with butter and jam later, I finally pushed back from the table.

'That was impressive, ma'am. Never saw a lady put it away like that. But you did say you were raised on a farm, I guess that answers it.'

'I do have a healthy appetite, Corporal, but this morning, I surpassed myself. I imagine my Aunt Dorothy would be appalled.'

'Not your mother?'

'Don't think she's that much of a hypocrite. You see, right now, she's sitting in jail charged with murder – not exactly a suitable place for a one-time belle of the ball.' I was surprised at my openness. I didn't know whether to blame it on fatigue, the traumatic series of events of the day, or perhaps, I was simply rebelling against the straitjacket of secrecy that accompanied my work. Probably a combination of the three but I certainly was sick of lies and deception.

'I'm so sorry. I didn't mean to pry. But . . . never mind . . .'

'What? You want to know if she did it? Because she did. She admitted as much. To me. To her lawyer. Even to the detectives. No doubt she'll go to prison. The only question is for how long.'

'Who . . . I mean . . . never mind . . .'

'Oh, please, Corporal, ask away. Unless it has to do with my work, I have nothing to hide. Just pay the waitress and let's head on home. I'll tell you more along the way.'

The sad saga of life at my birthplace from the death of my dad to the death of my stepdad filled a long stretch of the drive back. From the outset, Corporal Grant, who asked me to call him Sammy by the time I ended the story, demonstrated a remarkable amount of empathy for the situation which kept me talking until I told him more than I had planned. When I wrapped up, he said, 'Ma'am, that is a tragedy and I don't blame your mother one little bit.'

'You don't?'

'I wish my mother was that protective of me. My dad knocked me around a lot while I was growing up and all she wanted to do was advise me on how not to get him angry. But no matter what I tried, he'd smack me for any reason or none at all. Honestly, Miss Clark, I've come to believe that some men just deserve killing.'

I said nothing but had to admit to myself that if any man deserved to die for bullying and abusing his family, Ernest was high on the list. I wondered if my mother had weighed the positives and negatives before pulling the trigger or just acted out of a primitive, violent instinct.

When we were inside the gates of our home away from home, I thought about going straight to Y-12. Part of me wanted to update everyone and catch up on my work, but the rest of me cringed at the thought of walking through the lab door. All I really wanted was some sleep in my own bed. I turned down Sammy's suggestion of a stop in the cafeteria for lunch first and had him drop me at my flattop.

G.G. rocketed into the living room as soon as I stepped inside. He danced around on his tippy-toes and flopped down on his head. After giving him the physical affection he craved, I went into the kitchen to get him some food. There, I found a note from Jessie who wrote that she stopped by before her shift to play with G.G. and make sure he had food and water and she'd be back in the evening to check on him again. How, in heaven's name, did she know I was away? I didn't know it until it happened.

I climbed into bed and fell asleep smiling as I thought of my old school chum who had grown up to be a very fine friend indeed.

When I opened my eyes, it was dark outside but I had no idea if it was the evening of the same day or if it was already heading into the next morning. I stretched and G.G. pounced on my toes making me giggle. Then, I heard a small, soft moan. I was on my feet with no recollection of getting out of the bed. My heart raced. Did I see the lump of another body on the bed next to mine? Or was it nothing but a pile of pillows and my runaway imagination? I froze in place as an icy wave of fear washed over me. I held my breath as I bent at the waist, grabbed the chain of my bedside lamp and tugged. In the sudden light, the lump bolted upright and gasped. A startled Jessie rubbed her eyes and said, 'Oh, Libby, you're awake!'

I urged Jessie to go back to sleep but she insisted if I were up for the day, she was as well. While I fixed coffee and breakfast, she peppered me with questions about the events since we were last together. At first, she had a very difficult time wrapping her mind around Frannie's duplicity.

When she seemed to run out of steam, I asked, 'How did you know to come and check up on G.G.?'

'Your boys came to see me.'

'My boys?'

'You know – the lab gang: Teddy, Gregg, Joe and some big guy I didn't really know,' she said.

'That sounds like our Dennis,' I said, 'but they sure aren't *my* boys.'

'Really? They sure act like it, Libby. They were all kinds of upset when you weren't at home early in the morning. They said they were going with you to see Crenshaw to make sure you got out of his house safely, but when you weren't there, they panicked. You would have thought they couldn't breathe without you telling them when to inhale and when to exhale. Anyway, when they told me they didn't know where you were and they were worried, I volunteered to take care of G.G. every day before and after my shift. They made me promise to let them know if you came home and they swore they'd let me know if they learned anything. When they left me, they said that they were going to see Crenshaw before they went to work.'

'Did they talk to him?'

'Yes, they did. Teddy met me outside of K-25 at lunch break and said that Crenshaw asked them a lot of questions about what was going on in your life. When they explained to him about your mother's arrest, Crenshaw called someone in Bedford. Whoever he called told him they'd keep an eye out for you and send someone out to the farm to see if you were there.'

'Then what happened?'

'Before I came over here to check on G.G., I stopped at Town Square, got in line and called Mama.'

'Any news about the Bedford boys?'

'No. Actually, that was why I called Mama. All she said about that was that everyone was on pins and needles. She said all the mothers, wives and sisters of the men in the company were saying: "No news is good news" but she didn't think any of them thought it held any truth in this situation. She did have a lot of other news, though, about your mother.'

'What is it? Is she okay?'

'You're not going to believe what Mama witnessed in the courtroom, Libby.'

FORTY-FIVE

Mrs Justine Early put on her Sunday best and made the first visit in her life to an actual courtroom. Mr Coxe had told her that it was not necessary for her to be there since it was a simple meeting to set the trial date in the court calendar. Justine, however, felt an obligation to her old friend Annabelle and made a promise to little Ernie to report back on everything that was happening with his mother. She didn't feel she could do that without witnessing it all with her own eyes.

Justine was surprised to find that the seating in the room was a lot like what she found in church; nobody called them pews in court but the only difference she could see was the absence of the racks holding hymnals and bibles on the back. Everything started out as boring as could be, the two lawyers alternating in their offers of possible dates to the judge and the attorney on the other side claiming a prior commitment.

It got a bit contentious after a while and both of the men appeared more agitated with each passing minute. The sparks flew when Annabelle's lawyer, Mr Coxe, complained, 'Your honor, the state is deliberately suggesting dates when he knows I will be in a different courtroom with other cases. I suspect he is hoping not to bring this case to trial before the election because he is worried that my client will generate too much sympathy from the jurors that the outcome will not be to his liking.'

Mr Coxe and the prosecutor squabbled like a couple of eight-year-old boys until the judge banged his gavel three times and said, 'I don't care what either of you gentlemen think about the other. I don't care what you want. I don't want this trial dragged out for months. I want it all done in an expeditious manner. I won't tolerate anything less. So let's work out a reasonable date and stop all this unprofessional grandstanding.'

Annabelle chose that moment to rise to her feet. 'Excuse me, your honor, but I am afraid this is all a big waste of your honor's time.'

The quiet courtroom was suddenly filled with competing conversations. The judge banged his gavel like he was trying to drive nails into the bench. Mr Coxe threw an arm around Annabelle's shoulders and tried to get her to sit down but she shrugged him off. The prosecutor was shouting, 'Objection, your honor, objection.'

Mr Coxe joined in the fray with a plea to the judge to allow him a moment with his client.

The bailiff yelled above the clamor, 'Order in the court.'

Just like that, the whispering, fidgeting and arguing stopped. In the new quiet, the judge said, 'Ma'am, would you like to consult with your attorney?'

Coxe said, 'Thank you, your honor.'

Annabelle rose her voice above his. 'No, your honor, I would like to speak to you.'

'Very well. Sit down, Mr Coxe.'

'But, your honor—'

'Another word, Mr Coxe and I'll hold you in contempt of court. Ma'am, you may address the court.'

'Your honor, I want to change my plea,' she said.

'Have you discussed this with your attorney?'

'Yes, your honor, several times and we continue to disagree. I beg your forgiveness for disrupting the proceedings but I thought it was important to speak up on my own behalf.'

'Do you want to dismiss your lawyer and represent yourself?'

'Yes, sir, your honor, I do,' Annabelle said. She turned to Mr Coxe, smiled and said, 'I'm sorry, Wilford.' Then she faced the bench and said, 'Your honor, I plead guilty to the murder of my husband, Ernest Floyd. I got the gun. I pulled the trigger. And I meant to kill him.'

The uproar in the courtroom was so deafening that although Justine could see the judge slamming down the gavel, she could not hear the sound of it. The bailiff stood up on the row directly behind the prosecutor and shouted, 'Quiet down or the judge will clear the courtroom.'

That announcement brought a hush broken only by the last two hammers of the judge's gavel. 'Are you certain about this decision?'

'Yes, your honor. I was raised to tell the truth and denying it now will not serve any good purpose.'

The judge accepted her plea and adjourned the court to allow the attorneys on both sides some time to address the new situation they now faced.

Justine waved as Annabelle rose and started for the side door. Annabelle smiled at her friend and motioned to Mr Coxe. When he approached, she whispered in his ear. A moment later, a guard whisked her out of sight.

Mr Coxe walked over to Justine and said, 'Mrs Floyd asked me to tell you that she did this for her children. She didn't want Libby distracted from her work and she didn't want little Ernie to hear about the ugly portrait that would be painted of his father at trial. She asked if you would give her love to Libby and Ernie.'

'Can she change her mind again and change her plea back to not guilty?' Justine asked.

'She could try,' Mr Coxe said, 'but the judge might not allow it and even if he did and the case went to trial, the prosecution could use this guilty plea like a club to beat her over and over again. After that, the death penalty would likely be a certainty. Under these circumstances, though, it is possible that his honor will show her a measure of mercy.'

FORTY-SIX

Jessie and I went off in different directions that morning – she headed to K-25 and I to Y-12. My bitterness towards Frannie had not subsided over the night, in fact, it had grown. I keenly felt the absence of the car as I stood at the bus stop waiting for the rattletrap to screech to a halt and carry me across the reservation to work.

I entered my lab area and was greeted by cheers and dozens of shouted questions. I knew Gregg and Joe expected answers but now was not the time. 'I'm back. I'm fine. And I'm ready for work. Charlie wanted me to fill in for him, so I'm retreating to his office. Please give me some time to figure out just what I need to do. Then, I'll be glad to talk to anyone about their specific problems or concerns,' I said.

I was greeted by an uproar of objection but I went into Charlie's space and closed the door. The stack overflowing his in-box was enough to make me want to turn around, go home and bury myself under the covers. But I sighed, placed a hand on top of the stack and another under it and flipped it all over to start with the oldest first.

To my chagrin, much of the pile was requests for reports that required the information that I regularly provided to Charlie but which, in my serial absences, I had not been able to do. I set each one of those aside until I had time to get back to my own work or train someone else to handle it. Then, I sorted the rest.

First, I tackled the phone messages. I returned each call and explained in vague terms that Charlie had been injured, was currently in hospital and was recovering nicely. With as much diplomacy as I could muster, I batted away the questions for details. At this point, I was not at all certain of what was and wasn't public knowledge and I didn't want to disrupt my current peaceful relationship with Crenshaw by saying the wrong thing to the wrong person.

Next I handled the purchase order requests – fairly routine and easy to understand. I approved all but one that I set aside for the time being and took them down to the purchasing coordinator.

She would check the inventory for everything that was at hand and pass along the rest for approval from Charlie's superiors.

I had lost track of time and my surroundings and was quite surprised when a knock on the door caused me to look down at my watch. 12:30. Where had the morning gone? 'Come in,' I said.

Gregg and Joe walked into the room and Gregg asked, 'Don't you think you should take a break for lunch?'

At the cafeteria, we spotted Dennis and Teddy and drew them into our little group in a far, sparsely populated corner. I ran down the events since our meeting, interrupted frequently by questions.

Teddy was the most distressed by my tale. 'I should have walked you home. I should have gone into your house and checked it. It's all my fault.'

'Teddy, you can't blame yourself. If you had come home with me, it wouldn't have made a difference. She had a gun – either she would have left with two hostages or she would have left you lying face down on the floor and that would have been far worse.'

Before I could get them all to return to work, I had to give repeated assurances that I was okay. On the way back, Teddy asked if there was any news about my mother and I told them that story, too. I was more tired when I got back into Charlie's office than I was before my so-called break.

I plowed through Charlie's backlog for another hour before stopping to go to my station and start on my belated analysis reports of progress on the purity of the green salt. I had a lot of samples to extract and run through the process and doubted I could do more than make a dent in my own responsibilities.

Of course, on that discouraging note, I was interrupted by the arrival of Lieutenant Colonel Crenshaw and his cluster of uniforms. Did he always travel with a mufti-clad entourage? I led him back to Charlie's office where he positioned two men by the door before closing it.

'Miss Clark,' he began, 'we found your car.'

'You arrested Frannie?'

'No. But we did locate your car and someone is driving it back here now. We found it on the side of a highway between Little Rock, Arkansas and Texarkana, Texas.'

'Where is Frannie?'

'We don't know. Some suspect that she might have found other transportation and is headed for Mexico. The authorities along the border have been informed to be on the look-out.'

'Mexico?' I asked. 'But Mexico is our ally. Why would she go there?'

'I am surprised you knew that, Miss Clark. Most civilians are unaware that Mexico is working with us against the Axis but then, you have consistently surprised me – I imagine I should be more amazed if you didn't.'

'Why would she go hide in the country who is opposing Germany?'

'Miss Clark, I have come to hold you in high regard. Perhaps I should not completely explain the circumstances to you but I feel you have earned the right to certain information. However, I cannot risk sharing it with you, unless you give me your iron-clad assurances that you will repeat this to no one. Not to friends. Not to family members. Not to your secret group of whoever.'

His eyes seemed to pierce through the skin. The look on his face was intimidating and a bit frightening. For a moment, I was not sure if I wanted to hear what he said. Then I nodded. 'Yes sir, you have my word.'

'We are not certain if Ms Snowden was spying for the Germans or for the Soviets.'

'But sir, Russia is our ally.'

'For the moment, Miss Clark, but probably only until we defeat the Germans. Stalin and his gang will be on our side for only as long as it is to their benefit. As soon as they feel that time is past, many of us believe that they will be our new arch-enemy.'

That glimpse into international politics was a stunning one for me. I could not quite grasp that Machiavellian-sounding concept. I knew, however, that Crenshaw was convinced of it. The possible ramifications for the future were staggering.

'You've taken the secrecy oath, Miss Clark. And now, I am simply reminding you that you need to take it a step further. Not a word to anyone. I wanted to give a full accounting to you – and only you – and now I will leave you to your work.' He rose to his feet.

'One moment, sir. I do have a couple of questions. First of all, about the others involved in Marvin's murder and the spy operation . . .'

'We feel confident that we have everyone on the reservation, with the exception of Ms Snowden, under lock and key. They will have no communications with anyone for the duration of the war.'

'I'm curious, sir, how did you know Frannie was staying at the Andrew Johnson Hotel?'

'We didn't, actually. Initially, we thought she had to still be here inside the fence. Then, we started thinking about the possibility that she had slipped out unnoticed. We questioned everyone working at the train depot without finding any indication that she'd been there. After that, we blanketed the town. We focused, at first, on the places where black-marketers, thieves and other wrong-doers congregated, hoping to find someone there who'd seen her. Either they hadn't or they wouldn't tell us and we came up empty-handed. We sent a couple of teams to the different hotels – not because we imagined she'd gotten a room there but the possibility that her contact or a co-conspirator might be in one of them. We were quite surprised when we discovered Frannie Snowden in the Andrew Johnson.'

My eyebrows raised at this incredulous scenario. 'You're telling me, it was all just a coincidence?'

'That's the size of it, Miss Clark. Stranger things have happened before and will happen again.'

I didn't believe him. I suspected there was something more – some information or person that he was protecting. I knew if he was, he was not going to tell me. 'One last question: who is Raymond and has he been arrested?'

'We gravely doubt that is his real name. Agents have blanketed Manhattan and the surrounding area looking for any sign of him or his operation. There is little hope of identifying him, however, since we have no physical description. Nonetheless, the work will move forward.'

'Thank you, sir.'

'I hope, Miss Clark, that you have learned a lesson. Coming to me with any perceived criminal problem at the outset will eliminate the danger to you and your friends and make the quest for answers more efficient.'

I was not inclined to respond but he riveted me again with that icy blue stare that I knew would not cease until I did. 'Yes sir. I will bear that in mind.'

'See that you do,' he said as he spun on his heels and departed with uniforms in tow.

FORTY-SEVEN

A few days passed before Charlie returned to his post and relieved me of double-duty. He seemed a bit physically weak but in all other ways on top of the world. In another couple of days, I was caught up on my work and had turned another small container of the precious salt over to the courier for delivery to who knew where.

I was in high spirits when I returned to my home that night but an ugly bolt of apprehension coursed through me when I discovered a small package on my porch and a note wedged in my door. I went inside and opened the note first. I smiled when I saw it was from Corporal Sammy Grant reminding me that he'd be looking for me at the dance Saturday night.

I then tackled the package. Inside was a worn copy of *Sonnets from the Portuguese* by Elizabeth Barrett Browning. Puzzled, I opened the letter enclosed from Mrs Early:

Dear Libby,

Your mother asked little Ernie and I to retrieve this book from the farmhouse. She thought it would be meaningful to you. She told me to tell you to look at the inside cover.

Your mother also wanted me to inform you that she would cherish a letter from you when you have time to write but she does not want you to neglect your work to come to the dreary place she will not call home no matter how long she resides there. She further said that a visit would displease her since she has no desire to inflict any more sadness or pain into your life.

Ernie is doing well. He is doing his chores and more with eagerness and makes regular trips over to your farm to make sure your business is being well-managed. He is quite the little farmer.

With best wishes,

Justine Early

I opened the cover and my eyes welled up immediately. The book was inscribed: *To my dearest Annabelle, I love you dearly and always. May this token of my love serve as a demonstration of affection for you and heartfelt appreciation for the lovely gift you have given me – my beautiful little daughter Elizabeth Ann 'Libby' Clark*

The hard, cold spot I'd reserved in my heart for my mother was softening every day. I knew she said she did not want to see me again but her protests against visiting were her way of protecting me the best she could. One day, I'd find that I have forgiven her completely – maybe soon. It struck me that a big part of growing up and becoming an adult is developing the ability to see your parents' shortcomings and mistakes in context of their humanity – to accept that no parent is perfect and to understand that no human is without flaws.

AUTHOR'S NOTE

Spies wormed their way into the Manhattan Project at all levels including the facilities at Oak Ridge. Some worked for the Axis powers, others for the Soviets. Raymond was the actual code name of a Soviet courier. His identity as Harry Gold, the son of poor Russian Jewish immigrants, was not revealed until 1950. His confession to sixteen years of espionage led to the arrest of a multitude of espionage agents including noted spies Julius and Ethel Rosenberg who were executed for their crimes.

His wrongdoing may have never been known except for the arrest of Klaus Fuchs in 1949. Fuchs was born in Germany in 1911 and grew up to become a communist in opposition to the rise of Hitler's power. He moved to England in 1941 and worked as a scientist aiding the British in their exploratory efforts to build an atomic bomb. That country sent him with a delegation of his peers to the United States to advocate a merger of efforts in the production of nuclear capabilities.

From his base at Columbia University, Fuchs delivered information about electromagnetic separation at Y-12 as well as the gaseous diffusion method developed at Oak Ridge to the Soviets. He moved to Los Alamos where he continued to siphon off information for the communists.

Fuchs was arrested in 1949 and ultimately confessed on January 24, 1950, naming Harry Gold as his courier. He was sentenced to fourteen years but was released after he served nine. He died in 1988, but by then had also provided China with details about the plans for Fat Man (the bomb that fell on the Japanese city of Nagasaki in 1945,) enabling them to develop a nuclear program well ahead of schedule.

Harry Gold also pointed the finger at Al Slack, who was a shift supervisor at Y-12 in Oak Ridge. Before arriving there, Slack worked for Kodak in New York state, then transferred to Tennessee Eastman at the Holston Ordnance Works in Kingsport.

In that position, he gave the Soviets a sample of the RDX – or Compound B – the strongest explosive known at the time and more powerful than TNT.

Once Slack moved to Oak Ridge, Gold pressured him to provide information from there. The specific nature of the material he delivered from the reservation is not known but the FBI considered him a part of the 'Rosenberg Network'. Most people in that group were driven by ideology and principle. In contrast, Slack appeared to be another spy motivated by money, not belief. He was sentenced to fifteen years in prison.

Also at Oak Ridge was George Koval, who was drafted into the Army's Special Engineer Detachment where he served as a Health Physics Officer, monitoring radiation levels across the installation. That job granted him access to almost every area. Working at the city behind the fence, he passed secret information about the work on uranium and plutonium to a Soviet contact. When transferred to the Dayton, Ohio, facility in June 1945, he provided them with intelligence about the polonium-based work on an implosion bomb.

He kept his subterfuge hidden and was honorably discharged from the army in 1946. Two years later, he sailed for Europe and never returned to the United States again. He died in his home in Moscow on January 31, 2006 at the age of 92, bitter at the lack of recognition given to him for his highly productive espionage efforts. Thirteen months later, Putin posthumously awarded him the Hero of the Russian Federation Medal, that nation's highest civilian honor, acknowledging his courage and heroism in carrying out special missions and his important contribution to the Soviet Union's development of the nuclear bomb. The public had been unaware of his work until 2002.

On February 3, 1941, Company A of Bedford, Virginia, joined the war effort when the National Guard's 116th Infantry Regiment was activated. Ray Nance, Taylor Fellers and the Stevens twins, Ray and Roy – mentioned in this story – were real people who were among the thirty soldiers still in that company on D-Day, June 6, 1944. They engaged in the first wave of assaults on Omaha Beach. By the end of that day, nineteen Bedford men were dead including Ray Stevens and

Taylor Fellers. Two more lost their lives in the continuation of the Normandy invasion and then another two died before the war was over. Only seven of them ever made it back home.

Families in Bedford did not begin to receive notifications of their loved one's demise until more than a month later on July 17th. The town of Bedford suffered the most severe loss of life per capita of any city or town in the United States on the first day of the invasion of the European continent. For this reason, the National D-Day Memorial is located in Bedford at the foot of the Blue Ridge Mountains.

Many thanks to Oak Ridge historian D. Ray Smith for his help with historical background information on the Manhattan Project spies and to Alex Kershaw, author of *The Bedford Boys*, for details about the sacrifice made during World War II by the people of the town I now call home.